Books by Sue Henry

SUE HENRY

SLEEPING LADY

An Alex Jensen Alaska Mystery

AVON BOOKS

An Imprint of HarperCollinsPublishers

AVON BOOKS
An Imprint of HarperCollins*Publishers*
10 East 53rd Street
New York, New York 10022-5299

Copyright © 1996 by Sue Henry
Excerpt from *Death Takes Passage* copyright © 1997 by Sue Henry
Inside cover author photo by Greg Martin Photography
Published by arrangement with the author
Library of Congress Catalog Card Number: 96-2385
ISBN: 0-380-72407-3
www.avonbooks.com

First Avon Books Printing: May 1997

Avon Trademark Reg. U.S. Pat. Off. and in Other Countries, Marca Registrada, Hecho en U.S.A.
HarperCollins® is a trademark of HarperCollins Publishers Inc.

Printed in the U.S.A.

10

This one's for
Jerry Bunker
(aka Maule 9864 Mike),
pilot extraordinaire
and friendly source of much
valuable advice and information,
whose approach to life is *on the step,*
who has a knack for finding remote
locations to be put to fictional uses,
and who is always willing to answer even
the dumbest questions with a straight face.

Appreciation and thanks to:

The Abbott Family Proofreading and Promotion Service.

The Friday Night Adoption Society, as always, for their assistance, cheerleading, and essential sense of humor.

Cindy Schroeder (aka Jane Dyer), Special Agent, U.S. Department of the Interior, U.S. Fish and Wildlife Service, Division of Law Enforcement, Madison, Wisconsin, for enthusiastic long-distance assistance. And for the firsthand story of her hairraising participation in Operation Brooks Range, a successful international undercover investigation into the illegal commercialization of wildlife by big-game guides in Alaska, from 1990 to 1992, that resulted in the arrest of seven in Alaska, Arizona, Idaho, Iowa, and Washington, and the seizure of eight airplanes in Alaska, Idaho, and Texas.

The U.S. Fish and Wildlife Forensics Laboratory, Ashland, Oregon, and its amazing staff, for a remarkable tour of its facilities and for generously sharing technical information about the essential work they do.

Ken Goddard, its dedicated director, for the assistance necessary to write both fiction and nonfiction for publication in the United States and abroad.

Hank Rust, of Rust's Flying Service (flying Alaska's backcountry for over 30 years), for information and patient assistance on charter services and use of the call numbers for his Cessna 206.

Nancy Sydnam, M.D., for information on aviation communications and the use of the call numbers for her Piper Super Cub.

The Alaska State Troopers, the Scientific Crime Detection Laboratory, and its director, George Taft, for generous technical assistance.

Bill Farber, Alaska State Trooper, retired, for continued technical assistance.

Karen Boyer, Operations Assistant, First National Bank of Anchorage, South Center Branch, for information on the ins and outs of safe-deposit boxes.

Max Rothman, New York Life Insurance Company, Anchorage, for information on high-risk insurance for pilots of small charter services.

My sons, Bruce and Eric, encouragers and promoters, who—booksellers beware—have been known to stealthily rearrange the display of my books to best advantage.

And my agent, Dominick Abel—who must have an inexhaustible supply of patience in a cookie jar on one of his office shelves—for optimism and the support of his considerable talent.

It would be fitting, I think, if among the last man-made tracks on earth could be found the huge footprints of the great brown bear.

Earl J. Fleming, "Do brown bears attack?"
Outdoor Life, November 1958

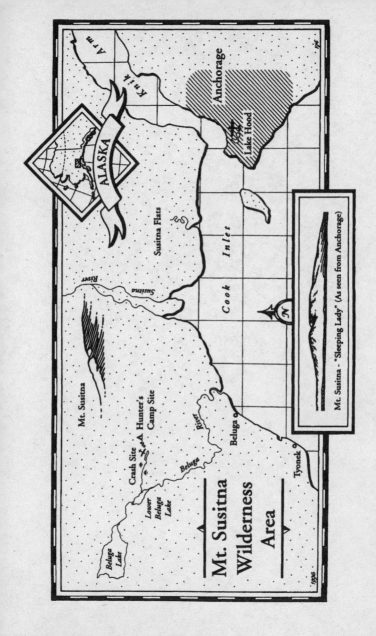

Mt. Susitna - "Sleeping Lady" (As seen from Anchorage)

Mt. Susitna
Wilderness
Area

Knik Arm

Anchorage

Lake Hood

ALASKA

Susitna Flats

Cook Inlet

Susitna River

Mt. Susitna

Crash Site

Hunter's Camp Site

Beluga River

Lower Beluga Lake

Beluga Lake

Beluga

Tyonek

N

AKLAK, THE GREAT BROWN BEAR, LAY ATOP A PILE OF dirt, brush, and vegetation he had dragged up as cover for his latest kill, protecting it from any predator or scavenger that, catching the scent of blood, might come looking for an easy meal. Partway down a narrow, tree- and brush-filled ravine, half-asleep and completely relaxed in his position on the heap, he was still highly aware of the sounds and smells of what went on around him. One ear twitched at the chirp of a ground squirrel, but, satiated with what he had gorged from a wolf-killed moose carcass the day before and the few bites from this fresh kill, he ignored it. He would lie here, or somewhere in the nearby undergrowth, until he had digested enough to be hungry again.

It was late in the year. Here and there on the north-facing slope, sheltered from the ineffectual rays of a pale sun that hung low in the southern sky for only a few declining hours each day, several thin patches remained of a premature snowfall. Aklak had already reconnoitered the den in which he had spent the previous winter, and to which he would soon return. In anticipation, he had raked a new pile of leaves and brush into the cave that lay beneath

1

two huge granite boulders, through the opening that would slowly fill with heavy snow and seal him in, warm and dry, to hibernate till spring.

For the cold half of the year, perhaps longer, if the winter was severe, he would not eat or eliminate, living off the fat he had accumulated during the warm months and the fluids stored in his body, losing 15 to 30 percent of the thirteen hundred pounds he now weighed. The summer just ended had been a bounteous one, during which he had gained well over three hundred pounds from a rich and omnivorous diet that included grasses, mushrooms, bulbs, herbs, birds and their eggs, wild honey full of bees, marmots and other rodents, seaweed, salmon berries, the underbark of trees, frogs, insects and larvae.

Existing primarily as an herbivore of more than two hundred types of plants, he was also a carnivore when opportunity presented him with an injured or newborn animal, or the carcass of one brought down by accident or another predator. He could as easily turn cannibal, ingesting any of his own kind that he killed or came upon already dead. Like other males, he would sometimes kill and eat bear cubs if they wandered within his reach, and their mothers if they were not quick or ferocious enough to elude him. Two thirds his size, females with cubs tended to avoid him, and other males, if possible.

During hibernation, eating nothing, he would require only about half the oxygen he needed when awake, and as he slept, his heart rate would slow from a normal ninety-eight beats per minute to eight or nine; his temperature would drop from ninety-eight point five to as little as eighty-nine degrees. If his body grew any cooler, he would rouse himself, *increasing his metabolic rate and his temperature along with it. Otherwise, safely removed from the harsh northern winter, he would curl up and snooze away the cold, foodless months, snugly unaware in his singular den. For Aklak, winter—even bitter Arctic winter with its howling blizzard breath and sub-zero temperatures that cracked trees and froze falling water before it hit the ground—hardly existed.*

Now, as he lay possessively, belly on the pile, the smell of still steaming blood and body fluids rose up through it and from his long, sharp claws. A hint of it remained in his mouth and he curled his long tongue up to where splotches of blood reddened the fur of his snout. The taste almost encouraged him to uncover the carcass he had buried, but he was sated and too comfortable to bother. The man would keep and would be better eating when he had tenderized a bit.

It had been an unusually easy kill. Before finding the man, he had been angry and frustrated with the whining, annoying thing in the air that he could not catch. Again and again it had returned, diving and circling, driving him at a run, always west across the rolling ground of the plateau. Furious and roaring, Aklak had stopped on three successive ridges to stand up on his hind legs, swiping high in the air with his claws, futilely attempting to reach and strike it from the sky. When it had fled from his last unsuccessful effort, thwarted, he had watched and snarled as it spiraled higher and away. Then, dropping to all fours, he had become aware of the scent of human blood and, following it to where the man lay on the ground, taken out his unsatisfied aggression.

There had been little resistance. No metal stick had barked fire as he charged, and the human did not stand up or run away, only struck at him ineffectively with its paws and made a high piercing sound when he took its chest between his great jaws and shook it hard. Closing his teeth over its head, he had swung it back and forth again and, all sound silenced, it had gone dead limp.

Usually he avoided humans when he caught their smell, retreating before he came in sight of them. Once or twice he had met them by accident and bluff-charged before leaving the area. He still carried an ache in one shoulder where fire from a stick had struck him. But this kill had been so simple that perhaps they had lost their power to hurt and in the future he might not go so far out of his way for them.

He had dragged the man carcass from the open ground of the ridge down into the ravine below it. As he went, he ripped the cloth covering from the body and left it where it fell. Finding a spot that satisfied him, he fed a little, and buried the man by scratching up the ground in a wide circle, breaking small trees, uprooting brush, heaping it over the carcass. Then he lay down upon it and drowsed.

Soon Aklak might be hungry again, but as he dozed a lethargy crept over him with thoughts of the den he had so carefully prepared. During the night he left the pile and crawled into the brush nearby, where he spent the remainder of the dark. He did not fully wake till late the following morning, and when he did, it was to a whitened world. Six inches of snow had fallen, covering everything with a cold, wet layer.

The great bear could still smell his kill, which he dug out and fed upon once more, tearing it apart as he did so, but soon he lost interest. The thought of his den, less than an hour away on another northern slope, was growing ever stronger in his mind. Half-heartedly scratching a few clawfuls of dirt and snow back over the partially consumed kill, he left it and headed east, dismissing it completely as he traveled.

That night the temperature dropped to well below freezing, where it stayed for the next week. More snow fell, until over a foot of it blanketed the plateau and its grizzly remains. In December, a fox dug up one rib where it had been tossed away from the carcass and stripped it of its few scraps of frozen flesh. Through the winter the rest lay as Aklak had left it, silent, still as the snow that covered it.

1

SHE CAME UP OUT OF SLEEP THE WAY A POWERFUL swimmer rises out of deep water . . . slowly, languidly, sensing the light over darkness, reaching for the surface with no anxiety . . . aware of the sensation of smoothness along the strong length of her body . . . anticipating the contrast of air on her eyes . . . but not yet willing to abandon the pleasant, silent suspension. Floating just below the surface, she resisted the impulse to analyze, clutching at wisps of feeling and her dream, unwilling to release it or the precious person in it who was no longer a part of her waking life. She did not dream of him often.

As soon as she recognized her own reluctance, she knew she was awake and was immediately aware of the dream fading as fog evaporates in sunlight.

The telephone rang.

She threw back the covers, sat up, swung her legs over the side of the bed, opened her eyes, and picked up the receiver.

"Yes?"

"Rochelle?"

"Ed."

"Chelle . . . the plane . . . they found the plane."

One image from the dream came back strongly

and she recalled for the first time in days just what his eyes looked like when he smiled. Abruptly, she closed her own, clinging to the image, refusing to breathe, knowing that the next breath she drew would fill her chest and face with the familiar agony. It came anyway—the loss—like a wave.

"Chelle?"

"U-uh." Then she could speak. "Where?"

"The plateau the other side of Susitna."

"I looked there."

"Yeah . . . well, you missed it . . . in some small lake. It was mostly underwater. Couple of hunters stumbled over it."

"And . . . ?" She could not force her lips to form the shape of his name.

"No sign of Norm. Just the plane."

"How soon can you be at Lake Hood?"

"What?"

"Meet me at the plane in an hour."

"Aw . . . Chelly," he entreated her with her childhood name. "Let them—"

Sharply, "No. I want to see."

"There's nothing of—"

"There's the plane . . . whatever was left."

"It's been over six months . . . all winter."

"Six months and thirteen days—a hundred and ninety-five. I'm going. Come if you like."

"All right. All right. But wait till this afternoon. Okay? Let me get the exact location. Do it right."

"One o'clock."

"Yeah. Okay. I'll meet you there, but—"

"Thank you."

At five minutes to one he was waiting when she pulled into the parking space beside the small stor-

age shed near her plane. Sitting on his heels by the
edge of Lake Hood, a leather jacket beside him on
the thin, new grass, he watched through a pair of
expensive reflective sunglasses as she closed and
locked the car door and walked toward him carrying
a blue flight bag. Rising, he flipped away a half-
smoked cigarette and took off the glasses . . . a tall
man with a handsome, narrow face that lacked signs
of humor, and watchful eyes that mirrored the water
colors of the lake. Her Cessna 206 rocked slightly
on its floats as he rested a hand on its tail.

A casual observer might not have immediately
noted the faint family resemblance in the color of
their eyes and shape of the wide brows, for in most
other ways they were dissimilar. Six inches shorter,
her otherwise slim frame was just a touch generous
through breasts, hips, and thighs. Thick cinnamon
hair, cut for convenience and combed back, was
lightly threaded with gray, giving it a frosted appearance, in contrast to her younger brother's dark
brown waves.

She came to a halt, looking up at him. "Thanks,
Ed."

He frowned. "They don't want you flying out
there, Chelle."

"They? Who exactly are *they*? I'm going, Ed.
They have no right to deny me permission in open
airspace. What have *they* done all winter?"

"Easy. *They* are the state troopers, after all, and
they have every legal right. They don't want you
there now. You can go later, if you still want to."

"Bullshit!"

"No. A good idea. Wake up. I'm not sure I want
to be in the air with you in this frame of mind. Let
them do the work, sis. Give it up. You don't really

want to go out there, and neither do I. Come on.''

Abruptly, she swung away, opened the door to the storage shed, retrieved and yanked on a pair of hip waders. Walking out on the left-hand float of the plane, she unlocked the door, angrily tossed in the blue bag, and began a preflight check.

''I do and I will,'' she snapped. ''I told you . . . come if you like . . . but I'm going, with or without you, little brother. And if you don't tell me where they are, I'll search those lakes one by one till I find the right one.'' Continuing her preparation, she took a hand pump and worked to remove any water that might have collected in the compartments of the floats.

''Then let me do the flying,'' he suggested. ''I *can* do that, you know. I'll go if you let me fly.''

The glance she gave him as she shook her head indicated this was not a new issue. ''You know the answer to that.''

''You're too damn picky.''

''Picky? This plane is mine, Ed. I worked hard for it—still do. What happened when I loaned you my car? Two thousand in repairs.''

He kicked at a rock in disgust. ''One minor accident that wasn't my fault . . .''

''A two-thousand-dollar accident is not minor, Ed. You promised you wouldn't drink. Whose fault was the DWI you got?''

''That's not fair. You're not being reasonable. I can fly this plane. I'm licensed.''

''This plane is my living, not a hobby I can afford to lose. No, Ed. No. You can't fly my plane. Forget it.''

''You can be a real . . .'' he started, then turned

sulky. "Whatever. I don't think we should go out there."

He took a step toward her.

"Don't try to stop me, Ed. What can they do, arrest me? You *do* know where it is, right?"

His expression told her he did. He glanced down, then out over the water, avoiding her eyes in obvious discomfort.

"What? What is it?" Stepping back onto the bank, she stood directly in front of him, looking up to search his face intently. "You're not telling me something. What?"

He shifted from one foot to the other and threw back his head to blow a puff of air at the sky. "Whu-u-h. Shit." Giving up, he faced her, irritation drawing two vertical lines between his brows.

"They *could* arrest you . . . and me for bringing you, sis," he told her. "It's not so simple. They didn't find Norm, but there's . . . ah . . . a body in the passenger seat of the plane. Someone was flying with him. A woman."

She caught her breath.

"Chelly . . . I'm sorry. But you can't say I didn't warn you . . . lots of times. They don't know who it is, or aren't saying, but she's been there all winter. They're investigating and they don't want anything disturbed till they get done. Please, Chelle," he almost whined.

She hardly heard. "A woman?" she breathed. "I want to know what woman he would take flying without telling me. Who? There was no one on the charter list."

"Lake Hood Tower? Cessna four five nine six uniform—south shore Spenard—with Information Charlie. Taxi for a west?"

"Cessna four five nine six uniform. Lake Hood Tower. Taxi for a west."

"Nine six uniform. Taxiing for a west."

Mechanically, through stiff lips, Rochelle Lewis initiated the communications procedure that would allow her Cessna 206 into the air from the water of Lake Hood, just north of Anchorage International Airport's runways for domestic and international jets. The shores of the long, narrow lake—the busiest small plane facility in the United States—were crowded with individual spaces for float planes that came and went constantly on two east-west channels of water, divided by an island. Toward the northwest end of the lake, conveniently located around docks, were the planes of numerous private services for flight-seeing, hunting and fishing charters—a marina for aircraft. There, a virtual air force of planes whisked a never-ending supply of Alaskans, tourists, and gear to remote locations unreachable by road, from luxurious lodges to bare survival camps. They might put a local fisherman down on a sandbar or a tiny pond in the midst of the wilderness for a day's or a week's angling, ferry rafters or kayakers to the banks of a wild river, or hikers to mountain slopes.

Beyond the water, on tarmac, hundreds of other small planes on wheels were parked, row after row, which made their arrivals and departures from a nearby strip. Through the summer months wheels and floats were de rigueur, but when cold weather came, freezing the lake and burying runways in snow, pilots were forced to either park their planes for the winter or convert them on to skis.

Rochelle ran quickly through a check of the instrument panel and throttled up to move away from the bank. A mother duck, followed closely by a rag-

ged line of early ducklings, paddled frantically away
from the huge, threatening thing that thundered in
their direction. Instinctively, Chelle swung out far
enough to allow them passage to the shore and left
the fuzzy yellow babies safely bobbing like bathtub
toys in the gentle wake of the slow-moving aircraft.
Ed, silently watched their escape from his seat on
the passenger side of the cockpit, acutely aware of
and irritated by his sister's pain and confusion, and
with his inability to alleviate or talk her out of it.

"Lake Hood Tower? Nine six uniform—ready to
go west. I'll be departing north—Point McKenzie."

"Hood Tower. Nine six uniform. Cleared for
takeoff west."

"Nine six uniform on the slide."

The radio crackled and the rising roar of the engine removed any possibility of conversation, letting
Ed off the hook for the moment. Moving into position midlake, Rochelle powered up and began her
takeoff, increasing speed over the water, till, suddenly, smoothly, the Cessna was airborne and rising
in a long, slow curve to the north.

Falling away below, the whole city of Anchorage
came into view, nestled against the Chugach Range
to the east, filling a triangle between the mountains
and the Y formed by Knik and Turnagain arms that
divided Cook Inlet. The bluffs of Earthquake Park
passed under them, a line of demarcation between
land and the waters of Knik Inlet, northernmost of
the two. The tide was out, exposing miles of shallow, muddy flats that challenged, and at times, all
but denied freighters and tour ships access to the
Port of Anchorage. Even at high tide, it was necessary for some to anchor out and lighter cargo and
passengers to the docks, with their limited space.

Flat-bottomed barges and ships with shallow draft had better luck, but entering both the inlets was further complicated by wicked bore tides with strong currents that surged regularly through the channels.

Ed ventured a look at his sister, but she concentrated steadily on flying out of controlled airspace, attentive to the chatter from the tower and other planes through the headphones that hugged her ears. As her eyes automatically swept the sky for other aircraft, however, her lower lip was caught between her teeth, a hint of tension beyond her usual concentration. A second set of headphones lay atop the instrument panel in front of him, but he left them there, reluctant to start a conversation. They did not agree on the circumstances of Norm's absence. She would talk to him when she was ready; she was tenaciously introspective, always finding it difficult to accept assistance or advice of any kind. The uncertain winter had been hard on her, he knew, for she would not let go, always so stubbornly determined to take care of herself—and, not for the first time, he wondered what had made her seem to assume some kind of blame for her husband's disappearance. He knew he could wait it out, but lately she had shut him out of her life, along with everyone else. He turned back to the window to watch the northern shore of Knik Arm slide under them, and they were back over land again.

Chelle, aware of his scrutiny, kept her attention focused ahead of the plane. She was actually feeling less tense than she had before takeoff. All it took was being airborne and some of the cares and stresses of her other, ground-based life seemed to slide away with the wind over the wings, allowing her to slip into the freedom and peace of the sky.

The world below grew small and insignificant, with
its confusion and clamor. Engine noise faded from
consciousness, became a consistent, white sound,
and there was the smooth, floating sensation of
flight. What she loved more than anything were the
solo flights, times alone in the air. Then she felt
whole and in complete control of her immediate en-
vironment, responsible for and dependent on no one
but herself.

"Hood Tower? Nine six uniform. Point Mc-
Kenzie—frequency change?"

"Roger, nine six uniform. Frequency change approved. Good day."

A line of electrical towers marched in a straight
line across miles of the Susitna Flats below them,
carrying power to Anchorage from Beluga, farther
west along the inlet, generated with natural gas from
the wells in the field that lay there. Crossing over
the line took them out of the airport's controlled area
and into open airspace. Chelle swung the plane west
into a heading that would take them just south of
the gently rounded slopes of Mount Susitna.

The mountain dominated the horizon, clearly visible across Cook Inlet from Anchorage, a silhouette
against the sky. Easily recognized and familiar, it
was a welcome landmark to the people of the largest
city in the state: a somnolent giant reclining pas-
sively, slumbering its way into legend.

According to stories, a race of giants once lived
among the majestic mountains and rivers of what
would become Alaska. They were well favored, but
the fairest of them was Nakatla, a woman as good
as she was beautiful, who was much loved by her
people. She had a tall and handsome lover, Kudan,
who adored her and was never separated from her

until one day an evil tribe brought war across the great mountains to this peaceful race of people.

Kudan, though reluctant to leave Nakatla, was one of several young men chosen as a peace delegation to meet with the warlike invaders. He left her to await his return at their trysting place, a slender pool of water that lay in a valley high on a nearby mountain. As she wept and waited there, she fell into a deep sleep and was not aware when news came that the young men, including Kudan, had been ambushed and slain. When the other women came to tell her, they found her peacefully dreaming of her lover and, filled with pity, begged their gods to let her sleep forever.

There Nakatla still reclined, a giant lady, covered in winter with a blanket of snow spread by the gods, and, in summer, clothed in green and brown shades of vegetation. Her hair seemed to flow down the southern slope, forming a long ridge that was called Ch'chihi Ken by the early Dena'ina people of the area, meaning "ridge where we cry," for in the past they would go there, where they could look down on their land below and mourn their ancestors. The legend was now largely forgotten, and most called the mountain Susitna, but those who appreciated the story called her the Sleeping Lady.

As Rochelle flew over the flatland toward the great mountain, she remembered how often during the last months she had wished she could just go to sleep like Nakatla and escape the pain from the loss of her husband. After the first few frantic, desperate days and weeks, it had seemed all winter as if she was half-asleep. Now she felt shocked awake.

She swallowed hard around a sour lump in her throat and felt her stomach twist in a knot of anxiety.

What would she find at that small lake where the plane had been located? Why was Norm not with the wreckage? Where was he? Impatient, she wanted to be there, to know, to see for herself, yet felt herself also wishing she could turn and run away, fly off into some other place—some other life—where none of this was happening, or had happened.

Glancing across at her brother, Ed, she found him looking at her with a frown, and was suddenly aware that her face was wet with silent, unrealized tears. Roughly, she swiped at her cheeks with one sleeve of the jacket she wore, then clung tightly for a second to the hand he laid wordlessly on her knee before she straightened, swiftly inspected the sky around them for other aircraft, increased her airspeed slightly, and guided her plane over Ch'chihi Ken, the long southern ridge of the Sleeping Lady's hair.

2

ALASKA STATE TROOPER SERGEANT ALEX JENSEN scowled in resigned displeasure as he watched the Cessna 206 circle in the east and set down to taxi across the waters of the long, narrow lake toward the plane in which he had arrived two hours earlier.

"Hell," he said to trooper pilot, Ben Caswell, "she's coming in all right. That's Lewis's wife, Rochelle. Damn it. I thought they told her brother to keep her away from here."

Caswell nodded, thoughtfully, as the floats of the Cessna came to rest against the bank next to those of his smaller Maule M-4. "There's a passenger, so he's probably with her. But I don't remember her as the type to take orders meekly, even from her brother . . . especially since he's younger."

Jensen half growled a reluctant agreement and strode off down the slope, intent on stopping Rochelle Lewis, who was out of her plane, walking on a float, headed for the bank. Caswell remained where he was to watch as the two met and were quickly joined by Ed Landreth. He could hear none of the conversation from where he stood, but it was obvious that Jensen's requests for her to leave were meeting with inflexible resistance. There was much head shaking on both sides.

After a minute or two, Landreth, who had seemed mainly to be listening, threw up his hands, palms out, and took a couple of steps away from his sister and the trooper. Turning, he spotted Caswell and began to climb toward him, leaving Chelle to the argument with Jensen, which, Cas considered, she was perfectly capable of continuing on her own and possibly winning, though Alex could be pretty inflexible himself at times.

As he waited for Landreth to reach him, Ben's thoughts drifted back to the previous fall, when Norman Lewis had first disappeared in his plane. Flying a supposedly routine charter, he had failed to report in at the time required by his flight plan and a search had been initiated between Anchorage and the landing strip at Gulkana, near Glennallen, a community a little less than two hundred miles to the northeast. No sign of his emergency beacon was ever picked up and no trace of his plane found.

Rochelle had joined the Civil Air Patrol search team, flying almost continuously every daylight hour. When a reasonable amount of time had run out and the effort was finally abandoned, she had continued, sometimes with the company of her brother, more often alone. On her own, she had expanded the determined search to anywhere Norm might have gone, rationalizing that, for one of the only times in his life, he might, for some unknown reason, have ignored his own flight plan. CAP pilots flew a well-organized, standard grid pattern, labeling anything outside it the ROW—the Rest of the World. Chelle had flown a lot of the ROW, finding nothing, before

the winter set in and ended the search by burying
the country in snow.

Cas had met her at the crash site of another Cessna
206, the popular, workhorse plane for charter pilots,
where she had gone to be sure it was not Norm
Lewis. He had flown Jensen in to investigate some
evidence of tampering that made the crash appear a
possible homicide. It proved an accident after all and
was not the Lewis plane. Case closed.

He had been impressed with her flying ability,
though she was obviously and understandably obsessed with the search for her husband. Even so, he
had noticed that she was levelheaded, practical,
highly skilled in the care and operation of her plane
and took no unreasonable chance in the air. Convinced that the *pilot error* listed for many airplane
accidents should actually be labeled lazy, sloppy,
and careless, Cas approved of Chelle Lewis as a pilot
and found he could not condemn her tenacious determination to find out what had happened to her
spouse. What a terrible situation not to know if
someone you loved was dead, or alive and hurt
somewhere, needing help. In Alaska it happened all
too often and was frequently unresolved.

Though people periodically lived through crashes
and survived for weeks and, at times, months in the
wilderness, there were thousands of square miles of
it and small planes were notoriously hard to find
from the air, even when you knew almost exactly
where they were. After an especially severe Alaskan
winter, it had been clear to all concerned that Lewis
must have been killed or seriously injured, and that,
injured, he could hardly have come through alive, or
he would somehow have found a way to return to
civilization or signal his location. Pilots had walked

out before, but not in the dead of winter. Now, it seemed their assessment had proved true, but without his body they could not declare him officially dead.

Though they did not know her well, both he and Jensen had come to respect Rochelle as, plainly, a good person doing the best she could in an unfortunate and stressful situation. During the winter they had occasionally checked on her.

Alex's musher friend, Jessie Arnold, had already known her slightly, for during the Iditarod each spring for the last few years Chelle had been part of a group of small planes—the Iditarod air force—that flew assistance for the famous sled dog race. Generous with personal support, Jessie had invited her for a weekend in Knik, and had visited her once or twice in Anchorage during the fall. With the new year, however, Chelle had seemed to close herself off and refused most, then all attempts at contact. Depressed and silent, she discouraged conversation, and finally, all they could reach was her answering machine. "I'm sorry," she had told Jessie once. "I can't. No matter where I am, it's not where I want to be. I'm just so tired of waiting for the snow to be gone so I can get back in the air."

It had been almost two months since the last contact, Caswell thought, watching her shake her head at Alex. Her face was full of the animation and color it had lacked the last time he had seen her. As Landreth scrambled up to stand beside him, he was thinking that it might be good to give her something to work on, to get her moving and focused again.

"He never was worth it, but she just won't give it up," Ed commented with an irritated grimace. "Hello, Cas."

Returning Landreth's greeting with a wordless nod, he wondered if it was the other man's criticism of his sister, or the familiar use of his name, that caused the stiffness he felt in his neck. Either way, Ben was not particularly enthused to encounter Ed again. Besides, he told himself, casting a glance at Landreth's well-polished but inappropriate dress boots, *he hasn't the sense to put on suitable footwear.*

There was something about the younger man that always seemed to put Caswell on his guard, reminding him of his own reaction when a particularly smarmy piranha at a local truck dealership had made the mistake of assuming he would be an easy mark. He had bought his pickup elsewhere. Somehow he couldn't quite buy Landreth either, and made no effort toward conversation as they stood together, looking down the bank while Jensen and Rochelle finished their discussion.

"I *have* to know, Alex," she told him again. "Have a *right*. Don't do this to me."

"I know you'll wish you hadn't, Rochelle," Jensen told her.

"But you said he isn't there. I've seen crashes before . . . helped with a couple of bloody ones."

"That doesn't improve the condition of this one. It's not bloody, it's bad. Real bad. This one's been here all winter . . . in the water and ice. Not an ordinary floater."

"I don't care. Not knowing is worse than anything. I have to see to make it real. You know? Who is it, anyway?"

"We don't know. As soon as the helicopter comes we'll get the remains to the lab and find out what we can. Fingerprints . . . dental records, maybe. Right now there's no way of telling.''

Chelle hesitated and looked out across the water of the lake before facing him again. When she spoke, her lips were stiff and he could see that her own reluctant struggle with what she was suggesting came at a cost to her pride.

''I might know her,'' she said. ''Might notice something you wouldn't.''

She might, at that, Jensen admitted sadly to himself, though there wasn't much chance; he was tired of trying to dissuade her. Without another word he gave in and, waving her up the hill, turned toward Landreth and Caswell standing above them.

''Thank you,'' she said as she brushed past him.

''I hope you feel that way later,'' he replied.

Detective Sergeant Jensen worked homicide out of Detachment G in Palmer, center of the Matanuska Valley farms and dairies. It was a spectacular location, surrounded by the majestic peaks of the Chugach and Talkeetna mountains, forty miles east of Anchorage, a morning's drive from Mount McKinley, and three hours from the fine fishing of the Kenai Peninsula, which he enjoyed as often as possible. He would not have been assigned to this case of a missing pilot and plane, except that, over the years, he had investigated more than one homicide that revolved around small plane crashes in the bush. So, when this plane had been located in a totally unexpected place within his detachment, with bullet holes, a dead woman in the passenger seat, and the pilot missing, he had been assigned the duty.

As he followed Rochelle Lewis up the slope, he was not at all happy about the situation, and still reluctant to have her at the site, much less for her to

see the horror that remained in the plane they had
found, even if it might cure her determination with
shock. He was, however, aware that, as a pilot and
as someone who was familiar with this particular
plane, she might actually make his work easier,
which, in turn, might make the whole thing easier
on her in the long run.

At the top, she paused next to her brother, greeted
Ben Caswell, and turned back to Alex.

"Where?"

He gestured to the west of where they stood and
stepped forward to lead the way. "Be careful to follow me. We want to leave the scene as uncontami-
nated as possible. That's why we didn't pull in right
beside it with the plane. It's just over the rise."

The four walked single file, Caswell bringing up
the rear, over the top and down the other side, where
part of the tail of a plane could be seen above a
screen of brush on the lakeshore. Landreth slipped,
slid, and swore a couple of times, but made it. In a
few minutes they were gathered next to a battered
fuselage, the nose of which was still partly sunk in
mud and water beyond the bank. A winch attached
to an outcropping of rock had been employed to drag
the wreck almost free of the lake, and its weathered
and dirty condition, except for the top of the vertical
tail fin and rudder, very much evidenced its season
underwater. The registration number, however, could
easily be read through the grime. It was definitely
the aircraft in which Lewis had disappeared.

Water still ran slowly from under it, tracing small
channels in the mud on both sides as it made its way
downhill and back into the lake. Both doors were
closed, and though the window glass was partially
opaque with sediment from the water, a human

shape could be seen inside. The broken fuselage smelled wet and dank, and underlying that was a cloying hint of something else that was grossly unpleasant.

"Don't touch anything," Jensen cautioned. "They've scrambled the lab boys out of Anchorage and they'll be here soon to get what they can, but it won't be much."

Chelle nodded, numbly, her eyes wide, but it soon became obvious that her mind was anything but numb. After a minute she moved without speaking, walked slowly around the plane, pausing twice— once to look up the slope to where the tops of three of four narrow spruce were broken off in a direct line with the ruined fuselage, and once when she reached the door on the left side.

Jensen stepped up beside her, pointing.

"Bullet hole," he said.

Without actually touching it, he drew a circle with one finger around a puncture in the metal below the window on the passenger side. The way the metal was creased, angling slightly, gave the impression it had been shot from below.

"Another. There." He pointed to a similar hole in the engine cowling. "This wasn't an accident. Someone shot this plane out of the air."

Rochelle's face was white and she looked sick, staring silently at the two punctures.

Ed nodded, slowly, frowning, but said nothing.

"Looks like he tried to set it down on this puddle, probably the closest possible, and couldn't quite do the job," Caswell commented.

"He tried, all right. And almost *did* make it." She spoke suddenly, in a tone louder than necessary, and swung away to gesture at the broken trees above them. "If it hadn't been for those, he would have. Couldn't see them from the other side of the slope till it was too late and he was right on top. The floats are up there, aren't they, Alex?"

He agreed and she continued her analysis.

"The branches and trunks took them off, slowed the plane down, and tipped it right into the lake."

Caswell nodded. She knew what she was talking about, had read the scene's clues as a pilot would, from her own experience of flying.

"Yeah, and whoever the passenger was, she didn't die as a result of the crash," Jensen said. "That bullet through the door couldn't have been better placed if she'd been a clear, unmoving target. Looks like it got her where it did massive internal damage. She may have been dead before she knew she'd been hit."

He looked speculatively at Chelle, who looked back with eyes in a frozen face, stiff, blinking tears. At the questioning lift of his brows, she took a deep breath, squared her shoulders, and nodded.

"You sure, Chelle? This is going to be pretty ugly."

"Sure."

"Here, then." He dug a small green jar from a jacket pocket, uncapped it, applied a fingerful liberally to his full mustache and into his nostrils, and handed it to her. Mentholatum, with its characteristic, strong smell. She followed suit, and took a handkerchief from one pocket to hold over her mouth and nose. The other two refused, shook their heads and took several steps back, a maneuver that did little good. When Jensen reached and opened the door, a wave of the foul odor of decomposition that had only been a hint before, enveloped them all.

Landreth swung away, coughing and retching. Holding his breath, Cas turned to walk swiftly out of range, having seen everything already, and having no wish to repeat the experience. Chelle turned even paler, gagged and looked sick, but held her ground. When Jensen waved her forward, she joined him to look quickly at the thing in the passenger seat.

Jensen knew that bodies that had been underwater for long periods of time were not pleasant, to say the least, waterlogged and unstable. Those that had been repeatedly frozen and thawed in that water could be hardly recognizable, depending on the length of time. This one was not the best, or the worst, though he was glad it had not been another few days, or a week.

The head was tipped back and to one side against the back of the seat, and what was left of the face was a dark, greenish-purple horror with visible teeth, almost defying identification. In amazing contrast, the hair, an ordinary light brown, had retained its color, though it had darkened with water, and was now drying in the air, even releasing a wisp or two of curl. It was long enough to have been pinned up high on the back of the head in a neat bun, the style probably intended to accommodate a dark western hat that lay on the floor by the woman's feet. The left hand lay in her lap, the right dangled by the door, and both were deeply wrinkled from long immersion but did not exhibit the decomposition evident in the face. Seat belt still fastened, the body was dressed in a pair of black denim pants tucked into laced leather boots, and a black down jacket over a blue sweater. The colors and textures of the fabrics were easily distinguishable, their hues only slightly muted with sediment.

The pilot's seat was empty, one end of an unfastened seat belt lying across it.

Chelle took it in at a glance, but as she started to turn away, her stomach churning, a gleam in the woman's lap caught her eye. Leaning forward a few inches, she pointed and spoke between clenched teeth. "There. What?"

Jensen shut the plane door and, taking her arm, guided her quickly away as she gagged and fought the results of shock and the breath she had taken in order to speak.

"It's a wedding ring. There's also a watch. We noticed them earlier. The ring has an unusual pattern that we may be able to track down. Did you see anything about her you recognize?"

"God . . . no. Nothing."

"You have no idea who she was? Why she was killed?"

There was a hesitation as she swallowed hard.

"No . . . none. Wish I did." She turned her head away, wiping her eyes and trying desperately to breathe enough clean air to clear her airways of the smell, the indescribable taste that clung in her nose and mouth, renewed with every breath. Jensen dug into a pocket and handed her a piece of peppermint candy that she sucked gratefully.

Without another word, she turned and walked up the hill toward the broken trees, slowing as she passed the twisted metal of the wrecked floats, but not stopping until she stood at the top and could look out over the rolling plateau, her back to the lake and the plane it had yielded up.

It was a broad, flat, Ice Age bowl, approximately forty miles from east to west, formed by some mighty glacier centuries earlier between Mount Su-

sitna and the Alaska Range. Filled with small lakes
and streams between swampy muskeg and low rocky
ridges, it would be difficult ground for anyone to
cross on foot. Many of the lakes were mere ponds,
too small to set a plane down or take off. Behind
her, unseen, not far to the west lay the much wider
waters of Beluga Lake, where Norm could have
landed his plane with room for hundreds of others.
Its cloudy beige waters were fed by the melt from
Triumvirate and Capps glaciers, and flowed in a
winding river of the same name over thirty miles to
the coast of Cook Inlet, passing through smaller
Lower Beluga Lake on its way.

Leaving the plane, Norm might also have climbed
this high to avoid the brush that tangled the lakeshore, she thought, focusing on him, trying to block
out the horror she had just witnessed. It was important to assess what he might have done, if they were
to figure out where he had gone, and she needed
something to take her mind off what she had seen
in the plane. Jensen was right—it had been worse
than she expected.

On the slope behind, a rock rolled from under a
boot and he stepped up to join her. After a minute's
silence, she began to tell him what she was thinking,
working it through objectively, out loud.

"He was alive, Alex. It's the only reason he
would leave the plane. He was alive and she was
dead, whoever she is. Otherwise he wouldn't have
left her there. Do you have any ideas?"

He shook his head and frowned. "They were flying low, or the bullets wouldn't have done enough
damage to disable the plane . . . or kill her. An extremely lucky shot. Planes are really hard to shoot
down." He was concentrating on what she could tell

him. She was an intelligent, insightful woman, and her initial observations were valuable. "What do you think about the way he came in? Cas says he hadn't much choice, pretty much just fell out of the sky."

"He's probably right. Not knowing how fast he was going and how far out the engine quit, I can't say for sure. It could have been several miles, or much less, but Norm was no dummy. This kind of terrain would be deadly to have to come down on— chew a plane to pieces. Floats or not, he would have headed for the nearest water of any size. From altitude he could have seen this lake, but from lower down, the ridge would likely have hidden the slope, and the trees between it and the water. They aren't very tall around here, or thick—but they're solid. By the time he committed and cleared it, it'd be too late to make any changes. No other choice."

"Wouldn't he be afraid of being trapped in the plane, or not being able to make it to shore in such cold water?"

"No. Not Norm. He knew better. Lots of people *are* afraid to ditch. Think they'll drown, or just don't want to risk losing the plane, but the odds of getting hurt in a water landing are much less than that kind of stuff." She waved a hand at the uneven ground that extended as far as they could see. "Most planes won't just sink like a stone. There's a lot of air—in the floats, the fuel tanks, and wings—to keep the plane afloat for a few minutes, long enough for you to get out, even if you're partly underwater. And, through the summer, these small lakes warm . . . a little.

"But he must have made it, though he *was* probably underwater when the plane stopped. So . . . *if* he wasn't badly hurt . . . and . . . *if* he was able to get the survival gear?''

Chelle swung around to look back down the hill, scanning the surrounding trees, brush, and an area of flat ground to the left of the plane.

"Have you looked for what'd be left of a fire? He'd have been wet. Getting dry would've been a priority, assuming he didn't need a lot of first aid. I'll bet there was at least a bump on the head. Nosing into that lake was no joyride. Even with the belts, he'd have been thrown around some.'' She frowned at the thought and the strain made itself evident in the pitch of her voice.

"We looked everywhere within a couple of hundred feet. No sign of anything burned. A fire would have left some evidence that wouldn't disappear over the winter. What else?''

"The cardinal rule is *stay with the plane*. Whoever looks, will look for the plane . . . and they *will* look.''

"But there wouldn't have been a plane to see, would there? And no emergency beacon, right? He'd know that . . . and that his flight plan said he was supposed to be the hell and gone the other side of Anchorage.''

"He had a transmitter, but ELTs don't work underwater. So, if I were Norm, and able, I'd be thinking about getting myself out of here. That'd mean walking . . . hiking . . . a long way.''

"Twenty, thirty miles to the inlet.'' Alex pulled a map from his coat pocket and began to unfold it.

"Yes, and as soon as possible, while he still had energy, because there wouldn't be much, or any food for a long, strenuous hike . . . just what was with the survival gear. Can't be more than thirty miles, and it's the closest place to go where there'd be people. Almost all downhill.'' With a finger, she pointed out a route on the map that led west down a stream into Lower Beluga Lake, then followed the Beluga River to Cook Inlet. "If he could reach the gas field, there's a gravel road that goes between its buildings and Tyonek to the west. It's where I'd head.''

When she raised her attention from the map, Jensen was looking at her with a frown of concern. "Rochelle . . .'' he began.

Uncontrollable tears welled up and spilled down her cheeks.

"Yes, damn it,'' she said, abruptly smearing them off on a sleeve. "He didn't make it. I *know*.''

But that doesn't mean I don't need to know where he is, she thought. If he's still in Alaska, he's got to be somewhere between here and there. I know it, and I'll walk every damn foot of it till I find him, or am sure he's not there. I've got all summer to do it, and I certainly don't need your help or permission.

Jensen went on. "There're other things about this, Chelle. Who shot the plane, and . . . her. Who is she? Why were they shot? Why is the plane here when Norm filed a flight plan that said he was headed for the Gulkana field at Glennallen? We've got some answers to find. They may help find him. We'll do the best we can and keep you posted.''

"I know. I hope you will. You should check to see if his survival gear *is* still in the plane. If he tried to walk out, it won't be there, unless he couldn't get to it after the crash. But it was in pretty shallow— if a hiker could find it. Shouldn't have been much of a problem to dive for it. And . . .''

"Yes,'' Alex told her, simply. "I will . . . whatever. And if you think of anything else, let me know. But . . . let's go down. Here comes the technical crew.''

Rochelle looked up and realized she had been half-aware of the pounding of helicopter rotors for the last few minutes. It hovered, now, over her head, beginning a slow descent to the only flat space large enough to hold it. The space Norm would have picked for a fire—the fire Jensen said he hadn't built.

She was suddenly exhausted . . . physically and emotionally. It was time to head back to Anchorage and leave the troopers to do the job she knew they would do well. But she would be back. Soon. Somewhere, Norm could still be out there, and, if he was, she *would* find him . . . herself.

3

CHELLE USED TWO KEYS TO OPEN THE FRONT DOOR of the house where she lived, off Jewel Lake Road, ten minutes from Lake Hood. One key for the dead bolt, one for the less secure lock in the doorknob.

From this area most of Anchorage spread out to the east and north, between the mountains and the sea, a city of two hundred and fifty thousand, more than half the population of the state. Jewel Lake Road was a busy north-south street that ran from International Airport Road to intersect with Diamond, a major traffic artery for the heavily residential southwest section of town. That the house was convenient to the airport had been an important factor to her husband, Norm, when he bought it. The streets around it bore a tangled brier patch of names: Loganberry, Raspberry, Strawberry, Huckleberry, and Elderberry, among others.

Chelle had moved in with him the year before, shortly before they married, almost reluctantly giving up the midtown apartment she had clung to with a superstition that annoyed him and at which she had been somewhat self-critically amused, but stubbornly refused to shrug off. Unreasonably, she had felt that prematurely moving her few pieces of furniture, pride of books, and small but good collection of Alaskan artwork—personal items that defined her—might jinx the relationship, a second marriage for her.

Norm had never completely recognized what Chelle felt about moving out of her place—if it was not done in the right way and time she might have to move back—and worse, that, when and if it happened, her apartment, the space that had become part of her image of herself, would be gone, leaving her no choice, no option, forced to start over, to search out a new and unfamiliar place to live. She was cautious, wary of starting over, but Norm had responded with irritation, as if she wanted to have her cake and eat it too, to live with him and to live alone.

Her uneasy irresolution had frustrated him for several other reasons he had not been hesitant to express. He owned the house and had viewed the rent she paid as wasted money that could have gone into the small but growing charter flying business they had started together. There was plenty of room for them both in the house, while her apartment was too small and had no storage space for their expanding collection of gear and equipment. The house was closer to Lake Hood and their two planes, with only one major traffic artery to cross, while the apartment was halfway across town. His last significant argument had been that most of their time had been spent there anyway. "You practically live here already, Chelle."

But she had adamantly refused to move in until they had set a date for the wedding. This was not with any intent to force him to formalize their living arrangement. In fact the idea of marriage made her even more uneasy. In a reversal of traditional roles, it had been he who encouraged the idea, and she who hesitated. It was because she knew that, reasonable or not, keeping the apartment was her security, her *ace in the hole*—the stakes in her intangible blind bargain with life in marrying Norm—trying again.

Now, each time she unlocked the door, as she did now, she was reminded with a fresh pang of emptiness that it was a wager she had lost. She had not been forced to find a new and separate place for herself, but she was once again—as she had feared and anticipated—alone. One way or another, despite his promises and rationales to the contrary, he was gone—*had* left her to ache with missing him, to be exhausted with her own anger at him and herself, her sense of betrayal, and the pain of his absence.

They had found the plane in which he disappeared eight months earlier, but he was not in it, and she had no sense of closure. All she could be sure of was that whatever had happened to Norm, wherever he was, it was not where he was supposed to be. He was still missing.

MIA, she thought, as the second lock clicked open and she reached to turn the knob. *Missing in action? . . . in air? . . . in affection?* Who was the woman— that thing—in the plane? Though Ed had hinted at it, she had refused to consider an affair . . . another woman. Had not believed it. She had always thought—feared—that she would know if *that* ever happened to her again. Considering her brother as the source, she had ignored his suggestions, knowing that from the time they met, he and Norm had taken an unreasonable dislike to each other, Ed behaving like a jealous child, Norm disgusted and wasting little sympathy on Ed's egotistical attitude and tendency to switch employment. *He's a goddamn grasshopper, jumping from job to job, trying to find some way to get paid for looking pretty. Thinks the world owes him everything.* Still, she couldn't easily accept the woman in the plane as proof of the infidelity Ed suggested of Norm.

She was also angry with her brother for his condescending attitude on their way back to Anchorage in her plane. Learning that she was considering a ground search for Norm, he had immediately ridiculed and criticized her plan.

"It's a stupid idea, Chelle. You haven't a prayer of finding him anyway—especially if he's as long gone as I bet he is. He probably panicked when he knew that woman—whoever she is—was shot—maybe left her in the plane to die and took off on his own. He's not worth looking for—probably not even there. You never should have married him. I warned you. He was a selfish bastard."

"That's not fair," she had retorted. "You don't know—"

"All he tried to do was turn you against me—the only real family you have. He couldn't stand that you should care about anyone but him. Can't you see that?"

"No," she had answered heatedly, "I can't. He never had anything against you that you didn't give him a reason for. I've got to find out what happened, Ed. Got to know."

"Well, it's a really dumb idea. And if you're going, you're going without me. I won't help this time. Not a chance."

"Don't remember asking you," she countered. Why should it be any different this time, she thought. You've always been more problem than help.

Poor Ed. Through her anger, she had still found pity for him, as usual. She had always felt that most of her only sibling's nature wasn't really his fault. Younger than she by eight years, Ed had the same last name that had been hers until she married, though they had different fathers. Chelle's had abandoned his unwanted family when she was born, and she had always felt responsible for the burden of her mother's silent, bitter resentment of his absence.

Working to support herself and her child, her mother had had little social life, and Ed had been the accidental result of a temporary relationship. Guiltily trying to make up for his illegitimacy, she had pampered and spoiled him, requiring Chelle to take care of him much of the time. He was given the best of everything possible because he was the youngest and a boy. "You'll get married. He has to be able to make a living." Chelle had chafed at the attitude, furious with the injustice, but kept most of it to herself and mothering Ed had become a habit. When her mother died of pneumonia, Chelle was twenty and working as a receptionist for a charter service, learning to fly. Ed was twelve and a problem that did not solve itself.

Arrogant, egotistical, and selfish, he expected her to take care of him, and continued to do so long past the age when he should have been caring for himself. He had trouble keeping jobs because of his inflated opinion of himself and a decided lack of patience with other people. He had dropped out of business college after one semester, not willing to do the work, or take a student loan, when Chelle couldn't afford to pay his way. Tall and good-looking, he insisted on expensive clothes and spent money extravagantly. Often he came to her for *enough to tide him over*, money he never paid back.

Norm had absolutely refused to bail him out and discouraged Chelle from doing so. Resenting this, Ed had angrily tried to talk her out of the marriage, insinuating that Norm wasn't true to her, or good enough, and was trying to break up her relationship with her only brother. From years of practice, he knew just how to push all the right emotional buttons and make her feel guilty, cheap, and mean when she resisted. Sadly, Chelle knew that they had never felt the same about each other since, and never would, whether or not she found Norm.

She almost wished it were the other way around and Ed was the one she needed to find. Norm, she knew, would have been doing everything he could to help, even if he thought her unreasonable and disliked Ed. How she missed his presence and support.

Damn. Damn him for forcing her into this situation.

Impatiently, she turned the knob, thrust open the door, stepped into the entry hall and halted abruptly, totally still, rigid with shock.

As the door closed behind her, she had taken a deep breath against her anger. That breath had slammed, tenuous and fragile, something hauntingly familiar into her unguarded awareness. There is nothing so poignantly powerful as the sense of smell, nothing to break the heart so completely, without warning or defense. From somewhere in the house, the fragrance of Norm's pipe tobacco lingered . . . had filled her consciousness as distinctly as if he had just left the room with it clenched between his teeth, trailing a wake of smoke.

It was not possible. It hit her with such emotional

force that she dropped the duffel she was carrying and froze in shock where she stood. A cramp of real physical pain in the pit of her stomach all but doubled her over. But it was nothing compared to the wave of psychological agony that arrived immediately after it. Ignoring both, she straightened and, against all reason, went swiftly through every room in the house, searching each, opening doors, even stepping out onto the back porch to sweep the wide expanse of yard with her eyes. White-faced and trembling, wet with sweat, she did not bother to reason, just looked, and found . . . nothing. The smell of that special blend of tobacco did not recur. It was gone as completely as if it had never been, as if she had imagined it, as, indeed, she decided, she must have.

There was no particular sense of anyone having been inside the house, only the scent—initiating a grief as exquisitely fine and sharp as the edge of a well-honed knife. A trick of the senses?

The last thing she opened was a closet full of his clothes—shirts, pants, jackets—and buried her face in a leather jacket that she knew still held a faint and fading suggestion of the smell of him, including the rich tobacco fragrance. It was painfully familiar because she had slept with it every night for weeks after he disappeared . . . still did periodically . . . hugging it to herself in the dark, staining its suede finish with her tears. Now she reasoned that the scent somehow must have drifted through the air of the house, drawn perhaps by the motion of a door closing as she went out, and hung in wait for her to walk, unwarned, unwary, into its agonizing trap.

Again, she breathed the odor of his body from the jacket and was, expectedly and at once, overcome by it and the reality of the day's discoveries. Dragging it from its hanger, she moved like an automaton to the bed she had left unmade that morning and curled up with it clutched against her face and breasts, pulled a down comforter over her whole self, and lay racked by heavy, dry, gasping sobs too deep for tears. All her accommodations and defenses, so carefully, painstakingly constructed during the eternal winter without him, were swept away. The hoarse sounds that tore from her throat were those of sustained loss, and also unintelligible resentment that she was vulnerable once more and it was all to go through again . . . the confusion, the grief . . . and the unendurable guilt of his leaving her.

4

THE COCKPIT LOUNGE WAS NOT THE CLOSEST BAR
to the airport or the busy waters of Lake Hood's
charter services, nor was it a tavern that attracted
tourists or business people in transit from regular
passenger flights. On Spenard Road not far from the
west end of the lake, a square box of a building that
exhibited numerous coats of paint—the last of them
brown—on its peeling, forty-year-old concrete block
walls, it sat behind a wide parking lot, twenty yards
from the street. The unpaved lot, though sporadically
graded and graveled, was full of a series of expanding chuck holes half-buried with mud or dust, depending on the season. It was the kind of place that
did not attract strangers.

For the most part, its regulars were airplane people—mechanics, hunting and fishing guides, the pilots of private and charter planes based around the
lake, and the baggage handlers and others who
worked behind the scenes to keep scheduled flights
in the air. The rest of those on a first-name basis
with one another were locals who lived within a few
blocks. There were also one or two of questionable
reputation who had frequented this particular water-
ing hole, since Spenard was a narrow, winding road,

crowded with massage parlors and notorious for its vice. They were accepted as part of the Cockpit's extended family, their past or continuing occupations never mentioned.

At almost seven-thirty in the evening, an originally green pickup truck, heavily dented and scarred, one front fender half-rusted off, bucked and rattled its way across the lot to pull into an empty space next to the building. The other fender had at some point been replaced with a red one which offered in structural integrity what it lacked in aesthetics. The windshield was cracked across just below a driver's field of vision, a condition common in a country of extreme temperature fluctuations that expand, contract, and eventually split glass that has been chipped by a flying pebble.

A short, husky man in a pair of greasy mechanic's coveralls, a bandanna knotted around his forehead to hold dark, stringy hair away from his eyes, climbed out, slammed the door to make it stay shut, and hurried into the bar. Just inside the door, he hesitated to let his sight adjust to the dim level of light that always seemed to be some uncertain hour of the night, due to the complete lack of windows. Searching the room, he spotted the man he wanted. Resting on his forearms, baseball cap pushed back on his otherwise bald head, a Budweiser bottle in front of him, he sat alone on the far side of the large horseshoe-shaped bar, casually aware of those around him, making eye contact with few.

The rest of the space was taken up with a mismatched collection of tables and chairs, a pool table, and a dartboard that hung on the back wall, possible peril for anyone injudicious enough to head for the rest rooms without first assessing the skill of whoever was pitching darts at it. Perhaps twenty people—a number that would swell to over fifty later in the evening—mostly men, sat at the bar or tables, several watching an ongoing pool game, or waiting to play the winner. A sports announcer, enthusiastically mouthing something no one cared about, filled the screen of a television set with the sound turned off. The murmur of conversation was augmented by a jukebox pulsing last year's country and western hits.

The man in coveralls walked around the bar, slowing once to grin and punch the shoulder of a friend who turned to greet him with an insult, nodding confirmation to the bartender's question of "the usual?" and slid onto an empty stool next to the man with the cap.

"Tom."

"Darryl."

Not until the bartender had drawn his draft and left change from the twenty he laid out, did he turn his shoulders toward the man he had come to see and speak intently and privately, in a low voice.

"They found Ace's plane this morning."

A frown. "Shit. Who?"

"Couple of guys from Kenai out for black bear. Water's still low enough in the lake to expose the tail section."

"Law go out?"

"Yeah. That trooper with the Maule and another guy. Had it hauled into town with a chopper late this afternoon."

A short silence ensued as the bartender moved to work at a sink near them and they waited for him to move away. Then, "Hear anything else?"

"There was a body in it."

"The bitch."

"Yeah."

"Then they didn't . . ."

"Guess not. Listen, you think maybe we should—"

"No." Tom interrupted. "We stay the hell away from it. Let it go on looking like an accident. Nothing to say it wasn't."

"They said the plane was shot down."

"That doesn't make sense."

"Right. But that's the rumor. Maybe we *should*—"

"I said no. Let it ride."

"Okay. Fuck, it was just a thought."

"A shitty one. I'll do a flyover day after tomorrow, when we run that guy from Dallas out to the camp. Just to check."

"Jesus, Tom. You still gonna take that guy out there?"

A savage look from under the baseball cap. "Shut up, stupid. Keep your voice down."

"Sorry. Just—"

"Just nothing. Haven't got the brains God gave a goose. You want to join Dale?"

"I said sorry."

"Then listen up. We sit tight. Already filed for that hunt. Got all the gear stashed at the lower lake site. Switching now would look funny. See?"

"Oh . . . yeah. Well, I just thought—"

"Just let me do the thinking. You *hear*. Keep your trap shut."

He shook his head in disgust and they sat in silence for a minute. Darryl drank half his draft and lit a cigarette, looking chastened.

"Anything else useful?"

"Ahh . . . Landreth went out there with his sister this afternoon. Came back a couple of hours later."

"Shit. She's nothing but trouble, that one. You talk to him?"

"Nope. Thought he might come in here."

"Hope he does. I wanna have a word. Going back to work?"

"Yeah. Got an engine to tune up for George before morning."

"Keep your ears open."

"Sure thing."

Ed Landreth showed up at nine o'clock with a red-haired woman wearing eye makeup to match a green dress that clung to her the way she clung to his arm. Perching on a tall stool at the bar, she tossed her hair, arched her back to thrust out an impressive chest, and ordered a strawberry daiquiri. Landreth sat beside her and it was clear from the wadded up handful of bills and change he pulled from a pocket to drop on the bar that the Cockpit wasn't their first stop of the night, and he didn't intend it to be the last.

When their drinks were almost empty, the man in the cap bought them another and, as Landreth looked across to nod his thanks, beckoned him over with a jerk of his chin. Landreth left his lady friend reluctantly, with a warning glance that told those sitting closest to her that he considered them a flock of vultures.

"Hey, Tom. How's it going?"

The two men moved to a table far enough away to avoid being overheard.

"Hear they found your brother-in-law's plane."

"Yeah. Out the other side of Susitna. Some woman in the cockpit who'd been there all winter.

Fuckin' sick.'' An expression of extreme distaste crossed his face.

"You go out?"

"Yeah. My sister's obsessed with finding out what happened to that bastard she married. Didn't help that he wasn't in the pilot's seat.''

"Any idea what happened to him?''

"Naw. Must have got out—took off would be my guess.''

Tom frowned, watching Ed's face closely as he considered.

"You know we got things going on out there.''

"How would I know?''

The eyes under the bill of the cap turned cold as he stared at Landreth for a few silent moments. "The law have any more plans, or are they through digging around?''

"Hell. They don't tell me anything. They were still at it when we came back. All I know is that my fuckin' sister is convinced that since he wasn't in the plane, he may have tried to walk out of there. Says she's gonna go to look for him.''

To make the conversation appear casual to anyone watching, the man in the cap had been listening from a relaxed position in his chair. Now he sat up sharply, inclined himself toward Ed Landreth, and made his voice as hard as his look. "Not a *smart* idea, Landreth. Make sure she doesn't try it. Not now.''

"Yeah . . . *right*. And she listens to *me*?''

"I suggest you *make* her listen. The next few days won't be a good time for her to be wandering around the Beluga Lakes area. I got this deal going with a lot riding on it. Keep her out of there. You hear me? I wouldn't like to have her get hurt.''

The implied threat filled the silence that hung in the air between them. Landreth scowled and shook his head, rubbing his hands together nervously. "I don't know if I *can* stop her, Tom. *Really*. What can I do?"

A pause, while the man in the cap stared at him with narrowed eyes. Disgust and resignation were evident in his expression and the sarcasm in his voice when he answered. "Baby brother, huh? Jesus H. Christ, Landreth. Grow up. You're pitiful."

Another pause for thought.

"All right. If you can't stop her, you *can* let me know if she decides to take off. And I want to hear the minute she goes. Got it?"

"Yeah. Yeah, Tom. I can do *that*. Right."

"Screw it up, you'll wish you hadn't. Got *that*?"

"Yeah. No problem."

"Don't forget you owe me, Ed. Big time, you owe me."

"I know. I won't."

Without another word, the man in the cap went back to his barstool, leaving Landreth with a concerned expression that deepened when he returned to find his lady friend in an animated conversation with the man next to her.

Collecting his bills, he left the change—two quarters—on the bar, earning a disgusted glance from the bartender. "Come on. We're getting out of here."

"Hey, honey," she objected, "we just sat down."

Grabbing her arm, Landreth pulled her from the stool to her feet, knocking over what was left of her drink in the process.

"Tough. We'll go to the Trophy. This place is dead."

"All right. All right. Don't get rough. I'm coming."

With something unpleasantly resembling a smile, the man in the cap watched them cross the room, stopping once to speak to a man holding a pool cue, before sliding his empty glass toward the bartender for a refill.

5

AFTER SIX O'CLOCK THAT EVENING, AN HOUR'S drive northeast of Anchorage, Jensen had swung off Knik Road and negotiated Jessie Arnold's long drive—full at the moment of potholes and the melt of breakup. Rocking and rolling over two hundred feet of uneven track to the open space in front of her cabin, he pulled his mud-splashed truck to a halt beside her blue pickup. A homemade dog box carrier filled the pickup's bed with transport for twenty sled dogs in neat, straw-lined compartments in two layers, a portable doggie motel. From a door at the rear, a narrow space between the two sections of condo-kennel provided storage for harness and other equipment. A light sled for sprint racing was secured to the top.

The sturdy two-room log cabin he had parked in front of had been planned by Jessie and built with help from friends a couple of years before she and Alex had met. Already it felt like home to Jensen, who had moved in with her less than six months before. Now he stepped out of the cab and stood for a minute, assessing his own feelings at arriving: pleasure and relief combined, with a bit of reluctance

thrown in at knowing he would have to tell her about
the day's activities.

The relief resulted from being temporarily away
from his job. He liked his work, but time to move
away from it and relax gave him a better perspective
on whatever case was currently occupying his mind.
These days he was finding it equally important to
spend time with Jessie, even sharing parts of his
cases with her.

But his pleasure in coming home wasn't all due
to their relationship. The cabin itself was satisfying
to him, secure and comfortable. Its walls were
slowly weathering from the naked yellow-white of
stripped logs to a pleasant grayish-tan which soft-
ened its appearance and gave it a natural look against
the white trunks of a small grove of birch—branches
still bare of leaves—and the few dark spruce scattered among them. It was a good place to live, four
miles from the nearest neighbor, though the cabin
was a little small for the two of them—especially
with the sled dogs and puppies Jessie rotated in and
out on a regular basis. Another room or two would
have been nice, but, for now, it suited them well
enough, with the assistance of a sizable shed behind
it that was half nursery for puppies, half storage for
their excess belongings and her mushing equipment.

Alex pulled a briar pipe from the pocket of his
wool shirt, packed it, and held a kitchen match over
the bowl till the tobacco glowed and a fragrant cloud
of smoke filled the air around his head.

Tank, the lead dog for Jessie's distance-racing
team stood as close to the truck as the cable that
tethered him to his kennel would allow. Several of
the forty-some other dogs in the lot yelped a welcome from their individual kennels, but Tank stood

waiting in silent dignity for this man to acknowledge his attention. Closing the truck door, a file of papers in one hand, Alex knelt beside the husky, rubbed his ears and murmured affectionate appreciation for the worth of such a handsome, intelligent canine, which earned him a sloppy lick that wet half his full mustache and the lobe of one ear.

Chuckling at Tank's enthusiasm and wiping his face, he was rising to his feet when the door flew open and Jessie stepped out to stand at the top of the steps, smiling down, drying her hands on a dish towel. An appetizing yeasty scent swept from inside and floated out into the still air.

"Hi, trooper. Short-legged member of the welcoming committee got you first, I see."

"Hope you don't have similar greetings in mind," he said, going up to sweep her into a hug. "If you do, aim for the left side. The right's already clean, thanks."

"Wash your own face," she told him, then warmly returned the kiss he gave her. "Hey, I missed you. Hungry? There's a drunk pot roast just about ready."

Jessie's drunk roasts, simmered for hours in Killian's Red Lager and carefully selected herbs, came close to eliciting genuflection from Alex. Shutting the door behind him, he took off his coat and boots, crossed the room, and stood wiggling his toes in front of a potbellied stove. A cast-iron kettle with a cover the shape of a dragon sat atop it, puffing humidifying steam from its nostrils into the room.

He glanced around the cabin, with satisfaction as always. It was full of warm colors and furniture chosen more for comfort than appearance. The log walls were relieved with a few pictures and a bulletin board that hung above a large desk in one corner. Like the desk, it was cluttered with papers that related to Jessie's racing and kennel business. Near the door, parkas, scarves, mittens, and other assorted cold-weather clothing hung on hooks. Under them, boots and mukluks rested on rubber mats to protect the wood floor. Here and there among the coats hung bits of harness and line for the sleds and dogs she drove.

Besides the heating stove, a deep sofa and a couple of easy chairs, worn with much use, a reclaimed dining table and brightly painted, mismatched chairs filled most of the space unoccupied by the shelves, cupboards, refrigerator, sink, and cookstove of the kitchen corner. Through an open door to the next room he could see one end of the large brass bed covered with a colorful patchwork quilt. Beyond his line of sight was a wall completely covered with shelves of books and his collection of mustache mugs. Another wall was lined with pegs, hooks, and shelves for hanging and holding clothes.

Glad to be home, he closed his eyes and appreciatively breathed in deeply the scent of the roast.

"The smells in here are good enough to eat, and I'm starved. Missed lunch when we had to fly out to Beluga Lakes this morning." Thoughtfully frowning, he contemplated the shape of his toes in the wool socks.

Jessie caught his expression and stopped halfway to the kitchen corner of the cabin. "What?"

He looked up to meet her question and shook his head. "Bad day," he told her. "Found Norm Lewis's plane the other side of Mount Susitna. Spent the day getting in and out with Caswell and the lab crew."

Her look changed to sympathy and she paused before asking, "Rochelle? Ah-h-h . . . I'll have to call her. Well, at least she knows now."

" 'Fraid not. Norm wasn't in it. A woman's body with a bullet wound . . . a passenger. But no sign of Lewis."

"A bullet wound?"

"And another that someone with very good aim put into the engine. No question the plane was shot down."

"Good Lord, Alex. Who'd want to kill Norm Lewis?"

"No idea. Don't know that he was hit, just the woman. There was no sign of blood in the plane, but it would have washed away before freeze-up last fall."

"Who was she?"

"Don't know that either. The autopsy may help. Rochelle said she didn't recognize her."

"She was *there*?"

Jensen shrugged. "You know how she is. Couldn't very well stop her from flying in with Landreth after he told her. She insisted on seeing it all."

"Including a body that's been out all winter? Yech!"

"Yeah."

"And?"

"And she didn't make an identification." He sighed and stuck the pipe that had died during the conversation back in his pocket. With the long fingers of one hand he rubbed the back of his neck and stretched to relieve the tension he still carried there. Besides the stress of an investigation, folding his long-legged form into Caswell's smallish plane was always anything but relaxing for the tall trooper. As usual, after flying with Cas, his spine felt permanently curved.

Now he recalled Rochelle's slight hesitation before she claimed not to know the woman in the plane. It bothered him again, as it had bothered him at the time. Had she merely been repulsed by what she had seen, or was it something else? He realized he was still holding the file he had carried into the house and tossed it into a rocking chair that stood near the stove.

Jessie came across to stand behind him, reached up and took over the massage of his neck and shoulders. "Oh, Alex. What a rotten day. For both of you."

"Well, Chelle seemed okay, considering. Made some pretty good suggestions, actually. If he'd been in the plane, I'd never have let her see it. She didn't say so, but I wouldn't be surprised if she intends to go back and hike from the site on down to the gas field by the inlet. Says that's where he would have gone . . . if he was able. She had that kind of look in her eyes."

"And you're going to let her?"

"Let her?" Jensen wheeled to face her. "Let her? Just what do you suggest I do to *stop* her? It's a free country and you know Rochelle as well . . . probably better than I do. I can't tie her up or arrest her, you know. I don't like it either, but. . . ."

As he vented his concern and frustration, Jessie wrapped her arms around his waist and leaned her forehead against the chest of his wool shirt. He sputtered into silence and held her close.

"Hey, I'm sorry, Alex. That wasn't a very smart question. I'm just worried, that's all. How much more can she take?"

"Well, get in line, Jess," he half laughed, without humor. "Rochelle Lewis is almost as stubborn as you are, and a pretty tough lady, too. But I'm not sure of her balance right now, after brooding over it all winter. It makes me wonder." Holding her at arm's length, he yawned. "What do you say we get some of that pot roast before I weaken and succumb to starvation. Feed me, woman!"

Spinning her around to face the cookstove, he held her shoulders and marched her, laughing, across the room toward the origin of the tantalizing smell of the drunk roast.

"Like I said about the greeting . . ."

"Yeah, I know. Feed myself."

Dinner over, they sat, companionably sipping at large mugs of coffee, at opposite ends of the enormous, overstuffed couch Jessie had once rescued from a garage sale. Layered with quilts, afghans, and fluffy pillows in a variety of sizes, it was wide enough for them both and expansive enough for Alex's long legs, a favorite place to relax, read, or talk.

After a few minutes of quiet, while they listened to the fire crackle and the soothing sounds of KLEF's FM classical music in the background, Jessie wrinkled her nose and brow in an unspoken concern that prompted Alex to give her a questioning look.

"Before dinner you said, 'It makes me wonder,' in relation to Chelle being at the plane today. What'd you mean?"

Thoughtfully, he stared at the red glow of the stove and drew on his pipe until he had it going well.

Jessie smiled. "You're doing it again."

"What?"

"That smoke screen thing. I remember you doing it when I first met you, during the Iditarod. When you wanted to think something out before committing yourself, or didn't really want to answer, you put out a smoke screen I could've cut with a knife."

He had to laugh, because she was right. Admitting it with a nod, he recalled their first conversation at the top of Rainy Pass, during that most famous of sled dog races. Looking at her now, familiar and very dear to him, he could also remember just how appealing she had been in the dark of that cold March night, with firelight reflections dancing in her eyes, hair tousled around her face.

Three mushers had died and the continuation of the race from Anchorage to Nome had been at stake. But Jessie had set herself in his path, a strong, self-assured, independent woman, intent on doing well in a sport at which she excelled, but also in helping to identify a killer if she could.

He had fallen for her immediately and completely, and it seemed, the response was mutual, for, one way or another, they had been together ever since. While she healed from a gunshot wound in the shoulder, he had helped care for her kennel of close to forty dogs, a not unwelcome chore in that it let them get to know each other.

"Well?"

"Well, what?" She was even more attractive and fascinating to him now, he thought, appreciating the openness of her expression.

"What don't you want to talk about?"

"Oh. That," he said, his attention returning to Rochelle and the afternoon's investigation. "Well. There was something about the way she reacted to the woman in the plane. It could have been just that the body's condition was worse than she expected, but it played off an idea I haven't quite been able to get rid of from the first.''

"Since Lewis disappeared, you mean?''

"Yeah. I've had this idea that it might not have been an accident. That he could have just meant us to think it was—or, at least, not something he had control of.''

"You mean he could have crashed the plane on purpose and walked away from it, going somewhere else? Meant to disappear?''

"Sort of, except, without the plane, I kept wondering if he might have flown out—maybe to the lower forty-eight. Finding it complicates things. Who's the woman? If he took off on purpose, did he have something to do with her death? Where the hell is he? Could somebody else have picked him up?''

"You don't really think he's dead,'' Jessie stated.

Jensen once again stopped to think before he answered, and the screen of smoke thickened. "I . . . don't know,'' he said carefully. "I haven't gone into it the way I would if I really thought he'd skipped out. Just wondered now and then. Haven't looked very hard for a motive. It's been a kind of nagging, back-of-the-mind sort of thing that floated in and out once in a while. Without the plane it was possible. With the plane, but without his body, it makes other alternatives possible.''

They looked at each other; he waiting for her reaction, she thinking hard. He noted the series of expressions—confusion, concern, assessment—that flitted across her face as she came to some conclusions, generated some questions.

Then, when she was ready, "You think Chelle knows something?"

He pursed his lips. "That's what I was wondering about her reaction today. Actually . . . well . . . no, I guess I don't really think so. I think she feels guilty about his disappearance, and I don't understand quite why. But I think she's sincere and really torn up over the whole thing. Either that, or she's a great actress. But I think something's bothering her that she's not saying."

Jessie got up to refill their coffee cups and didn't say anything until she had settled back in her place on the huge couch.

"I think that's pretty natural, don't you? Especially when there's no explanation for it? We all get the guilties now and then. Maybe, when . . . if . . . she finds that he's really dead, it'll ease that for her. But she's always going to wonder if it could have been her fault somehow. You know, the if-I-had-only stuff?" She paused, then went on in a gentler voice. "You still do it yourself . . . sometimes. Over Sally."

He sighed in discouragement. "Sorry. I . . ."

"It's okay, Alex. Just an observation. Really. I don't want you to worry about or hide what you feel. Just make sure you know what it is—not your fault—and keep it straight. I think you do."

He nodded, remembering the fiancée who had died years before he and Jessie met. It had taken him a long time to know that though he could get over it, along with a certain amount of unreasonable guilt, he wouldn't forget . . . didn't want to.

"You know?" Jessie went back to the subject of Chelle Lewis. "I wonder if she isn't really afraid Norm *is* alive. That he may have left her because of

something she did . . . or didn't do. That he may not
have loved her enough to stay, and that must be her
fault. It wouldn't have to be reasonable. That could
account for her sort of off-beat reactions, couldn't
it? That brother of hers doesn't make things easier,
either.''

Jensen nodded slowly. ''Yeah, and what if he did
stage all of it and leave? He might have let her know.
Still might. There could be insurance involved, but
. . . without a body . . .'' He gestured toward the file
he had dropped into the rocking chair. ''That's why
I brought the paperwork home. Thought I'd go
through copies of the file one more time. See if
there's anything that doesn't fit—now that I've got
some distance on it—in light of today's discoveries.

''The other thing's the plane being shot down.
That's almost impossible to do—from the ground or
otherwise. Whoever did it would have to have been
one hell of a marksman with a large-caliber rifle.
Somebody who had what he felt was a really important reason to even try.''

Jessie held up an index finger to interrupt, and
from her intense look, something new had occurred
to her.

''Have you thought . . . I mean could it possibly
be that . . . Do you think it might have been the
woman they were after? Not Lewis? He could have
just been in the way.''

''Hm-m. Yeah, that's possible. I think I've got a
lot of digging to do.'' He reached across the gap to
the rocking chair and picked up his file. ''Maybe this
will tell me something to get me going.''

With one hand, she searched through the pillows
at her end of the couch, looking in vain for the pa-
perback mystery she had currently been reading and

retrieved a book on sports medicine instead.

"Well, good luck. I'd rather have this, thanks."

They settled into reading, but before he was half through his file, she had climbed, yawning, to her feet, kissed him lopsidedly, and shuffled off to the bedroom, mumbling, "G'night, trooper."

Temporarily distracted, Alex watched her go, suddenly aware of his physical and emotional satisfaction in this small, somewhat crowded house, and how much it was inspired by the woman with whom he lived. It was good to have a *cave* of one's own, in which to be one's own *bear*. It was more than good to have someone like Jessie to value and share it. At this particular moment in time, he realized, he was surrounded with just about everything that gave him comfort, peace, and pleasure. What a contrast with the distasteful duties of the afternoon.

It was the reality of the woman in the plane that had tired him more than usual. That much he knew. Jensen hated floaters. Though there weren't too many ways of dying that he hadn't seen, bodies that had passed long periods of time in water were the kind he detested most. In training, he had been told that he would become inured to all kinds of death, come to see only the details that forwarded his investigation, solved the puzzle. But from experience, he now knew it wasn't completely true and never would be for him. Some officers seemed to become used to the husks left by the grim reaper, however violent—even joked about them. He had never been able to reach their level of immunity. Floaters were the worst. The smell was always bad, but there was something about the unnaturally clean quality of the skin that set his teeth on edge, made his stomach roil. A shudder hunched his shoulders and he forced himself back to his reading in escape.

He studied his paperwork for another hour and, when he turned out the light, was thoughtfully contemplating a new idea he meant to check in the morning—one that had resulted as much from Jessie's comment as from the information in the file.

IN HIS DEN, DEEP INSIDE THE CAVE INTO WHICH HE had retreated the fall before, Aklak slowly roused to the first sounds of melting snow, spring once again softening the wilderness. For several days he remained lethargic, alternately dozing and waking as his metabolism increased, raising his temperature and the rate of his breathing, making him less and less sleepy. He uncurled himself, rolled over, stretched his legs and back, and reversed his position so that his head faced the entrance to the cave. Fresh air blew in where the deep snow had melted enough to uncover a space at the top of the opening, waking Aklak further. He sat up and yawned several times, then began to lick and groom himself, and scratch his belly furiously with one paw. Leaning back, he rubbed his back up and down against the rough edges of a granite boulder.

Awareness returned as appetite. During hibernation he had lost three hundred and twenty-five of the thirteen hundred pounds he had weighed in the fall, one fourth of his earlier body weight. His first concern was food. The need for it finally drove him staggering to his feet and to the entrance tunnel, where he easily dug away the icy barrier with claws that had grown sharp and long from lack of use during the winter. The thick callused parts of the pads of his paws had sloughed off during hibernation, and what was left was now soft and tender, highly sensitive to irregularities under his feet, and made walking initially difficult.

The first time he pushed his way through into the outside world, a cold wind was blowing a thin, late snow through the air, and he retreated into the den. Two days later, when he came out, the sun was shining and this time he stayed, though he wobbled slightly on his unexercised legs until he had walked far enough to strengthen them. Thirsty, ravenous, and ill-tempered, he headed downhill in the direction of the gurgling sound of a creek.

Drinking his fill of the ice-cold flow, Aklak turned to a south-facing slope, where a few blades of new grass were just above the surface of the damp ground. These he dug up and swallowed roots and all—only a mouthful. Food would be scarce for the next few weeks as it grew steadily warmer and more plants began to grow. For a hungry bear it was slim pickings and kept him on the move, searching hungrily.

A ground squirrel, also just up from a winter nap, exploded from its hole, practically under his feet. Still groggy, he pounced, but missed, and it vanished between two rocks. Soon he would easily be able to catch or dig out almost every one he saw.

Aklak wandered on, over a rise and down the other side, single-minded in his hunt for something to fill his empty belly. Soon, hungry or not, he would grow tired and crawling into brush still bare of leaves, he would sleep a few hours until his appetite woke and drove him again.

*   *   *

Miles away, in another den, dug into another north-facing slope, under a five-thousand-foot peak of the Alaska Range, Aklak's female sibling still hibernated with her two new cubs. They would sleep for perhaps another month before emerging, when the grass was already long enough to eat and other food easily found.

Aklak would neither have recognized, nor had an interest in, his sister grizzly, for it had been almost ten years since they were two of three cubs following their mother through a first summer in the world. Should they ever meet, she would see him only as an adversary, one of the most dangerous threats to her new cubs, for he would view them as food. If she could not avoid him, she would fight to the death to defend them, with no hesitation or knowledge that he had once been her brother and playmate.

Soon this mother bear would wake to an even more important hunger than his. She would have to feed not only herself, but the cubs that had begun to nurse when they were born in the den and would depend on her milk at least four times a day through the next six to eight months of Alaskan summer, until they were well established on other foods. Her milk, rich in fat, protein, and carbohydrates, would provide them with all the nourishment they needed when they emerged from the den.

For now, she still slept on her side, deep in the den, her two cubs humming and trilling softly as they fed. In a few short weeks, they would be scrambling along in her wake, yawning and stumbling, as they struggled to keep up through the last grainy heaps of sublimating ice and snow.

6

ROCHELLE LEWIS SLEPT THE EVENING AWAY AND woke up just before eleven o'clock with an aching head, so hungry she felt sick. Lunch had been as nonexistent for her as for Jensen, and it was long past dinnertime. Refusing to think of anything but food, she threw back the comforter and staggered toward the kitchen, stiff from hours in one position.

Once there, she reached blindly into the refrigerator for a half-gallon container of milk. Groping unsuccessfully, she finally leaned in to look and found it in a spot a shelf lower than it usually occupied. Careless, she thought. I just don't pay attention anymore. Thirstily she drank a large gulp from it without bothering to find a glass.

From the sparsely filled shelves, she rounded up a scrap of slightly green cheese, two eggs, a few pieces of a pound of bacon, and an onion. Pulling two slices for the toaster from a half loaf of stale bread, and ignoring a questionable collection of salad dressings and condiments, she tossed the bacon in a skillet to fry, followed by half the onion, chopped. While they sautéed, she salvaged the cheese by paring off the mold, then grated it. In the freezer compartment, she located a package of hash

brown potatoes. In a few minutes, leaning over the
sink, she was wolfing bites of a farmer's omelet and
toast, washing it down with more milk from the car-
ton.

Haven't been eating right, she thought, stabbing
at a scrap of bacon with the fork. It's why I'm so
tired all the time . . . why I'm not thinking straight.

She had hardly noticed as the winter passed that
what she brought home from the grocery—when she
remembered to stop—had grown monotonously similar: bread, eggs, milk, cheese, cans of soup, chili,
and tuna, once in a while a pound of ground beef,
or a chop. When she had felt hungry, she had eaten
. . . something . . . whatever she came upon first.

I've been living out of cans and frying pans.

Filling a mug with cold water, she added a tea
bag and thrust it into the microwave. As she watched
it go around hypnotically, she continued her contemplation of food. If what she had eaten at home was
inadequate, so was the other half of her winter's diet
of fast food: hamburgers, sandwiches, French fries,
cups of coffee from cafés she hardly remembered.

It's a wonder I don't resemble a baby whale, she
scowled, pinching at least an inch at her waist. Going to have to get some fresh vegetables and exercise
. . . if I'm going to find Norm.

As she flinched from the thought, the bell on the
microwave dinged. Lifting out the cup of hot tea,
she discarded the limp bag, dumped in some milk,
skipped the usual sugar, and headed back to the bedroom.

Leaving the adjoining bathroom clouding with
steam from the hot water filling the deep tub, she
stripped off the clothes she had worn flying earlier
in the day, and tossed them toward a pile of others

to be washed. In a drawer she found a pair of flannel pajamas, then retrieved a terry cloth robe, creased from weeks on a hook in the closet.

How long has it been since I did more than keep moving till I was exhausted, drop whatever I was wearing on the floor, crawl into bed and collapse, she wondered, pouring lavender bath salts into the tub, shutting off the water, and climbing in. It was enormous, large enough so she and Norm had been able to soak in it together.

Norm.

Once again her thoughts went skittering off, frantically scrambling for another subject. This time, however, she determinedly drew them back and purposely let ideas about her missing husband fill her mind as she slid down till the warm suds came up under her chin. Closing her eyes, she lay back and let her body go limp, luxuriating in the heat and sensation of floating that always reminded her of flying. But her mind continued to whirl, sorting through the day's revelations.

She realized that she was feeling awake and clearheaded for the first time in months of existing half-asleep—half-alive. With winter's arrival, charter flying ended since the planes she and Norm flew remained on floats year-round and were pulled out of the water before the lake froze over. She had retreated into her house, read dozens of books, watched one videotaped movie after another—anything to keep from thinking—going out only when necessary, mainly when she ran out of food or to eat something she didn't have to cook for herself.

Now she knew that during her last unconscious hours in the bed, something had changed. What? Why? The only difference was that they had finally found the plane . . . with its repulsive passenger. Who *was* that woman?

Frowning, she let herself slide down even more to submerge her face, tipped her head back and lifted it, hair streaming water, back into the cooler air. The feeling was faintly familiar, and after a minute, she recalled slowly waking that morning and the tangent smoothness of the sheets in the warmth of the bed. The memory fled as she continued to assess her feelings.

It was odd that, somehow, the fact of the plane and Norm's absence from it seemed to have released her from the grip of her agonizing lack of ability to think . . . to act. Since winter had locked the county in the frozen grip of snow and ice, and increasing darkness reduced the daylight to a few narrow hours around noon, she had felt powerless and stunned. Retreating into the sheltering confines of the house like an animal into hibernation, she had been only marginally aware of her surroundings. Except for Norm's jacket, she had left almost everything of his the way it was the day he'd disappeared, pretending he would be back at any minute.

Turning her head, she could see his toothbrush and shaving gear, neatly lined up by the bathroom basin, his towel still on the rack, laundered without thinking when she laundered her own and replaced. Why? He had gone. What had she done . . . what sin committed . . . to make him leave? What personal failing had she exposed that he could not accept? It had to be something. What? She wasn't enough for him? . . . *pretty* enough? . . . *young* enough? He would not have left her for nothing . . . would he? Could she possibly have misjudged him? She desperately wanted to know.

For a few seconds she fell back into the hole the winter had been, then, suddenly, she was angry. Stop it, she told herself savagely. It's useless . . . wallowing. Some people leave, with or without justification. You know that—or should by now.

It wasn't your fault, even if it was because of you. Your father left because he was weak, because he couldn't stick it out with a child—any child—because he didn't want you, or your mother . . . didn't know how or want to be a father. Bill left because he was a bastard, plain and simple. You knew that from the bruises and married him anyway. Men leave—one way or another. It's what they do finally. That's all. And sometimes they do you a favor when they do.

With a sudden furiousness that splashed water over the side of the tub, she stood up, stepped out onto the mat, and grabbed a large towel. Drying roughly and wrapping herself in it, she took another, turbaned her wet hair and moved to the basin. In one impulsive motion, she yanked open a drawer directly under the toothbrush, razor, and bottles of shaving cream and lotion and swept them all into it with one motion of her arm. Norm's bathrobe hanging on the back of the bathroom door and the towel on the rack, she wound into a bundle which she took into the bedroom and threw on the pile of clothes to be washed. Discarding her own towels in similar fashion, she put on the pajamas and robe and, instead of finding socks, went hunting for a pair of slippers that had not been worn in so long they had lost themselves in the back of her closet.

They weren't there.

Well, maybe they were in Norm's. Their things had often mixed, especially things like slippers that

tended to clutter the bedroom floor and get tossed
into the first open door. Opening his closet, she
dropped to her knees and, using her sense of touch
as well as sight, in the dark recesses under the hanging clothes, searched through the disorderly collection of shoes and boots.

Ah! No . . . only one of his socks that had escaped
the laundry pile. Nothing. Damn. Maybe they were
farther back. Pawing into the last corner, her fingers
hit the edge of something cool and square. Not the
shape of shoes. What the hell was it?

Pushing aside some of the clothing on hangers,
she reached in and lifted out a gray metal box similar
to those used sometimes for cash boxes. Though
they had two that were used for the charter business,
this one was not familiar, or the same. It was larger,
new and unmarked, not scratched and battered as
were the others that had been in and out of trucks
and planes for months. Those had carried paperwork
mostly. Cash went promptly to the bank. What could
this one possibly hold? Why had it been hidden?

Abandoning her quest for the slippers, Chelle
spotted them under the foot of the bed, got up and
went barefoot across the room to the small table
where she had placed her mug of tea, collecting the
footwear on the way. Sitting down on the edge of
the bed, she stared down at the gray box on her
knees and frowned. It was not as much like the others as she had originally thought. This one had a
combination lock and was stronger, much heavier,
and fireproof, from the look of it. She would have
been able to break into the others, had a key been
lost, with a pry bar or a sledge, perhaps. Not this
one. In fact, it had a different kind of lock entirely
. . . that required a combination. What the hell? She

shook it and heard the muffled rattle of something within.

With shaking hands, she tried, unsuccessfully, to open it. The three small rings of numbers that were dialed to a position that would release the lock had been turned to obscure the correct combination. Vividly, she remembered Norm thumbing similar rings on the lock for the storage shed near his plane. The last thing he had always done was turn them to be sure it could not be casually opened. "Lots of people forget," he had said. Obviously habit had not failed him on this one.

All right. What combination of numbers would he have used then? Something he could remember easily. His birthday? August 7, 1952. In order from the left: 8–7–2. Nothing. His plane identification had four numbers. The first three: 5–9–6? No. The last three: 9–6–8? Wrong. The first three numbers of their phone number: 2–4–3? Damn it.

The thing sat almost smugly in her lap, resisting her efforts to break its code. What was his driver's license number? His social security number? Had to look, since she had trouble even remembering her *own*. She carried it down the hall to their shared office and scrambled through records till she had both numbers and tried them both in several different orders. Nothing worked.

"Damn it, Norm," she finally swore aloud. "How could you do this to me?" She shook the box again, listening to the intriguing rattle. It sounded like something hard—metal, wood, plastic?—as it hit the sides. Perhaps more than one thing. Click. . . . clink.

Back in the bedroom, she tossed the box down on the comforter and plumped herself down against a pile of pillows at the head, scowling angrily at it as she drank her lukewarm tea. They had no secrets. *I thought! Everybody has secrets.* Not important ones. *You do.* That's different. *Is it?* She shrugged. So what was this? *And who was the babe in the plane?* What would he have wanted to hide from her? *Damn you, Norman Lewis!* How could he? *And the plane you flew in on!* But he hadn't wanted her to open it, had he? *If you had, you'd have used . . .*

Slowly she sat up and reached for the box. Pulling it back onto her lap, she sat rigid in heart-stopped stillness. Was it possible? Could he have . . . ? Carefully, with unsteady fingers, she turned the numbers, one by one, till they lined up in a very familiar group, indeed. Then, as easily as if it had never been locked, she opened the lid of the box.

9–2–9. September 2, 1949. He had used *her* birthday.

She sat looking into the box for several long minutes before she could make herself reach in. There wasn't much, it was almost empty. Lying on the metal bottom were two things: a key and some folded papers.

The key, when she laid it in the palm of her hand, was solid—had weight and reality. Chelle closed her fingers around its uneven shape, closed her eyes and sighed, realizing she had been holding her breath. She looked again, not recognizing its type immediately. Longer and thinner than most, it was a one-sided key, the square cuts deeper than those on a house or car key. It was unlike any she had ever held before.

Turning it over, she saw that it was numbered, 548, and on it was printed, "Action Locksmiths" and "Do not duplicate." So it was for something important. What? Could be anything, she thought, but no ideas were forthcoming.

Tears welled up when she reached trembling fingers for the papers and turned them over. A message? Could there be something for her after all? Shuffling through them, she quickly identified documents with which she was already familiar: the deed to the house, tax statements, the notes for both planes, titles to her car and his truck, life insurance policies—all the paperwork that had anything to do with the financial side of their lives. There was no letter among them to explain why, after much procrastinating on buying a fireproof lock box to protect them, he had suddenly done it without telling her and hidden it away in his closet, where she was least likely to stumble over it.

In confusion she turned over the pages to find a yellow sticky on the back of the first one. On it were a series of numbers written in black ink: 6082645732. What the hell?

They looked like the account numbers she wrote on checks for the payments on loans for her plane or the house mortgage. Usually those were hyphenated, but she supposed they might not have to be. She compared it to the number of the policy—not the same. What she knew for sure was that it was a number she had not seen or written before on any regular basis, a number that seemed to have been Norm's alone. What could it mean? Obviously it identified something for him and had been attached to the pages for a reason. What?

Registration numbers for cars or planes were similar. Did they have this many digits? She counted them. Ten. A long-distance telephone number? Three, three and four. It fit. Without hesitating, she

lifted the receiver from the phone on the bedside
table and dialed. In a moment she could hear it ring.
Once . . . twice, then, with a click, a woman's voice
spoke in her ear. "Two-six-four-five-seven-three-
two. Talk to me," then the beep of an answering
machine and the slight hum of its recorder, waiting
for a message. Chelle hung up and sat staring at the
phone. A woman. *The* woman?

Any ten-digit number might reach someone,
somewhere . . . wouldn't it? This one still might not
be a phone number. And, if it was, where and who
had she reached? Six-o-eight. Flipping through the
phone book from the drawer of the table, she located
the page that listed area codes. Slowly she searched,
checking each state, and finally found it in the next
to last one: Wisconsin. *Wisconsin?* As far as she
knew, Norm had no connection with, had never been
to, or so much as mentioned Wisconsin. Three cities
were listed with that area code: Beloit, Janesville,
and Madison. The rest were either four-one-four or
seven-one-five.

Picking up the receiver again, she dialed the six-
o-eight long-distance information number.

A recording, "Thank you for using AT&T." Then
an operator, "What city, please."

"I don't know," Chelle told her. "I have an area
code and phone number that I can't identify. Can
you tell me what city it's for?"

"What is the area code and the first three digits?"
Chelle told her.

"That would be Madison."

"If I give you the rest of the number, can you tell
me who it belongs to?"

"I'd have to have a last name."

"Is there any way I can find out?"

"I'm sorry. You'd have to call the number and ask."

Chelle hesitated, stymied, then gave up.

"Thanks anyway."

Have to have a last name? If she had a last name she wouldn't need to ask, would she? Well, tomorrow she could call again . . . see if someone real and nonmechanical answered.

What did the insurance and the number mean? What was Norm trying to tell her? Was he trying to tell her anything? Why hadn't he left some explanation?

She was suddenly exhausted again. And still angry with Norm, though his use of her birthday for the combination to the box had brushed against the part of her that had responded to and remembered his warmth and caring attention. He *had* meant her to open it—was attempting to care for her somehow, to tell her . . . something. She felt emotionally wrung in opposing directions. Information. She needed more information and she was too tired to try for it tonight.

Putting the key and papers back in the box, she closed it and turned the numbered rings, as she knew he would have done. After all, she wouldn't forget the combination. The box, however, she did not replace in his closet, but set down on the floor at the foot of the bed. Tomorrow. She would deal with it tomorrow.

Would Jensen be able to help with what she had found? Probably. But the way she had found it— hidden away in the back of the closet—made her feel that caution was indicated. She needed to find out all she could about both things first, she decided. Maybe she wouldn't tell anyone anything yet. Def-

initely not Ed, and maybe not even Jensen, or anyone.

But her feelings were subtly different than they
had been. Before she went to bed, she carefully hung
Norm's leather jacket back in the closet and reso-
lutely closed the door. Then she set her alarm for
six o'clock, turned out the light, and went quickly
and soundly to sleep.

7

WHEN THE ALARM CLOCK WENT OFF AT SIX THE next morning, Rochelle Lewis wasn't there to hear it. By the time she returned from a three-mile run, breathless and rubber-legged from exercise too long ignored, it had shut off its own insistent, repetitious beeping.

"Damn," she panted. Laying down yesterday's mail, picked up from the box as she came in, she stripped off her blue sweats and headed for the shower. "I'm a physical wreck."

Later, clean and dressed, she made herself breakfast for the first time in weeks: eggs and bacon, toast, juice and coffee. It even tasted good.

When she had finished the last bite of the toast wiped in yolk and loaded the dishwasher with the plates and pans she had just used, plus those from the night before, she dumped in soap and went back to the bedroom, leaving the machine to slosh energetically without her company. Grabbing the still unopened mail, she took it with her and sat on the end of the bed to flip through it. Two bills, a flier for a new restaurant, a community newsletter, and the bank statement, which reminded her that a payment on her plane would need to be made in the next few

days. She had not bothered to look at a statement
since . . . last fall, knowing what there was and automatically paying bills as necessary. Tearing back
the sticky flap, she took out the report and small
number of canceled checks she had written in the
last month, glancing at the total in the account, and
stopped cold. The amount was unexpectedly much
less than she anticipated. . . . several thousand dollars less.

The figure had to be wrong. She and Norm had
carefully calculated what payment must be made on
her plane during the slow winter months and deposited one payment more than enough to cover them
until business picked up again in the spring. Now
there was less than enough to cover the minimum
amount almost due, let alone two months after that.
Had she somehow paid them twice? Had they mis-
calculated? No. She knew neither of these answers
were right. Some other error was at work here.

From a pigeonhole of her desk in the office, she
took unopened statements for the last few months
and began to go through them, searching the with-
drawals. March back through October there were
none at all, nothing larger than her usual check for
payment on the plane. Then in September's statement she found it—a withdrawal for five thousand
dollars, the slip written in Norm's handwriting. What
the hell was going on? He had said nothing about
the missing money, and it made no sense. If anything
he was more conservative than she, carefully ac-
counting for every dollar, working toward a business
owned free and clear. He had borrowed only when
absolutely necessary and paid loans back as soon as
possible, making inroads on the principal with anything extra.

Chelle sat at the desk, staring at the statement, thinking hard. Could it have anything to do with the key she had found in the lock box? Had he hidden the money somewhere? Why? No interest would accrue if it weren't in the account. It didn't seem likely. Could he have bought something . . . lost some bet . . . owed someone for something he didn't want her to know? It didn't feel right. Or—she finally let in the thing she didn't want to think about— had he needed it to leave?

With that, she stopped turning it over in her mind and went back to the bedroom. She would find out what that key—and the number she had found— meant. Right now. Picking up the strongbox from the floor and putting it in her lap, she took out the key and the papers. Once more she dialed the number on the slip of yellow paper and listened to the phone ring in Wisconsin. As before, she reached only the answering machine that beeped at her, demanding a response she was unwilling to give.

Maybe it wasn't a phone number at all, she thought, hanging up and putting her mind to work on the puzzles provided by the box. Letting the number go for the moment, she turned to the key. What could it open? Who could tell her? Where would Norm hide money that needed a key? A storage locker somewhere? The airport? No, they cleaned out lockers on a regular basis. It didn't seem that kind of key anyway.

Well, if one wanted to know about something, one went to someone who would know. Who would know keys better than a locksmith? She had the name of the one who should know all about it, Action Locksmiths, on the key itself, right? In the yel-

low pages, she found an address on West
Forty-eighth.

Taking her wallet and a jacket, she dropped the
yellow paper with the number and the key into a
pocket, locked the door of the house, and headed
toward midtown in her battered Subaru station
wagon.

"A safe-deposit box key. You're sure?"

The bored locksmith nodded, handing it back to
Chelle. "Only kind looks like this."

"Which bank?"

"Da'know, and couldn't tell you if I did. If you
got the key, you should know."

She knew, faced with his bored expression, that it
was the truth. He wasn't being helpful, but he didn't
know. Now what? Check every bank in town? Well
. . . how many could there be?

There could be a lot. Not counting the credit un-
ions and mortgage companies, the phone book contained the names of eight banks with between one
and seventeen branches listed for each. How would
she ever find the right one? Frustrated, she ripped
the page from the phone book and headed out to try.

Picking one she considered a low possibility, she
drove to Denali Street to see what she could find
out—a practice run. They might very well refuse her
any information at all, or worse, take away the key.
Approaching a counter behind which she could see
a vault with safe-deposit boxes, she waited until a
woman stepped up to ask how she could be helpful.

"I have this," Chelle told her, indicating the key
she had laid on the counter. "Does it belong to a
box at this bank?"

Picking up the key, the woman gave her a questioning look. "Isn't it yours?"

"Well, not really. It was sort of left for me."

"I'm sorry. We can't give out any information unless your name is on record as renter, or renter's agent. Are you listed?"

"No . . . I don't think so. Well . . . maybe . . . I don't know. I think it was my husband's key. I found it in his things."

"Oh," said the woman, misinterpreting, "I'm so sorry. What was the name?"

Chelle let it go, since she now seemed more accommodating.

"Lewis. Norman Lewis."

"And your name?"

Rochelle told her, and taking the key, the woman went to check a box of cards on a desk behind the counter. In a minute she came back.

"Sorry. No Lewis by either of those names."

"No Lewis?"

"Not by those names. Sorry."

Hesitantly, Chelle held out her hand, afraid of a negative reply. "Can I have the key back, please?"

But the woman was completely cooperative. "Certainly." She handed it over.

Turning to leave, Chelle swung back with one more question. "Is there any way to find out which bank or branch this belongs to?"

"Not that I know of. Could be any one. Nobody puts location on the key, for obvious reasons."

"Thanks, anyway." Frowning, Chelle left to consult her list and delete one bank from it.

Street by street, bank by bank, she traversed midtown. Leaving the rest of Anchorage till later, if necessary. Response was similar at the next six banks she tried: no Norman or Rochelle Lewis on file. Discouraged and disconcerted, she began to feel she was hunting the proverbial needle. Could he have listed it under another name? Maybe. But he had used a number she could discover easily for the box in which she had found the key. Didn't that mean he wanted her to find out what it fit as well? Nothing. She found nothing.

There were still a lot of banks to check, and she learned quickly, began to make her requests less hesitant. She stopped admitting that she knew nothing about the key.

"Lewis," she stated with assumed confidence at the counter of a branch of the First National Bank of Anchorage to a dark-haired woman with a pleasant smile, who peered over reading glasses with bright eyes the color of weak tea. "Norman Lewis. My husband."

The South Center Branch was where she and Norm did most of their banking, where the statements had originated, and which carried the half-paid loan on her plane. Norm had been inclined to keep all their business in one place when possible. If he wanted her to find it, he might have thought she would assume this too, or was it too obvious. She could hope, and did, while waiting for the woman, who soon returned with another smile, a file card in her hand.

"Norman Lewis," she said, indicating the card. "Can I see some identification please?"

Rochelle's heart leapt into her throat, and she fumbled her wallet open to lay her driver's license on the counter between them. Carefully, the woman, Florence Gouge, from her name tag, compared the signatures and nodded. "Yes, you're listed as agent."

Agent? Chelle wanted to ask, but maintained her confidence in silence. Let the woman assume she already knew this.

But, when Florence looked up, her friendly smile faded slightly at the flushed appearance of Chelle's face.

"Are you all right, dear?"

Holding out an unsteady hand, Chelle forced herself to relax and smile, though it felt as unreal as it probably looked on her stiff face. "Fine. I'm fine. Could I see that, please?"

Florence laid the card down on the counter. "See? You're right here." She pointed.

There in front of her, on a line at the bottom of the card, in blue ink, incredibly, was her own name: Rochelle J. Lewis. *In what looked almost like her own handwriting.*

She stared at it numbly. It was a forgery. She had never signed this card. What the hell . . . But . . . if she wanted to know what was in the box it belonged to, she couldn't say so, could she?

"Would you like to access the box?"

"What?"

"Open it? Do you want to get into it?" the woman explained, as if she was speaking to someone with a retarded ability to understand. Her smile had disappeared entirely and she looked concerned.

This wouldn't do. Rochelle shook herself mentally and forced her cold fingers to pick up her wallet and snap it shut efficiently, dropping it into her jacket pocket.

"Yes, please. I would."

"Sign here, please." Another card, once again

signed in her handwriting, another signature that
wasn't hers. Below it a section labeled "Log of Box
Entry," with lines and spaces for date and signature.

Slowly, she signed and, as her hand shook
slightly, thought, with dark amusement, that the
name looked less like her own than the forgery
above it. Florence, however, was satisfied.

"Come this way." She held open a gate and led
the way to a vault familiar in appearance to the others Chelle had seen. Stopping in front of box number
548, she inserted the bank's key and stepped aside
for Chelle to do the same with the one she had. It
fit, turned easily, and allowed the box to slide forward, exposing a covered top with a hinge that
would allow it to fold back.

"There." Florence was once again smiling. This
was correct and normal procedure. The keys worked
and all was well. "Call me when you're finished,"
and she was gone, leaving Chelle alone with a box
she had never seen but was evidently supposed to
know all about. Who had forged her signature on the
card? Norm, apparently. Did the bank care? Probably not. As long as their rules were followed they
were covered and had no reason to care.

But she cared. And Norm had cared . . . hadn't he?
What was going on here, anyway? What do you
want from me, Norm? This is not fair. You could
have clued me in. I loved you, damn it! What the
hell are you doing to me?

With a flash of yesterday's anger, she flipped back
the lid to the metal box, took a deep breath, and
looked inside. Then, for a long moment, she stared
silently down into the rectangular cavity.

An envelope, sealed, and there was nothing—not
even her name—written on it. She took it out, tore

it open and removed the legal-sized pages. Spreading them open, she saw immediately that what she held was not a letter, but an insurance form. It was a policy—with her name as beneficiary. Someone—presumably Norm, since it was his policy—with a yellow marker, had highlighted portions concerning the amounts: death benefits of two hundred and fifty thousand dollars, and double that amount in case of accidental death.

For a time she stared at it, uncomprehending. *Five hundred thousand dollars?* The figure was meaningless in its size. But it would pay off her plane . . . give her a living? He had meant her to be taken care of—to be able to get along without him.

But didn't death have to be proved? Didn't they have to have a body in order to prove it? And there was none. Was he even dead? What now? Did this make any difference at all? Where had he got the money to buy this policy? From what was missing from the account? And why was there no letter—no explanation? Why hadn't he left her something personal?

She pocketed the papers and closed the lid on the box. Then she swore. Long and without reservation, she hissed words through her teeth that would have deeply offended Florence with her sweet smile—had she been present to hear. But she wasn't. No one was. So Chelle ended up swearing at Norm again, until she finally ran out of words and burst into tears.

8

AS SOON AS HE REACHED HIS OFFICE IN PALMER THE next morning, Jensen called the Scientific Crime Detection Laboratory in Anchorage to ask about the autopsy on the body of the woman from the plane.

"They're on it now," a lab clerk told him. "A rush job yesterday afternoon bumped it to this morning."

"When'll it be done?"

"You could check back about noon, I think."

"Better than that, I'll come in. Tell John not to take off for lunch till I see him, will you?"

The next step was to present his idea from the night before to the commander of his detachment.

"So you finally located the Lewis plane. Really thought that was a lost cause," Swift commented as Alex settled into a chair in front of his desk.

Ivan Swift was a short, compact man, built like a V, with heavy shoulders and a narrow waist. With his long thin nose and bright, intelligent eyes, he had always reminded Alex of a fox. His dark hair was graying at the temples. He barked his words and wasted none of them.

Different in style, but similar in their belief in the

86

value of the details of crime, the two men respected each other, got along well, and Jensen was allowed much leeway in his investigations for the department.

"What's the story on the woman?" Swift asked abruptly.

"Not sure yet. The autopsy's still under way, but I've got some thoughts on it."

"Go."

"Remember that Fish and Wildlife undercover agent from outside who disappeared in the Arctic National Wildlife Refuge sting last year?"

"So? You think this is her? Why? It's a long way from ANWR."

"That's why I'm waiting on the PM, but it's a possibility. The timing for one thing. Also, because she was the only one shot. There wasn't a sign of Lewis. Gone. Vanished."

At the tone of Jensen's voice, the commander's eyes narrowed and a pair of creases appeared between his brows.

"On his own?"

"Could be."

A pause. Then, "You think he set her up?"

Swift's thoughts were jumping ahead as fast as Jensen had anticipated they would.

"Maybe. Don't even know it's her yet, but . . . possible, if it is."

"Guess we'd better find out. Enough left for prints?"

"Yeah. The body's bad, but it was pretty well protected in the cockpit. They started on the ID last night."

"Okay. You're back on it full-time. Need help?"

"Becker?"

"On the Oppner case."

"Caswell? We may need his plane."

"Done. I'll call and set it up. You tell him."

"Thanks, Ivan."

As Jensen drove the forty miles to Anchorage from the Mat-Su Valley, he remembered all he could about the ANWR operation in northern Alaska that had resulted in the arrests of many people involved in the illegal hunting and transportation of big game—moose, caribou, grizzly, sheep, wolf, and musk ox. After working three years to set up the sting, Fish and Wildlife agents and other law enforcement personnel from inside and outside the state had come down like hawks on the guides, pilots, and managers of two guiding services they had infiltrated and on whom they had succeeded in collecting evidence of wrongdoing. People had been arrested as far away as Georgia.

Wisconsin Special Agent Karen Randolph, like several others from out of state, had been an undercover plant. Her assignment had been one of the hunting camps of Dale Stoffel, a notoriously crooked and so far unconvicted pilot and guide. Sometime during the hunt she had supposedly arranged with him, she had disappeared and there had been no sign of her since. Stoffel insisted she had never showed up for the hunt, and went on claiming it consistently throughout his arrest and conviction for two other operations. He had been sentenced to eighteen months and had lost all the planes, cars, and equipment related to the crimes. Still in jail, he continued to allege that Randolph had been his client on paper only—a no-show for the actual hunt. They had not been able to prove otherwise, or locate conflicting evidence, or Randolph's body, if she were dead, as they knew she must be.

Alarm bells were now ringing in Jensen's mind, telling him something concerning this case needed attention. If the dead woman from Lewis's plane *was* Randolph, the whole thing blew up significantly as more than the murder of a woman and a missing pilot. It would mean that Lewis had also been involved. What else would explain the presence of a federal agent in his plane? Could he have been part of the illegal activity? Part of the sting? His name had not been in the paperwork that Jensen had seen, but he had been brought in only at the last, to assist in the arrests, and knew a minimum amount about the case. Lewis might have been included, but how? Was it possible he had killed her? And, dead or alive, where the hell was he?

His plane had crashed not only far from where its flight plan indicated it should have been, but far from ANWR as well. Why? Other illegal hunting locations had been identified, one suspected in the Beluga Lakes area, though the focus had been farther north. Still . . .

But it was no use leaping ahead. He must wait for the coroner's results. It all hinged on that. If the body turned out to be someone else—and it certainly could—there was nothing to connect it or Lewis to Stoffel and his poaching operations.

Lewis might possibly have been having an affair with someone his wife knew nothing about. Jensen assumed that Rochelle Lewis had wondered about it, though she had said nothing to indicate it. That could be what made him feel she was hiding something, could explain her obsession with finding Norm. He needed to talk to her again, soon, get a better reading. But first—the autopsy and fingerprint results.

He pulled into the parking lot of the crime lab to find Ben Caswell leaning against a fender of his truck, waiting. A satisfied grin spread over his face when he saw Jensen and stepped forward.

"Hey, you pulled it off again, huh?" he said as Alex climbed out of his truck. "Got us both out from behind a desk, for which I am humbly grateful." Snatching off the out-of-uniform baseball cap he wore, he pretended to sweep the ground in front of Jensen's advancing feet. "Thank you, thank you, oh mighty emancipator of slaves."

Alex chuckled at the unusual antics that were a contrast to Caswell's more customary watchful, quiet demeanor. He was hardly ever silly, though he sometimes displayed a wicked sense of humor. It said volumes of how tired he was of being a desk jockey for most of a winter that had been more than normally lacking in crime investigations requiring planes and their pilots.

Ben Caswell was not the sort to enjoy pushing paper. He found most of his pleasures in life outdoors and they usually involved his compact Maule M-4. Alex always enjoyed working with him because he didn't waste time running in speculative circles. Sparing of words, he worked ideas through carefully in his head before trying them out verbally. Whatever he was asked, his commonest response was "Let me kick it around a little," or "Can I get back to you on that?" He had a talent for sorting through the facts of a case and separating items worth consideration from the trivia that could just as well be ignored. His memory was phenomenal, and there was something of the bulldog in his stubborn pursuit of ideas and solutions to the cases on which he worked. In addition, he could fly rings around a lot of other pilots, a detail that had more than once saved their bacon, Alex remembered thankfully.

He was proud to count Caswell as a personal friend, and it pleased him that not only did Cas and Jessie like each other, but Ben's wife, Linda, had become a friend as well. The foursome frequently went to movies or got together for dinner or a weekend of hiking or fishing.

Now he laughed at Ben's clowning and laid a hand on his shoulder as they turned to walk toward the crime lab.

"Give it up, Cas. You'd have found some other excuse for yourself if I hadn't needed you on this one."

"Yeah, you're probably right. What's the deal, anyway? Something about yesterday and the Lewis thing, right?"

"Right. I've got this feeling I can't get rid of that Norm Lewis—"

"Took off on his own?" Caswell interrupted.

"You, too?"

"Well, I've been kicking it around off and on. Then finding the plane and no Lewis yesterday really got me going. What's your take on it?"

"I took the file home last night and went through it again," Alex told him. "What I came up with is that . . ."

He paused as they went through the door to the lab and into the front hallway, where they turned left, headed for the director's office.

"I think the woman in the plane . . ."

As he was about to complete the sentence, a wheelchair came whipping around a corner, cruised up to the two troopers, and stopped bare inches short. A fuzzy-haired man with a frown beetling his dark brows looked up at them accusingly.

"Where've you been, Jensen?" he demanded in a deep voice that reminded Alex of someone shaking gravel in a can.

"And good morning to you, John," he nodded. "Driving in from the valley. You got something?"

"Thought you were in a hurry for ID on that woman you gave me yesterday."

"I am. But, short of using the siren, I got here as fast as I could. What've you got?"

"More'n you probably expected." The growl of an answer drifted back over his shoulder as he spun the chair and started swiftly back down the hall. "Let's hit my office and take a look."

Jensen and Caswell exchanged amused glances as they hustled to catch up. Both of them were well acquainted with John Timmons, who had worked as assistant to the coroner at the lab for longer than either of them could remember. He had not always been a prisoner of the chair he handled so well. A skiing accident had deprived him of the use of his legs five years earlier. It had not, however, significantly changed his attitude toward life, which pretty much amounted to hurling himself at it headlong, work or play. Wheelchair racing had replaced skiing in his quest for speed and challenge. Some Machiavellian mechanical genius—or madman—had built him a four-wheeled version of a dirt bike, and he now raced off road, as well as on, whenever he got the chance, though winter restricted his opportunities. When cold weather and cabin fever set in, he turned to a luge run he was designing for the *vertically challenged*, as he termed himself, and which, so far, perhaps luckily, remained on paper.

The chair he used at the lab was fitted with a lift that brought him up to a level at which he could work. This, plus powerful arms and shoulders, and a set of braces that held him rigidly in a standing position part of the time, allowed him to continue doing autopsies as always. Since no one could do them better, or come up with more accurate results and creative ideas from them, he would have been sorely missed had he been forced to change occupations.

As they made a left into his office, Alex remembered this and found himself once again grateful. If anyone could unlock the secrets of the body of the woman from the plane, it was Timmons, and he had a hunch there were several secrets to be unlocked.

There were. The woman in the plane had not only been shot, from the evidence of massive bruising on the body and two broken fingers, she had also been savagely beaten as well.

"Happened not long before she was shot," Timmons informed them. "That's all I can tell you after this amount of time. It was done with something hard and heavy, a little over two inches wide. I'd guess a club of some sort—maybe a gun stock. There are signs of some sharp ninety-degree edges. There are also restraint marks on her wrists from some kind of cord about half an inch in diameter. You can make your own speculations, but I'd guess it was an attempt to get information, or force some action, not one to beat her to death. There is no sign of her being hit in the head, and that's one area that indicates intent to kill. She was pounded repeatedly in the stomach and chest area. Must have been pretty painful.

"She died of a ruptured spleen, result of the beating, but it took a while for her to bleed out internally . . . after she was airborne, I'd say. Lividity occurred in a seated position. I'd be willing to bet she was already dead when the bullet hit her. Could have been just a lucky shot."

An hour later, Jensen and Caswell sat down for a quick lunch at O'Brady's, the nearest restaurant to the crime lab and offices of the state troopers, and a frequent stop for officers and personnel who wanted to get back to work in a hurry. The food was good and the atmosphere of green curtains and brass rails cheerfully suggested an Irish pub.

"So," Caswell mused, frowning around bites of a Reuben sandwich, "Karen Randolph. You were right. What made you think it might be her?"

"Something Jessie said last night, to be honest. She suggested that whoever shot down the plane might have been after the woman, not Lewis. I knew that Randolph disappeared about the same time he did and just put the two together. It seemed likely, and stranger coincidences have happened. I couldn't say for sure, but John made the same connection and came up roses with her dental records, then the report on the prints confirmed it."

"That'll bring the feds sniffing around, won't it? What the hell was she doing in his plane?"

"Now that's the stopper. I haven't a clue and it's got to have something to do with his disappearance and the fur-and-feathers sting. The possibilities are practically endless, but we can start with the assumptions that either he was involved with her, her investigation, or—barring that—with who she was investigating."

"The guides they were setting up, you mean?"

"Specifically Dale Stoffel, I mean. He was the one she was assigned to, was supposed to have gone hunting with, but he keeps claiming she never showed up and we couldn't prove otherwise because she was never found. Just disappeared."

"But I thought that whole thing was supposed to have happened up north—ANWR."

"Most of it was, but there were several other suspicious sites under consideration, including west of Susitna, where some inconclusive evidence was located. She almost had one guy on Kodiak—an independent, not connected with Stoffel's bunch—but a bear got him. Obviously she wasn't up north when Lewis's plane went down, was she?"

"So they're related."

"Looks like it. We need to find out how."

"What do you propose?"

"Another conversation with Stoffel would probably be a waste of time." Alex scowled. "Now that we can prove she was beaten and shot, he might change his story, but I doubt it."

"John said the slug was too messed up to be any good."

"Right, but it came from a heavy piece, something used for big game, for instance. Nothing small-caliber. Had to punch through the door of the plane before it hit her, and it didn't kill her, remember. But Stoffel wouldn't know that, or that it was unidentifiable, and they confiscated most of his guns along with the planes and other related stuff. We might get lucky, if he knows the right gun was among them. It's a long shot for later, maybe."

"And Lewis?"

"I'd be willing to bet he's either as dead as Randolph, or somewhere almost impossible to track down. Possibly both. Stoffel isn't the kind to take chances on informers, and Lewis just doesn't seem to have been the type to take off on his new wife.''

"Like to wager?''

"Nope. Not until it's a sure thing. But I want to talk about it with Chelle Lewis again—and, sometime down the road, I suppose, to Stoffel. For now, we'd do better to take a look at who was connected that we couldn't jail. Might be a lead there somewhere to tell us who may still be in business.''

"Where's Stoffel?''

"Spring Creek facility in Seward. Not due to be released till August.''

"You want to fly down there?'' Caswell grinned his eagerness to get into the air, but Jensen shook his head.

"Not yet. One of his people made a deal and spilled a few names, if I remember the reports. And wasn't there a cousin we didn't have enough on to convict? We need to hunt him up, but even more, to go over the trial transcripts and get all our ducks in a row before seeing him. Maybe he'll have something to give us a lead. Then Stoffel might jump, if he thinks we know something more than he anticipated. Besides that, I don't want to give *him* any information at all. I seem to remember there were threats made toward some of the witnesses—including some of the feds—*after* he was locked up. And not all his flunkies were corralled in the sting.''

"Yeah, you're right. I sat in on the last day of his trial and the way he expressed it was that, win or lose, he would *straighten out* whoever had *framed* him.''

"Framed him? Ha! Why don't you go pick up a

copy of the transcripts, while I check with Fish and Wildlife on a couple of things. Later this afternoon I want to hunt up Rochelle Lewis, so I'll leave a message, or meet you back at your office after that.''

''Curses, foiled again. Back on the ground, just when I thought I was liberated. If we miss each other, don't forget you and Jessie are coming over for dinner tonight.''

''And miss one of Linda's fine meals?'' Alex went on to promise, ''We'll get this show in the air soon. Okay? I didn't spring you just to sit around on the ground.''

9

WITH CASWELL HEADED DOWNTOWN TO RETRIEVE
a copy of the trial transcript, Jensen returned to head-
quarters for information from the Fish and Wildlife
service. In less than half an hour he was back in his
truck, heading west with the names of several poaching suspects, and one in particular that interested
him, Tom Greeson, the cousin of Dale Stoffel whom
he remembered from the Brooks Range case.

"He's never been arrested?" he had asked the
Fish and Wildlife agent.

"Oh, arrested, yes, several times. Never had
enough evidence to convict, but we know he was,
and undoubtedly still is, involved in the same illegal
activities as Stoffel—hunting the same day they fly,
and taking game inside protected areas like ANWR
and Denali National Park for the most part. We
didn't catch him in the Brooks Range sting because
when it went down he was playing flunky for Dale
back in town, wasn't seen in any of the hunting
camps we sent undercovers into to get firsthand evidence. He slipped through the net and has kept his
head down ever since, as near as we can tell. Pretty
quiet, but that doesn't necessarily mean clean.''

"So he could be back in business—just being more careful?"

"Or running a very small, tight operation. Sure. Anything's possible. We haven't anyone following him around. Can't afford the manpower to anticipate violations. Unfortunately we have to be more reactive than anything else—following up on cases where the damage has already been done. My guess would be that, with Stoffel inside, Tom's got a chance to take up the slack and will probably take it this season. But he's nowhere near as smart and twice as mean. He'll probably make a mistake we can get him on if he tries to fill Dale's boots."

"If you wanted to find him, where would you look?"

"Well, Stoffel's got a ranch in the valley where he runs some of his business. Tom's there sometimes, I guess, but usually he hangs out in town. Out at the airport, or at a couple of the bars nearby—the Cockpit, maybe. They're the hub for a lot of stuff."

Jensen had thanked the agent and gone. Now he headed for the Cockpit and hoped to get lucky and find . . . well . . . he wasn't quite sure what, besides Tom Greeson, but perhaps something that might give him direction or a clue to solving the problem of the death of the Randolph woman and the disappearance of Norman Lewis.

It was still early in the afternoon, when Alex pushed open the door of the Cockpit. Its hinges whined their need for lubrication, setting his teeth on edge. The contrast of a day full of sunshine with the interior darkness of the building caused him to blink and pause while his eyes adjusted, as had Darryl, the mechanic, the day before.

The place was all but empty, a couple of hours

away from the arrival of the usual late-afternoon bar-
flies. An elderly man, with a fringe of white hair in
need of a trim around his ears and skinny, corded
neck, sat nursing a draft beer on the far side of the
large bar. A pair of cues lay on the green felt of the
pool table next to a rack of balls, ready for some
players to come and start a game. On one of the tall
stools closest to the door, a barmaid in a miniskirt
and tight sweater waited to go to work. Perched at
the bar with a cup of coffee and a cigarette, she
swiveled to watch Jensen walk across the room, her
expression carefully neutral, a look that he knew
meant she had identified him as law enforcement.
Some people seemed to have a sort of sixth sense
about police and were cautious as a result.

As he approached, the bartender on duty came
through the door of a refrigerated room into the area
behind the counter, carrying two cases of Coors to
restock the glass-fronted cooler. The space seemed
suddenly smaller in the presence of this tall, heavy-
set man of about thirty-five, though he moved easily,
without haste, not a threat to the abundance of glass-
ware and bottles around him. Glancing up, he nodded, recognizing Jensen, set the beer down on the
floor by the cooler, and stepped across to hold a
massive hand out which engulfed the one Jensen offered in return.

"Hey, Alex." He grinned. "Haven't seen you for
months. How you been, buddy?"

The barmaid visibly relaxed. The stranger might
be John Law but he was an acquaintance at least,
therefore provisionally acceptable.

"Johnny Raite. Hey. Didn't expect to find you
here. Last time I saw you you were leaving
O'Brady's to go outside last fall. You get enough of

the lower forty-eight and decide to come on home where you fit in better?''

"Yeah, well. The *old country* isn't what it used to be. Too many people and cars in not enough space. I came back up right after the holidays and this's the only place needed a booze jockey. I worked here a couple a years ago, so they took me back when their other guy busted a leg falling on the ice on his own front step."

"Good to see you."

"Hey, you too. Whatcha doin' in here this time of day? Anchortown given up on crime?"

"Naw, I'm just looking for some information on a couple of guys that may or may not hang out around here. You know a Tom Greesor? Ever come in here?"

The grin faded as Raite cast a swift glance at the barmaid, who straightened slightly and returned his look with a frown. Turning back to Jensen, he nodded.

"Yeah, he's in and out pretty regular. Why? He got a problem?"

"Don't really know," Alex told him. "Lots of rumors about illegal activity in the hunting arena. I was told this might be a place to locate him for a few questions I have about a case I'm working on."

"Isn't hunting in the fins-and-feathers department?" Raite asked. "Thought you were on the homicide squad."

"Yeah, well other things sometimes tie in."

"This about that plane that you guys found over by Susitna yesterday?" the barmaid suddenly asked, turning to face him and combing her fingers through her hair to pull it away from her face. As she turned, Jensen caught the scent of her perfume, some kind of pleasant floral aroma that seemed out of place in the present surroundings. Her hair was bottle-blond, but she had honest eyes and an easygoing attitude.

"Could be," he allowed cautiously. "Where'd you hear that?"

"Heard it was there all winter, right?"

A slow, nodded confirmation.

"And there was some woman in it?"

"Can't say much about that. But it's interesting that you heard about it. Who told you?"

"Oh, just something I overheard last night in here. Couldn't really say who, just talk."

"Was Greeson here last night?"

"Oh yeah." She shrugged, a motion that suggested she might have been happier had he been elsewhere.

Raite agreed from behind the bar. "He was here most of the evening."

The barmaid frowned. "I remember. It was Ed Landreth who mentioned the plane. Remember, Johnny? He came in with that flaming redhead?"

"Yeah. That's right. Only stayed for a couple of drinks and took off right after he had a short conversation with Greeson. Didn't hurt my feelings. He looked like he was ready to tie one on."

"Right. Well, he was on his way out and stopped to talk to Tim Cole. I was taking beers to the guys playing pool."

She pointed across the room and Jensen noted that she would have had to pass between the bar and the door to reach the table. She went on.

"As I went by I heard him telling Tim about a plane they found in some lake out there, and the woman in it. Said he'd been out there and seen it. Makes my skin crawl. Think of being there all winter and nobody knowing where you were. Yuck.''

"That all he said?'' Alex asked.

"Well—I don't know because I had to come back for another round, but he left before I got back, so he couldn't have said much.''

"But he talked to Tom Greeson. How long? Did you hear any of it?''

"No. I stay as far away from Greeson as I can get. He's a mean SOB—drunk or sober.'' She wrinkled her nose as if she had caught an unpleasant odor, and tapped her long fingernails against the side of her coffee mug. "Trouble. He's trouble. Makes me uneasy, the way he watches people all the time, playing big shot, and setting up deals.''

"What kind of deals?'' Jensen asked.

"Oh, I don't know. He's sort of slimy-acting. The sort of deals that make you feel they're mostly in his favor. Anything with cash attached, I guess. He's got a vicious temper. Put a girl in the hospital once a couple of years ago. She refused to press charges— too scared, I think—but she left the state as soon as she was well enough to travel.''

"Hey,'' Raite interrupted. "Can I get you something? Beer?''

"No thanks, Johnny. I got work to do.''

"Coffee, then? Coke?''

"Sure. Coffee'd be great, thanks. You know any more about this guy?''

Raite shook his head no as he set a mug down on the bar before Alex and filled it with coffee. "My opinion's about the same as April's. Not a very nice person, our Mister Greeson. Ah . . . watch that. I just made it and it's hot.''

"Thanks, I will. Ever hear his name connected with Dale Stoffel?''

"Yeah, that's old news. They're related somehow. But Stoffel's still in jail, isn't he?"

"Yes. For the next few months. He'll be out in August."

Across the bar, the old man, who had finished the beer he had been drinking since Alex walked in, suddenly pounded on the bar with his glass. As Alex jumped, both Johnny and the barmaid smiled at his reaction.

"That's just old, deaf Charlie," Raite told him. "He can't hear and when he drinks he thinks nobody else can either. Lets me know he's ready for a refill by banging. We're used to it."

He went to draw another draft for Charlie. April got down from her stool, went behind the bar, and began transferring bottles from the case of Coors into the cooler.

Jensen sipped his coffee thoughtfully and wondered if any of what he had learned in the last half hour would fit into the equation he was trying to solve. When Raite returned from serving the draft, he changed the direction of his inquiries.

"You acquainted with Norm Lewis?" he asked.

The bartender stopped to look questioningly at him. "You mean Norm Lewis that disappeared last fall on some flight to Glennallen, right? Yeah, I knew him. Hell of a nice guy. Used to come in here in the old days, but I hadn't seen him for a long time when I heard he'd gone missing. Ever find out what happened to him?"

"Haven't found him. No." Alex saw no reason to include the information that the plane they had been discussing had belonged to Lewis. They hadn't found *him* after all.

"He ever have anything to do with Greeson that you know of?"

"Shit no. Walked two different sides of the street, those two. Don't think I ever saw them so much as say hello. Nothing shady about Lewis. He was building a neat little charter business with his lady friend. Working hard at it, as far as I heard."

"You mean his wife, Rochelle?"

"They got married then? I heard they were pretty tight, but didn't know about the wedding."

"So Lewis hung out here?"

"Naw. Only came in once in a while, with Jeff Bunker. Neither of them fit in much with this crowd. The location is just handy to Lake Hood, where they both kept their planes, so they'd stop once in a while for a quick beer after a flight."

As Jensen paused, trying to think of anything else he wanted to ask Raite, the door squealed open and three younger guys tromped in.

"Hey, Johnny. Couple a Buds and a Heineken, okay?"

"Time to earn my check." Raite grinned and, as Jensen stood up to leave, dropping a dollar on the bar, added, "Good to see you. Stop in again. It's pretty slow this early."

"Thanks. I'll do that. Keep your ears open, will you?"

"Sure. No problem."

The door protested once again as Alex went through it and out into the dusty, unpaved parking lot. He had almost reached his truck when it squealed again and he heard Raite call his name.

"Where'd you find that plane, Alex?"

"Lake the other side of Susitna. Why?"

The big man walked across to speak in a lower

tone, as a pickup pulled in and the driver got out near the door. He frowned, concentrating.

"Well, Greeson has a way of carrying on a conversation that doesn't get overheard, and I don't even try to eavesdrop—too much to do anyway. But yesterday I did hear him mention Beluga Lake to one of the bunch that hangs out with him. Didn't get anything as to what it was about, just the location. That mean anything?"

Shaking his head, Jensen thought for a second before answering. "I don't really know, Johnny. But thanks just the same. It may tie in somewhere. There was a woman in the plane, and she didn't die of the crash. That's all I can tell you. Keep it to yourself if you can, but I'd appreciate anything you might pick up that relates."

"Like I said . . . sure. Don't forget that Greeson is a mean SOB," Raite cautioned. "April sure nailed that one right."

As Jensen drove away, heading for Rochelle's, he thought about Greeson and people like him. Greedy, egotistical bastards. Somehow he connected to what was going on, he was sure. Now to figure out just how.

10

As soon as Alex parked in front of the Lewis house, he felt that Rochelle wasn't there but went to knock anyway. For some uneasy reason, he still half expected her to come to the door. The house didn't feel empty somehow, but she didn't answer and all remained quiet.

What was it, he wondered, that made a knock sound different when there was someone inside a house? Could even one human body within four walls create a variance of sound, and exactly how was it not the same if empty? Could it be a subtle change of heat, or sound and motion, almost beyond one's ability to detect? It was similar to the way you could at times intuit that someone driving ahead of you was going to make a turn or change lanes long before he switched on a signal or reached an intersection. Sometimes you just knew and found yourself driving accordingly, though it hardly made conscious sense.

He knocked again, almost as an experiment, listened, then, lost in thought, started down the wide cement driveway to his truck. He had expected to find her home. From the way she had made a recluse of herself for the last few months, he had assumed

she would be. Gone for groceries, maybe, or . . .
damn. What if she'd gone back out to the crash site
to begin her search for Lewis? Could she have got
it together that fast? Doubtful, but . . . just possible.

Nearing the street, he picked up his pace, intending to head for Lake Hood to see if her plane was
in its usual place, when a car, traveling too fast,
turned from behind a wall of bushes into the drive
and screeched to a rocking stop just short of hitting
him.

Good reflexes and an adrenaline-assisted leap carried him off the cement and onto the brown, winter-
matted lawn on all fours, soaking the knees of his
pants. From where he landed, he looked back over
a shoulder to ascertain the identity of the driver and
knew immediately that wherever Rochelle had been
it had not been the grocery store.

Though her eyes and mouth were wide in shock
at the near accident, there was something else about
her face that caught and held his attention as he
clambered to his feet. Surprise had not erased the
frown that drew her brows down and impressed two
vertical lines between them, or a less than subtle
tension that paled and pinched her face. She looked
ready for fight or flight. It would not have amazed
him if she had jumped out of the Subaru wagon and
threatened him with fists or four-letter words. She
seemed angry and ready to blame someone for more
than just a close call.

Instead, as she saw he was whole and uninjured,
she dropped her forehead onto her hands on the
wheel and her shoulders started to shake. Her posture did not astonish Jensen. He had expected an
emotional response when he saw the expression on
her face. That she should be overcome by tears was

anything but surprising, but he wondered, as he approached the car with its rolled-up windows, what else had complicated her day.

"Rochelle," he instructed loudly, "roll down the window. It's all right. I'm not hurt."

When she did not move and continued to tremble, he opened the door and reached to lay a hand on her shoulder in sympathy.

"It's all ..."

At his touch she straightened abruptly, throwing her head back, and he realized she was not crying, after all, but laughing. Uncontrollably, and with very little sound, almost hysterical, she rocked back and forth with a mirth so strong it left her almost unable to breathe.

"S-s-or-ry," she gasped. "I'm-m s-s-s ..." As she swung her feet out onto the cement of the driveway, another wave of laughter overcame and bent her double. Gradually she regained control of herself and looked up at his astounded face, which set her off again. Momentarily swallowing her reaction, she reached a hand to grip his arm, partially bracing herself upright.

"I'm sorry. Really ... I ... You looked so ... ridiculous ... funny ... all knees and elbows flying through the air. Scared the hell out of me ... but ..." She choked again.

Alex recalled his giant, uncoordinated leap and tried to picture it from her angle. In spite of his concern, he had to smile.

"I do that sort of thing best with no warning," he told her. "It's not so easy to throw around my extremities that way when I have to make an effort."

She looked up at him with a grin, clearly glad he wasn't angry with her reaction. Then, as suddenly as she had laughed, she fell apart, dissolving into tears. As though every emotion had gone crazy at once, she now shook with sobs almost as intense as her gales of laughter.

"Hey. Chelle. What's wrong?"

With hands on her shoulders, Jensen half lifted her from the car to a standing position. Automatically pulling her toward him to comfort if he could, he grew more anxious when she shoved him strongly away with both hands.

"No . . . no. I can't stand . . ." Leaving him beside the car door, she turned and, in an odd, crippled sort of run, fled up the driveway to the front door of the house, where she fumbled with the locks and disappeared inside, leaving it wide open.

Jensen stood looking after her for a minute, then got in and pulled her car up close to the garage, locked it, and went slowly to the house, giving her time to gather the pieces of her scattered emotions. As he reached the front door, she came back through it, almost at a run, barreling into him hard enough to carry them both a step or two into the yard. Her tear-streaked face was white with anger and shock as she yelled something almost incoherent and wrenched herself around to wave an accusing arm toward the house.

"Bastards . . . damn them."

Jensen grabbed her by the shoulders and forced her to stand still, though she continued to gesture.

"What, Rochelle? Is somebody in there?"

"Don't know, but there obviously was. It's trashed. The place is trashed. Damn it. Who the hell . . . ?"

Immediately all law enforcement officer, Jensen hurried her to his truck and yanked open the door.

Retrieving his off-duty Colt .45 semiautomatic from
the glove compartment, he turned back to Rochelle
and thrust his keys into her hand.

"Get in here and stay till I check it out. If I'm
not back in five minutes, or anything bad happens—
you hear shots—call dispatch for backup. You know
how to use the radio. If you've got to use it, use it
fast. If there's any threat, get out of here. Got that?"

"But, I want . . ."

"No. Get in and lock it. You're holding me up
and maybe letting the perp get away."

Without another word, she obeyed his directions,
climbed in and shut the door, looking furious, re-
sentful, and scared. Before she had it locked, Jensen
was halfway across the yard, moving swiftly, on full
alert, toward the house.

Quietly, carefully, weapon leveled and ready, he
stepped through the door and stopped, back to the
wall, while he swept the room visually before moving cautiously through the rest of the house in the
same manner, room by room.

It was, as she had said, trashed, but not vandal-
ized. The furniture—tables, chairs, lamps—had not
been tossed about vindictively. To his experienced
eye it was clear that the place had been systemati-
cally searched. The drawers in every room gapped
open, or had been pulled free and dropped by someone who didn't mean to waste time, their contents
dumped on the floor and pawed through. Closet
doors hung wide and everything that had been on
their shelves was now scattered outside on the rugs,
jumbled with clothing that had unmistakably been
stripped from hangers an article at a time.

The office was the worst, with paper strewn everywhere from the desk, file cabinets, and storage cup-

boards. Every book in the room had been removed from its shelf and evidently flung down when ruffling through it proved unrewarding, as had others elsewhere in the residence.

As he cursorily examined the clutter, it occurred to Jensen that it had been accomplished with an order of sorts. The perpetrator had gone about it in a planned and semicoordinated way, never bothering with nonessentials. The search had been conducted only where it would have been possible to hide whatever had been the object of the hunt—something specific. It must have been small and thin enough to fit within the pages of a book, or, perhaps, between or behind them. Judging from the pages and sheets scattered around, it could have been paper. This was no burglary for gain. The VCR, television, music system were all untouched. A gold bracelet of Chelle's lay on top of a chest in the bedroom. Something else was at work . . . a desire for information of some kind.

The back door, he found, had been kicked in, splintering its frame. At the extreme outer edge, a line of trees separated the backyard from its nearest neighbors, effectively assuring that no sound or unusual behavior would have attracted attention, though they were still without their new leaves. The intruder had been reasonably safe in assuming privacy, but it wouldn't hurt to ask a few questions concerning strangers anyone had seen in the area. It was also reasonable to expect that such a professional searcher had worn gloves and there would be no fingerprints, but that, too, would have to be verified.

What had been the goal of this flagrant, determined disturbance? If anything was missing, it would take Rochelle days to figure out what . . . if she could. Only the kitchen and the large double garage, half full of gear from the Lewis charter business, seemed undisturbed. A number of cardboard bankers boxes stood on garage shelves, the kind you would fill with paper . . . records. These had not been touched. Had his knocking on the front door interrupted the intruder short of these last two rooms?

Alex had little belief in coincidence, and this break-in seemed too well timed to be one. Did it somehow relate to the disappearance of Norman Lewis? To Karen Randolph? If so, how? All his intuition told him there was a connection in this to the whole puzzle, and whoever had broken in here had, or was, at least part of the answer. Did Rochelle know more than she was telling? It was time to do some real digging.

Leaving everything the way it was, touching nothing, Jensen quickly assured himself that whoever had caused this chaos was no longer on the premises, then returned to the truck. Rochelle Lewis waited, unmoving, in the cab, hugging herself with folded arms, a frozen expression on her face that betrayed no single emotion. She watched him cross the yard and climb in on the driver's side.

"No one," she stated flatly.

"Gone," he admitted, and frowned, picking up the microphone to contact dispatch. "Got to get the crime unit on it. You won't be able to get in for a while. They'll want to walk you through to see if you can tell if anything's missing. Then it'll be closed off while they do what they can to salvage any evidence."

"When?" she demanded, when he had finished the call.

"When can you go in? Couple or three hours, probably. Depends on what they find . . . or don't. You have somewhere to go? Someone I can call?" He thought briefly of Jessie in Knik, but decided to keep her out of it for the moment.

Chelle shook her head and asked an unexpected question.

"You check the garage?"

"Yeah, why?"

"Was it a wreck?"

"No. Doesn't look like whoever it was got in there . . . or the kitchen."

"Can I stay and work in the garage?"

"Why, Chelle? Give yourself a chance to catch your breath somewhere else."

He could understand her wanting to stay near her own space and possessions. The police investigation of a crime like this often seemed like another intrusion to the victims of such a break-in. Already feeling violated and upset, some responded with exaggerated possessiveness, protecting what they had left. Others wanted nothing except to be somewhere else. But . . . the garage? What could she want to do there?

"I need to get some gear together. I've got to get ready for . . . a charter. Everything I'll need, except for the plane and a few clothes, is in the garage or kitchen."

Something about it didn't ring true. He began a protest. "I don't think . . ."

The look on her face was grim, as she shook her head and raised a hand to halt his comment.

"Look, Alex. This is the first . . . ah . . . reservation of the year. I can't just stop my life now, can I? If there are jobs to be done, people to fly, then I have to do it, to keep the business going. If Norm's not here, I still have to live somehow and what money is left in the bank's supposed to go to finish paying for my plane. Without more, I could lose my wings and the business too. Then where would I be? Just let me get on with it, okay? I'm okay. Really.''

An hour later, Chelle was, as she had requested, in the garage, sorting out a pile of equipment and supplies for what she estimated would take at least a week.

Jensen was in the kitchen, speaking intently to Caswell on the phone. From Ben's impression of her, he thought she was probably right and could take care of a reduced charter business alone, if that's what she had in mind. He wasn't convinced, however, that it was. But, it wouldn't hurt to keep track of her for the next few days, just to make sure she didn't do anything stupid—like going off alone to look for her husband's body.

11

———◈———

BY THE TIME THE POLICE FINISHED GOING OVER HER house, Rochelle had all the supplies and equipment she would need for at least a week in rugged country neatly piled in the center of the garage. From a tall stool, elbows on the kitchen side of the breakfast bar, a mug of black coffee warming her palms, she watched without speaking as three officers carried out their cases of investigative technology, photography, and print lifting, knowing they had little to show for their efforts. Shaking their heads when she nodded at the coffeepot, they thanked her politely, and closed the front door as they left.

Ten minutes of thumps from the rear of the house stopped about the same time and Jensen came back to the kitchen, a hammer in one hand, to tell her the back door was solidly secured until she could get someone to repair the frame.

"Couldn't get through it without waking up half the neighborhood," he assured her, and from the number of nails she had heard being pounded, she believed him.

"You sure you want to stay here tonight?" he asked, perching his long-legged frame on another of the stools, facing her across the bar.

"I'll be fine, Alex. Really."

"Well . . . I think you might feel better in a hotel, but I'll ask the APD to drive by every hour or so. Okay?"

It's my space, she thought. Nobody—damn it—is going to take it, or scare me out of it tonight. I've got too much to do.

She looked up at his concerned face and agreed.

"Okay. If it feels bad, I'll let them know and go to a hotel, but I'd rather stay here." Without asking, she filled another mug with coffee and pushed it across the bar. "Take five. You've been at it for hours. Sorry"—she smiled crookedly—"no mustache cup."

"Thanks." He returned the smile and smoothed his expansive handlebar mustache. "Only five, though. I've got to get on down the road. We're supposed to be at Caswell's for dinner and I'm already going to be late."

Good, she thought. Something to keep you occupied—your mind on someone other than me.

"Tell Jessie hello for me, will you?" she asked, looking down at the counter, but the expression on her face—distracted and unhappy—said something else to Alex.

"Sure. Ah . . ." He paused and a frown creased his forehead. There was something . . . several somethings. She was exhibiting concern and stress.

"What?" he asked. "What is it?"

Though she appeared worried, her overall attitude had changed slightly. She seemed less fragile, more focused, as if she had made a decision of some kind. He suddenly felt uneasy about leaving.

She looked up at him, frowning. "You said it

didn't seem like whoever broke in had searched the kitchen, or the garage. Right?''

"Didn't seem like it. Nothing scattered around like the rest of the place. Why? You find something?''

She nodded. ''A few things missing, but nothing else was disturbed. I can't really say how long they've been gone.''

"What's missing?''

"As far as I can tell there's a sleeping bag, a flare gun, a set of rain gear, a first aid kit, and a heavy hunting knife.''

"That all?''

"No. There's a radio transceiver gone, too. There were two old ones we used as spares on the shelf and now there's only one.''

Alex's forehead wrinkled thoughtfully. ''How long since you remember them being there?''

"God, I don't know. Weeks. I haven't had charters—haven't needed anything.''

"How about before. Could Norm have taken them for some reason last fall?''

She hesitated, trying to remember. ''I don't think so. I did a lot of flying—going in and out of there—after he went missing. I think I would have noticed, but it's possible, I guess.''

"No way to tell then, but we'll keep it in mind. Listen, Chelle. About that charter . . .''

She didn't wait for what she knew he would say next.

"Don't bother, Alex. I can't let people down, so I'm going.''

Can't let *Norm* down? she wondered. ''I promise I'll be careful. Besides, I'll file flight plans, so you'll know where I'm heading.''

But not till I'm already gone, she decided. Probably a round robin, giving them an estimate, since I'm not sure about the return and won't be able to say when I'll close it out. Try for a week.

"Don't *worry,*" she told him. "I'm a big girl, okay? Been doing this for a long time."

He bit his upper lip like a child determined to hold his tongue, and nodded once, stiffly, not completely satisfied, but respecting her right to decide. Let her fly the charter. It would be something to keep her busy, at least . . . maybe out of trouble. What was she *not* telling him?

"Okay. I give up. Just check in once in a while. This break-in concerns me. Do you have any idea what he . . . she . . . oh hell . . . it . . . was after? Don't forget that it's possible—if this try was unsuccessful—it might happen again. Don't take chances."

At his frustrated attempt at political correctness, she had to smile, as she shook her head. "Not a clue." But suddenly she remembered the milk, found that morning on the wrong shelf. No. Silly. My own dumb mistake. As he went on, she forgot it, to focus on what he was saying.

"Now. I need your reaction to some things we found out about the crash."

For a second she froze, then waited with wary, close attention.

"The survival gear was still in the plane. I'm sorry, Chelle, but it all seemed to be there: sleeping bag, emergency supplies, first aid kit, flares, rifle, ammunition . . . the lot. Either he couldn't get to it, or didn't try. There was no way to tell much from the instruments. Doesn't matter much anyway, does it? We know what brought it down."

Her frown narrowed her eyes with concentration as she nodded. Norm had always carried survival gear in his plane, never removed it, only replaced what he used, or added to it. The gear missing from the garage was almost a duplicate of what he normally carried. Had he taken it? Why? She drew a deep breath.

"What else? Who was she? Do you know?"

He nodded. "Did Norm ever mention a Karen Randolph?"

"Randolph? No. Never. Who was she? What was she doing in his plane?"

"Nothing on your charter books?"

"No, and I know them almost by heart. Never heard of her . . . from him, or in writing. Who *was* she, Alex? Tell me, damn it."

"You've got to keep quiet about it, okay? For now, we don't want it known that we've found her body."

"Yes. Okay." With one important exception he didn't need to know about, she would comply.

"Randolph was a special undercover Fish and Wildlife agent. Up here from Wisconsin as part of a sting on illegal trophy hunting. You remember that big bust in the Brooks Range—ANWR—last year? She was part of it."

"Wisconsin?" Rochelle breathed. Another piece of information clicked into place. The Madison number in the lock box could be hers. Why? What? Norm? Special agent? Her head spun with confusion and she hardly heard Jensen's question.

"Yeah. Does that mean something?"

When she glanced up, he was looking at her with a glint of suspicion in his eyes. It shook her. For the first time she suddenly felt like a suspect of some kind.

"Ah . . . I don't know. Two days ago I would have said it meant nothing at all, but . . . well . . . I found something strange yesterday, Alex."

"What?"

She told him about the metal box in the closet, the papers and key it had contained, and her search for the safe-deposit box that led to the insurance policy. "When I tried the number on the phone it reached an answering machine with a woman's voice that the operator told me was Madison, Wisconsin. But she wouldn't tell me who it belonged to. Could it be Karen Randolph? But why would Norm have her number? Why Wisconsin?"

"I can't answer about Norm yet, but it's interesting that he had her number, if that's what it turns out to be. Give it to me so I can run a check on it. I'd like to see that insurance policy, too. You brought it home?" She nodded, and he went on. "Randolph came in from outside so she could go undercover as a hunter after big game—someone they wouldn't know or recognize. Get evidence that they were running an illegal hunt—taking game from restricted areas, hunting with planes."

"They? Who're they? Is that who trashed this place?"

"Now, here's where it gets sticky. We don't know. Those who were caught in the trap are still in jail, but there were others who were probably involved that we didn't get. It could be one of them, on his own, or for someone who's still doing time at Spring Creek in Seward. Dale Stoffel, maybe. He was the biggest fish. His guiding business was behind most of it."

She slid off the stool to pace back and forth in the kitchen, talking as she thought.

"Stoffel. Now there's a name I *am* familiar with. Everyone who flew or guided talked about him. Word gets around . . . rumors. He's had a bad rep for years. Had a plane confiscated once for guiding a hunt on federal land. Wasn't shy about letting people know that the law wouldn't get another of them— that he'd blow it sky high before he let it go to the feds, and did. Saw them coming again and couldn't get off the ground, so he stuck a rag in the gas tank, lit it, and ran for cover."

She wheeled around to face Jensen, realization and anger spreading across her face as she put the rest of the pieces together. It wasn't *her* he suspected.

"You . . . *think* . . . Norm was in on it somehow . . . the illegal stuff. You've got to be kidding, Jensen. *Never*. He wasn't a greenie, or a wolf-hugger, but he found the idea of trophy killing distasteful. Only took that kind of charter—into the hunting camps, I mean—for a good client, or when there wasn't someone else to fly. He thought hunting should be limited to subsistence, not allowed for sport. I'm not so committed, one way or the other, so I flew most of the hunters."

She stopped walking suddenly, as a revelation of another kind floated to the surface of her consciousness. This one she did not comment on aloud. Norm had not turned over a hunting charter to her for several months before he disappeared. He had flown them himself, and there had been several. Why? It had not occurred to her before, but now she thought back, mentally counting on her fingers. Six? . . . seven? No. It wasn't possible. Not Norm. But could

he have been helping the feds? It would explain the
Randolph woman in his plane . . . the secrecy . . . her
number in his lock box . . . perhaps, somehow, the
missing money. Had he known something . . . kept
some kind of record? Was that what her burglar was
looking for?

"What?" Jensen demanded, behind her. "You remember something else?"

His questions were beginning to be an irritation.
Should she tell him that she intended to go hunting
for Norm? No, she decided. Not till she knew where
this was leading her, what it all meant, and she still
didn't know much. Not all. Not yet. Later . . .
maybe. If she could clear Norm. He didn't need to
know she meant to go out there tomorrow . . . probably wouldn't let her go alone if he did. Carefully
she composed her face before turning.

"Nothing. Just trying to remember. But you're
wrong if you think Norm could have been part of
that kind of thing, Alex. It simply wasn't in him.
You'll see. I'll get you that phone number and the
policy to look at, but I want to keep it here. Okay?"

He agreed, but, as she headed for the back of the
house, he knew from her expression, or lack of it,
he would get no more from her. There was something she wasn't telling him, but he knew it would
do no good to press for it. Whatever her reason, she
felt justified in keeping it to herself, and it would
probably be better to leave it alone . . . for now . . .
but not for long. She'd had enough thrown at her
today. Tomorrow would be soon enough.

But he was concerned with it as he drove across
town to the Glenn Highway and most of the way to
Knik to pick up Jessie. He was glad he would be

spending the evening with Caswell. They needed to talk.

But his mind . . . and sympathy, mixed with irritation . . . were back with Rochelle. He believed that, alive or dead—and probably the latter—Norm Lewis was gone—had left her—and wouldn't be back. He had wished badly that there was something he could say . . . could give her to alleviate some of the hurt. Knowing from personal experience the confusion and guilt grief could inspire, he found himself more than usually concerned and quite helpless. She would not let him in. Clearly did not completely trust him . . . or anyone.

Losing someone shook your confidence and judgment. made you want to . . . atone? . . . for things you had no control over. *You,* after all, were still alive, while the person you grieved for was not. What else could elicit more guilt, more effort to make up for it? She was an attractive, talented, strong woman, intelligent, with a mind of her own. All right—stubborn. That brother of hers was no help—more of an albatross, if what Alex had seen of him was any indication. She was pretty much alone in all this, determined to know, and capable of trying to find out on her own.

Frustrated, he wanted to turn around, go back and shake her awake . . . or give her the support she didn't seem to realize she needed. Knowing that she would welcome neither didn't afford him much relief. Damn it, anyway.

Rochelle waited till he was gone long enough to be sure he wouldn't be back, then threw on a jacket and transferred the pile of equipment and supplies to the Subaru and headed for Lake Hood. A quick

phone call had told her she would have some waiting
to do and might as well get her plane loaded while
she did it.

Gassed and ready, the Cessna sat rocking slightly
on its floats when she reached the lake. Long shadows darkened the water, cast by the evening sun, still
far enough from the horizon that she was tempted to
fly up and watch it set from the best of all possible
vantage points. Afraid she might miss her objective
if she did, she carried gear to the plane instead and
stowed it neatly, ready for the morning. Aware, as
always, of the empty space next to hers that would
normally have held Norm's familiar 206, she pretended to ignore it, concentrating on the job at hand.

Preparations complete, she had occupied a log on
the bank for over half an hour, watching the dark
increase and the water change colors, when a compact Maule M-4, similar to Ben Caswell's, slid out
of the sky, set down smoothly on the waters of the
lake, and taxied toward the space next to Norm's.
She got up and walked across to stand solidly, arms
akimbo, head tilted slightly, waiting.

Close to shore, the pilot of the small craft killed
the engine and let the plane coast to the bank as he
stepped out onto a float and peered through the gath-
ering dusk.

"Chelle? That you?"

"Yeah, it's me, Jeff. Got a minute?"

"Sure. Let me tie up first."

While she watched, he pulled a pair of waders up
over the legs of blue coveralls and walked into the
water to swing the plane around to face the lake
before tethering it. Though not a tall man, he was
very fit and it was obvious from the ease with which

he maneuvered the Maule that he had done it often and had plenty of muscle left over.

The last rays of the departing sun stained his prematurely white hair gold as he stepped back onto the bank and came toward her with a grin.

"Great day to be up there," he said. "You just down?"

"No. Going up tomorrow though. Weather's supposed to hold."

"You're waiting for me, then. What's up?"

His smile faded as he searched her face for clues to what she had to say and found no good news.

She hesitated for a second or two, knowing the information she brought and the questions she must ask would disappoint and trouble him. She liked this man who was a special friend to her husband—his best, almost family—and who had grown to be her good friend too. Though she had already known how to fly when she met Norm, he had insisted she take a lesson or two from Jeff. "He can smooth off any rough spots—teach you more than I could. He's the best."

And he was.

Easygoing and generous of spirit, Bunker was universally respected as a pilot's pilot by those who flew off Lake Hood. She felt privileged to know him, appreciated his cheerful confidence, and tried to emulate his responsible attitude toward what he clearly felt was the *gift* of flight. By no means a simple man, he thoroughly and without reservation enjoyed living, criticized little, openly appreciated much, and had a healthy sense of humor.

He hadn't tried to minimize his frustration and concern over his friend's disappearance and continued absence—had flown hours of search patterns—

but was predisposed to optimism. Throughout the winter, he had not let a week go by without checking in. Respecting her independence, not attempting to take care of or smother her, but letting her feel his consistent presence and support, for which she was more than simply grateful.

Now he stood, patiently waiting, with a questioning look, so she told him quickly.

"They found the plane and Norm wasn't in it. Still missing."

"Damn. Where?"

"Beyond Susitna. In one of those lakes on the bench before you get to Beluga. The bad thing . . . there were bullet holes in the fuselage, and a dead woman in the passenger seat. Jensen . . . you know . . . the trooper? Says she was an undercover agent for Fish and Wildlife on that Stoffel Brooks Range thing last year. She came up missing about the same time, but nobody associated her with Norm. Still don't know what the deal was. They want it kept quiet."

She stopped, interested in his reaction, which was stillness—utter watchful stillness—and exceptional attention. He knew something.

"And?" he prompted.

"And . . ." She pulled a hand from her jacket pocket and passed him the envelope from the safe-deposit box, closely watching his expression. ". . . this. He left it for me to find. Do you know why? If he told anyone, he'd have told you. Did he?"

Jeff turned it over twice, took the insurance policy out and read it before looking up with a frown, shaking his head.

"No," he said slowly, "Norm didn't tell me anything about this."

But there was something going on behind his eyes that she couldn't identify. Straight as they come, she'd never known him to dissemble, but she was abruptly aware that he was choosing his words with care. Jeff wouldn't lie, but he was avoiding the whole truth by answering the question literally.

"All right. If he didn't tell you about this, what *did* he tell you? Is he alive, Jeff? Did he expect for me to somehow cash in on this policy and get part of it later? What the hell is going on? Where is he? There's other money missing. Have you known all winter that he wasn't dead—that he set it up and took off somewhere? How could you . . ."

"Hey." As her voice rose in anger and pain, he stepped forward to grasp her by the shoulders, paper pages crackling under his hand. "Chelle, hey. Stop it. No, damn it. He didn't tell me anything of the kind. Whatever gave you that idea? He loved you. You know that."

"Do I?" She looked him straight in the eye, challenging.

"Yes. More than anything. He'd never have put you through this."

"Convincing me, or yourself?"

His expression changed, as if he had suddenly come to a decision. He handed back the papers and stepped back. "I had no idea he left this, Chelle. He didn't tell me much of anything. Nothing that would help, or I would have told you sooner. He gave me something and made me promise."

"What? For God's sake, what, Jeff?"

"I'll show you. It's for you anyway. Wait here."

He went to a shed similar to the one by Chelle's plane, opened the door and rummaged around for a minute. When he came back, he was carrying another envelope that he handed to her. It was sealed, like the first.

"Tell me," she demanded, holding it without attempting to tear it open. "What did he make you promise?"

Her eyes in the half-light were wide and her face haunted with stress. The envelope trembled in her hand.

"Come and sit down first."

They sat on the step to his shed.

"Okay," he told her, "here's the thing. Last fall, sometime in September, because we were both down here getting the planes ready for winter. He was doing something with your radio . . ."

"It had been cutting out on me. He found a loose wire."

"Yeah. Well . . . when we were through, he came with a pair of beers, sat down, and said he had a favor to ask. Said if I agreed to do it, I couldn't ask questions, and that it was important. I said I would, of course. He'd have done the same for me. It wasn't like Norm to need favors, or ask them, so I wondered, but I *didn't* ask. Then he gave me that envelope, sealed, just like it is now. Asked would I keep it for him and not tell anyone, even you."

"Especially me, I think," she whispered. "Why?"

"He didn't say that. Said the reason he couldn't explain was because it was someone else's confidence, but that this would make it okay for you, just in case."

"In case . . . what? What is it?"

"That's what I don't know and couldn't ask, see? He told me to keep it sealed and locked up, and give it back when he wanted it. The only exception was if one of two things happened: Either you came with questions, or I was very certain he wasn't coming back to get it. Then I was to give it to you, unopened.''

''Is that exactly how he phrased the last part?''

''Yes. If I was very certain he wasn't coming back to get it. Your coming tonight qualifies for the first of those two things, doesn't it?''

It did, but the thought that she was struggling to force from her mind was that it might qualify for both. He hadn't said *if you know for certain that I'm dead,* but rather, *if you are very certain I'm not coming back to get it.* Had he actually left intending *not* to come back for it? Giving himself time to disappear—to cover his trail? Was he somewhere else, alive and well, meaning to stay gone, no matter what Jeff said? Jensen thought so. It was part of his attitude, although he hadn't come right out and put it in words.

This was the nightmare all over again. Chelle sat staring at the envelope in her hand. It was not thick and weighed little, but its shape suggested money and something else. A letter?

Intolerable. The old guilt swept over her in a wave, but she fought it furiously. What was it? She did and didn't want to know. Would it tell her that he had knowingly left her? Why he had? Or would it give her a clue to what he had been doing? Why he had taken the trouble to lay down this evidence trail with obvious forethought?

This would make it okay for her . . . *just in case,* he had told Bunker. What could possibly make it *okay*? If he was gone for good—or even if he was alive—it would never be *okay,* and he had to have known that. A few dollars or pieces of paper would change nothing, mean nothing.

Jeff sat silently beside her, solid and supposedly trustworthy, waiting for her reaction to cue his response. But could she trust him? Could she trust anyone . . . even herself? He was first and foremost loyal to Norm, not her. Was he still keeping promised secrets?

With a flash of anger, she ripped off one end of the envelope and shook it, open end down, ready to catch whatever slid out. A folded, plain sheet of plain white paper landed in her hand, and fell open to expose a thin stack of bills held together with a red rubber band, the top bill a hundred. The money missing from the bank account? It didn't feel very thick.

There was no letter . . . no message. The unfolded white sheet lay in her hand, empty of writing . . . and of Norm's reasons for this *just-in-case* contingency he had entrusted to his friend.

AS THE WEATHER GREW WARMER, AKLAK WAS MORE and more on the move, each day devoted primarily to eating. From the time he left his den in the spring and till when he returned to it in the fall, he might range as far as a thousand square miles in his never-ending search for food. Early in the year, this would consist mainly of grass and sedges, and though he could eat a wide variety of vegetation, he preferred anything that was high in protein—energy food that would add fat to his body. Through the largesse of the summer, he would often eat close to ninety pounds of food each day. Later in the year, when cold weather made edible things more scarce, his range might increase as he attempted to find food and store fat for hibernation.

Through the warm months, when there would be plenty on which to browse, he would never go hungry and would have a wide variety of choices. Under rocks and fallen logs, he would scratch up worms and grubs. Few mice or ground squirrels would escape him, for if he did not catch them aboveground, he would scrape them out of their burrows with his sharp claws, his strong shoulders and forearms being well adapted for digging up yards of earth al-

most effortlessly. But rodents would be only a side dish to his predominantly herbaceous diet of roots and greens.

Aklak was particularly fond of the sap and cambium layer of tree bark. Standing high on his hind legs, he would bite into the bark, catch a strip in his teeth to tear away from the trunk, then lick up the sweet sap and chew at the inner bark.

In his prime at ten years old, he might live twice that long, though his sibling sister would probably outlive him, since female bears, as with many species, tend to live longer than males. Aklak was larger than average. From the bottom of his front paw, when it was flat on the ground, to the highest point of his shoulder, he stood five feet six inches, and from his nose to the tip of his tail, just over nine feet. Though in others of his kind color varied from blond to almost black, his coat was a beautiful warm brown, with pale-tipped guard hairs that gave him the grizzled look for which his kind was named: grizzly, from the Old French word grizel, *meaning somewhat gray or grayish. Those hairs extended beyond the heavy thickness of fur, adding the frosted, or silver-tipped, appearance.*

His face was broad and slightly dished, his dark brown eyes small and close-set, his ears small and rounded. To increase the distance of his sight, to reach upward for something, or to posture or fight, he could stand on his hind legs unaided, but he did not walk while standing. When he traveled, it was on all fours, and because, like all bears, Aklak did not have a separating clavicle to hold his shoulder bones apart, he moved with a curious shuffling, pigeon-toed gait, his shoulders working as he alternately moved his front feet one at a time. The hump between his shoulders provided the muscle for his remarkable digging ability and the exceptional power of his forepaws to strike—quite enough to decapitate a man, or dispatch a moose with one swipe.

His paw prints, with their swirls and whorls, were as unique to him as were a human person's, and the tracks they made looked remarkably similar to those a human would make, though larger. His toe prints formed a relatively straight line, with marks of his long claws several inches in front of them, twice as long as the toe pads. He walked on the front part of his forepaw, which left a track seven inches long and eight inches wide. His complete hind paw measured a full fourteen inches long and nine inches wide.

Capable of speeds up to fifty feet a second at full charge, he could maintain them only for a few minutes, but could easily run half again as fast as a man. His vision and hearing were reasonably good, but Aklak's sense of smell was his most important asset, for no other animal's was more acute. He could pick up the scent of prey from several miles away.

Strongly built and extremely healthy, he was susceptible to very few diseases and challenged by nothing in his world but other brown bears and the weapons of man.

His name, Aklak, had been given to his species by the Eskimo people. But his kind had other names in North America, given by other peoples: the beast that walks like man, bruin, enemy of man, fur father, grand old gladiator, great bear, grouchy, king of brutes, lord of the woods, Moccasin Joe, monarch of the mountains, Old Caleb, Old Ephraim, old man of the mountains, silvertip, that which lives in the den, and Uncle, among them. Those given to him by

Native-American peoples were more admiring and personal: big hairy one, chief's son, colored bear, cousin, elder brother, fine young chief, four-legged human, grandfather, old man, old man in a furred cloak, real bear, that which went away, and the unmentionable one.

Unconscious of any of these, secure in the world in which he lived, Aklak would spend the spring wandering the great plateau at the foot of Mount Susitna, unaware that it, too, had a name given to it by man—simply accepting what came, as it came, expecting nothing.

12

"YOU'VE BEEN SOMEWHERE ELSE ALL NIGHT," JES-
sie said as she hung her jacket on a hook by the
cabin door. "What's on your mind, trooper?"

Alex turned to smile at her and the question. She
could read him better than he expected at times.

Dinner with Ben and Linda Caswell, followed by
two rubbers of bridge, had been pleasantly relaxing
and, for the most part, full of friendly humor and
conversation. Early in the evening, Alex had brought
Cas up to date on the break-in and what he had
learned from Chelle, while Linda and Jessie dis-
cussed a gardening project they were planning.
Later, however, he had not been able to put it away,
found it hard to keep his thoughts from drifting back
to the case and Rochelle Lewis. It was a distraction
that felt more important than it seemed from the
facts, but he hadn't been able to shake it off.

Once, he had slowly become aware of his hand of
cards—and the other three players regarding him
quizzically—with no idea at all what he had just bid.
When he lost two obvious tricks in a row and Jessie
had threatened to make him sleep in the storage
shed, they had conceded the game and headed for
home.

It was a clear, cool night with a new moon hanging like a silver scythe in the sky in front of them as Jensen aimed his truck east into the Mat-Su Valley. Pioneer Peak loomed in dark southern silhouette as the road curved left to cross the twin bridges of the Knik and Susitna rivers. Content to listen quietly to the country and western music from the radio without conversation, Jessie had leaned lightly against his shoulder and laid an affectionate hand just above his knee as they traveled. In the lights from the dashboard, they had exchanged smiles. And, before they were ten minutes out of Eagle River, Jensen was once again considering the Lewis case.

Most of his contemplation had a familiar feeling. Collecting bits and pieces of evidence, seemingly related, or not, was part of what challenged him professionally. He enjoyed solving the puzzles, and was exceptionally good at it. At a certain point in most cases it often appeared that most of what he knew or suspected was a crazy quilt of partially defined shapes, full of holes and designs that didn't match. He had learned that it was better not to overexamine the parts that frustrated him but, rather, to relegate odd scraps to the back of his mind, where they could gradually work their way into a pattern that made sense. Through years of investigation, he had grown confident in this method, took it on faith, knowing he could leave some things alone to come together on their own, while he focused his attention on others.

Even after arriving at the cabin, however, Alex wasn't quite comfortable enough with the process to abandon his thoughts. While Jessie made them each a cup of tea, he added wood to the stove, and when she handed him his large, brown mug of fragrantly steaming liquid, he was ready to talk about some of it.

"Just can't get this case to leave me alone tonight," he told her, finally settling into a chair on one side of the kitchen table.

"How do you mean?" On the other side, she leaned on her elbows, holding her mug in both hands, reminding him of Chelle at the breakfast bar earlier.

"I feel like there's something going on that I can't get hold of and it bothers me. It's kind of like when you know something that must be done is potential trouble. You can't make it any easier, but you sort of walk all around it, checking out everything that could go wrong and planning what you'll do if anything does.

"This one has me on that kind of an edge. I don't have enough information yet. So it's like the usual loose ends, but more than that."

"What exactly makes you feel that way?" she asked. "Can you identify the causes?"

He frowned. She was right. He needed to go back to the foundations of the feelings. Narrowing his eyes, he nodded slowly and thought aloud.

"Yeah . . . part . . . maybe. Chelle's a big reason. I *do* think she's building herself up to go hunting for Norm. But her outlook has changed somehow . . . something subtle. She's focused on something and isn't saying what. I think she knows something, but I couldn't get her to tell me. This afternoon she got a sort of listening look on her face—like she was trying something on mentally to see how it fit—but when I asked, she denied there was anything."

"This afternoon?"

"Yeah. Somebody broke into the Lewis house this morning while she was out. Kicked in the back door and did a pretty thorough job of tossing most of the place. It was definitely a search for something I have a hunch they didn't find. I think we interrupted whoever it was before they could finish. The kitchen and garage were untouched—though Chelle says there are some things missing from the garage— but the office was ankle-deep in paper and books that had been thrown off the shelves."

"You think she knows what they were after?"

"Or thinks she does, maybe, but that doesn't fit quite right either. It's more like she knows something she didn't know until yesterday, or today . . . something she's thought over and decided to act on. There's a confidence she didn't seem to have before. You know? But she's afraid of something, too. I could almost smell it. Hard to explain."

"Well, you're probably right. You're pretty good at reading people. But why keep it to herself? Doesn't she see that it might help more if you knew what she knows, or is worrying about?"

"I don't know. There's some reason she thinks it's important, I guess. What I'm getting more sure of is that Lewis isn't coming back. He may be dead. He may have taken off. But she hasn't come to terms with that. Suspects—maybe, subconsciously, but doesn't let it in. This afternoon, early, she almost ran over me, and was so upset she couldn't decide whether to laugh or cry, so she wound up doing both. Hysteria. But, by the time I left, she was refusing to stay in a hotel for the night—calmly packing for a charter with determination and organization—cool as you please."

"She covers up a lot."

"I know. But there's a lot going on. Angry? Scared? Depressed? Determined? Can't put my finger on the right combination. I don't know. She's going to come down hard when she has to face what I think is coming. She can be angry as long as she convinces herself he took off on her. When, and if, she knows for certain he's dead? Wish I could help, but that's a real loner space."

With concern of her own, Jessie watched a confusion of concern and emotion flicker across his face. It was unusual for Alex to allow himself to become so personally wrapped up in a case. His objectivity was very important to him, so he made special efforts to remain a step away emotionally from those he investigated, or who were perceived as involved, victims or not. She knew the situation played on his understanding of loss and grief, that he recognized himself in it, but it didn't explain his depth of distraction with this case. There was something more.

Well, she thought, whatever it is, maybe if I play his game and leave it alone, it will come to me.

When he looked up, noticing her silence, she was studying his face thoughtfully.

"Thanks, Jess," he said suddenly, in appreciation he couldn't separate into distinct and describable pieces.

She was *so present* when she listened. Not judgmental. Seldom critical. Never demanding. Just there . . . as if nothing else mattered as much, whatever it was, and there would be all the time needed to attend to it. He thought that lately he had come and gone from their relationship with utter, unquestioning confidence, but with little thought to its nurturing or

care. Have I been taking it . . . her . . . for granted?
he wondered. Probably.

"You're welcome," she told him, "for . . . whatever."

"Hey,"—reaching for her hand—"you're a long
ways away over there."

She smiled. "And you're a long ways away up
here," she said, tapping the top of her head. "It's
okay. I'm getting used to the law enforcement mo-
dus operandi. It's a sort of mental merry-go-round
you climb onto and go in circles, trying to catch the
gold ring, and can't get off till you have it and the
music stops."

Alex chuckled. "That's not a bad description,
lady. All you forgot is the dizzy part, the feeling that
the rest of the world is whirling around while you
stand still."

"Yeah? Well, whirl, or stand still, to your heart's
content, if it helps solve the thing. I'm going to
check on Black Dog's cut foot once more before I
turn in. Back in a minute or two."

He watched her step into boots, slip into her
jacket, and go out the door. Through the window in
it, her honey-colored hair, backlit from the porch
light, glowed like gold silk before she disappeared
into the dark.

How different, he thought, from Chelle's thick
reddish-brown.

Then he got up to rinse their tea mugs clean and
get the coffeepot ready for morning.

13

THE EARLY-MORNING SKY WAS CLEAR WITH ONLY a few scattered clouds on the western horizon, the air, still, perfect for flying, exactly what Chelle Lewis needed. As she finished transmitting the ritual departure exchange with the tower, lifted the 206 from the water of Lake Hood, and swung away to the north, once again her breath seemed to come deeper and easier.

Automatically, she squelched the communications frequency and tuned her second radio to the upbeat contemporary music of KFQD's AM station with its powerful long-range transmitter. The rhythmic tones of Stevie Nicks's "Leather and Lace" filled her ears as she watched the Automatic Direction Finder swing around to indicate the broadcast's position of origin to the east. As it set her foot tapping, she realized it was the first time in months she had listened to popular music with more pleasure than pain, especially this nostalgic station that seemed to play, on a rotating basis, the music that had meaning to her life. Before Norm disappeared she had never noticed how every song was one of love or loss, many some of both. Those that didn't reflect the joys and sorrows of togetherness were almost as bad. Listening had seemed an intolerable masochism that turned pain into what felt like shards of glass in her chest and stomach. Now, as she reached to turn it off, some obstinate, new strength drew her hand back and she went on half listening, ignoring most of the words. This morning it was not unpleasant company, as long as the tempo was upbeat.

Still tapping, she banked the Cessna west toward Mount Susitna.

A blanket of snow still covered most of the Sleeping Lady, though it was looking more and more moth-eaten as the temperature grew ever warmer and patches of dark rock melted out, absorbing the heat of a sun that hung longer in the sky each day. By the summer solstice on the twenty-first of June, it would be light almost all night.

Fall in Alaska was brief, and winter came in like revenge, but spring seemed to take its time, stretching and luxuriating in the renewal of warmth, swelling from stark, bitter browns to lush, new greens that hung like a haze in the alders and birch everywhere you looked, an enlivening promise of summer. It was Chelle's favorite season.

Shortly before dawn, she had dropped a note in her brother Ed's mailbox, avoiding the confrontation she knew would be inevitable if she told him she was going out alone to start a ground search for her husband. Tired of such confrontations, and his condemnation of Norm, she had kept her plans to herself. There was also the shadow of doubt in her own mind that she had no desire to share, knowing it would be taken by him only as a confirmation. She had not called to tell him about the break-in, had spoken to no one since leaving Lake Hood the night before.

She had returned to a house that felt invaded, but empty, and had occupied the evening hours rescuing books from the floor, resentfully smoothing creased pages and sorrowing over the broken spines of old friends. Though not really frightened, she had been cautious, going through each room to assure herself she was alone, checking the security of the back door, locking every lock, closing all the curtains and blinds.

From the gun cabinet in the hall, she had taken her big .375 Weatherby Magnum, carried it to the bedroom and leaned it against the wall by the bed. It was her usual go-along gun: the rifle she took most often in the plane, especially in bear country, which included most of the state, and much preferred over handguns that took up less space. Intending to take it with her the next morning, she felt safer with it close at hand, though it was considerably more firepower than she would ever need on a housebreaker. Used competently, it could stop a Kodiak brown, a charging moose, probably an elephant.

Even knowing the rifle was loaded and within easy reach, there had been only interrupted naps during the hours of darkness. She had found herself waking to check each sound she couldn't immediately identify, indoors or out. Twice she had seen an APD squad car pass the house. Once she had peered out a rear window to watch the shadowy bulk of a large bull moose amble across the backyard in surprising silence.

She had not noticed a motionless but watchful shadow within a shadow next to a small garden shed at the back of the property, and went back to bed unaware that it remained watchful most of the night. Regardless of the lack of sleep, now that she was in

the air on the first stage of her mission, she felt alert
and more energetic than she had in weeks.

There seemed to be a thin hint of reddish-yellow
in the alders on south-facing slopes near Alexander
Creek at the foot of Mount Susitna on the eastern
side. It was only a hint, but it pleased her to think
that bursting energy would soon spread to everything
that still looked gray and tired. With extra hours of
spring daylight, trees in the north seemed to virtually
explode with leaves between one day and the next,
then grow as fast as possible. Wilderness Alaska
might display a wealth of pearl, diamond, and opal
in the snow, ice, and aurora borealis of her winters,
but during the warmer half of each year, she wan-
tonly lavished a thousand hues of jade, emerald, and
sapphire in munificent extravagance over her forests,
tundra, lakes, rivers, and coastal waters. It was good
to anticipate.

Except for an Alaska Airlines 737 completing a
wide turn south toward Seattle from the runway at
Anchorage International, the sky was momentarily
empty at almost seven o'clock in the morning. Its
brightening blue looked scrubbed clean and the air
was so clear she could plainly see four of the vol-
canoes that formed part of the Alaskan edge of the
Pacific Ring of Fire. Spurr, Redoubt, and Illiamna
on the mainland, and Augustine, on its island at the
outer edge of Kamishak Bay, rose in a majestic line
at the upper end of the long mountain range that fell
far beyond her sight to the south and west, sweeping
into the scimitar of Aleutian Islands that divided the
Bering Sea from the North Pacific.

In a few minutes, Mount Susitna fell behind her
on the right and she was floating back over the plateau where she had been only two days before. As

she silenced the music on her radio, she frowned, suddenly recalling the glitch in her usual takeoff routine that morning. The radio had been set on the wrong frequency.

All pilots had their own idiosyncrasies and habits in performing the necessary flying chores. One of hers was almost automatically setting the radio to the frequency she would initially use on the next flight. After completing her landing communications with the tower, she always switched to the frequency that carried all the details on weather and conditions important to pilots: "Information Alpha."

This morning the radio has still been turned to tower frequency, an annoyance that suggested to her that perhaps she had been more upset over the discovery of Norm's plane and irritated with Ed than she had realized. It annoyed her to lose track of her normal routine, especially in connection with her plane. Consistency was, after all, the key to safe flying. An easily altered radio frequency was no threat, but what else might she have forgotten or missed that could make an important difference? And it was not the first time since Norm disappeared that it had happened. Twice before the winter had set in she had neglected to make the change and been just as bothered by the mistake.

But she had let her concern slip away as, less than an hour from takeoff, she had dropped out of the sky and was drifting in for a landing on the narrow, nameless lake where Norm's plane had gone down. Not a breath of breeze so much as rippled its mirror surface, so still it reflected like a piece of sky fallen between the hills, making it impossible to see where air stopped and water began. Confident that the surface was there nonetheless, Chelle leveled out above it and let the Cessna slowly lose altitude until, at last, the floats brushed and revealed it with twin wakes of visible disturbance.

Pleased with the perfect smoothness of the landing, she was powering down when the shadow of something in the water ahead made her instinctively swing the rudder hard to the left. The Cessna responded decently, like a boat in the water, and there was only a small bump she could hardly feel as the right float nudged against a heavy log suspended and almost invisible just below the surface.

Chelle heaved a sigh of relief at just how close she had come to disaster. A punctured float would fill quickly, destroying buoyancy, possibly making it impossible to take off, depending on the size of the hole. The bump had, thankfully, not been hard enough to create such a hole. She would have no trouble remembering to locate this particular hazard and avoid it when she left.

Taxiing to the shore, she pulled up near the empty spot where Norm's plane had rested. The helicopter had lifted it out, swinging on a strong cable, and flown it back to the lab in Anchorage. Only a few scrapes remained where it had initially been dragged out of the water by the winch. In the mud around these were the footprints of what looked like an army. Had there been as many people as there were prints, she thought, they could have picked up the plane and walked away with it.

Floats resting against the bank, Chelle cut the engine and automatically reset the radio as usual. From this location, she was too low to receive radio signals from Anchorage, but setting the radio anyway made her feel she was wiping out her earlier error. Half smiling, she opened the door and sat looking around

her for a long minute before climbing out. In the
sudden silence she heard a raven's raucous call and
saw it swoop from the branches of one of the stunted
evergreens on the ridge, inky-black wing tips feath-
ering the air like fingers. The big ravens looked
blacker than black, noisy holes in the world where
light seemed to disappear. Ripples caused by the
plane dispersed on the lake, leaving it flat and still
once again. Somewhere, unseen, a fish jumped with
a distant splash. A squirrel's alarmed *tic . . . tic . . .
tic* betrayed its presence in the brush and she imagined its fluffy tail twitching in time to that warning
sound.

It was cool in the early sunshine, so she pulled on
a down vest over her turtleneck sweater before walking the float and hopping off with an armload of
equipment. Her waders over wool socks squished in
the mud near the water's edge, but farther up the
ground was bare and drier, where she expertly fastened a *come-along* to a tree and ran a cable back
to the plane. In just a few minutes, she had reversed
the Cessna's direction and pulled the back third of
the floats out of the water and onto the bank. Around
two other trees, she looped additional cables that
ended in safety slip-hooks, tethering the hooks back
onto the cables through their spring latches, securing
the plane solidly to the shore. Later, it would be
relatively easy to loosen and push it down the bank's
gentle incline into the water again.

Satisfied with the results of this chore, before un-
loading her gear, she climbed back into the plane,
pulled a handful of USGS maps from the door
pocket and sorted through them till she located the
one she wanted: Tyonic B-4, Alaska. Tucking the
rest away, she spread it out on the passenger seat,

leaning to examine it in the sunlight that fell through the window.

The rolling hills of the plateau it pictured around this small lake rose and fell in topographic lines between five hundred and a thousand feet above sea level. One of the lowest and largest of dozens of unnamed lakes and ponds in the area, it was easy to identify, in the lower right quadrant, by its slightly more than mile length and elongated shape. Approximately seven miles away to the southeast, the plateau ended and fell steeply away to flatland near the Cook Inlet.

Four miles west, Lower Beluga Lake widened the Beluga River, giving it the appearance of a snake that had swallowed a particularly large dinner. It was this direction Chelle felt Norm would have chosen if he had tried for the coast. Following Olson Creek, which began just over a ridge east of the crash scene, would have been shorter, but essentially more difficult, as it swept through a narrow, heavily forested ravine that fell off to the flats below. Beluga River was large enough to float a raft, even a log, over parts of it, reducing the required walking time and effort. Olson Creek was too small for this possibility.

The area between the two lakes was an obstacle course of rocky ridges between patches of low, swampy ground, also rough hiking at best, but more open, less tangled with trees and brush. Looking closely, she found that a nameless creek drained from the west end of this lake to the shores of Lower Beluga, between fairly low and consistent ridges. Its north side looked most passable, and there would be no creeks to cross, though some low spots would be swampy.

Chelle knew that surrounding most of the lakes

and rivers was a wild quarter-mile tangle of alder, willow, and spruce so thick it would be a nightmare to fight her way through. Avoiding as much of this as possible made sense, not only for her own ease of travel, but because Norm would also have chosen the path of least resistance. She determined to climb the ridge above the lake and head west on higher ground, parallel to the creek and away from the worst of the trees and brush. Since there was no trail to follow, she would pick her own path.

Satisfied, she folded the map to fit into a waterproof envelope, tucked it into a pocket of her jacket, and turned to transfer her remaining gear to the bank. Climbing from the plane, she walked the float with three loads before locking it up and double-checking the cables that secured it. On top of the instrument panel inside the cockpit, she left a note, printed in large letters that could be read through the windshield. It included the date and that she had headed west to Beluga River expecting to return in four or five days. No one would report her plane abandoned and initiate an unnecessary search.

Before shouldering the pack she had prepared the day before, she changed into hiking boots and fastened her waders to the back of it. There was some water to cross and she would rather carry them than suffer wet boots that would be difficult, if not impossible to dry.

In one jacket pocket, she stashed a large can of pepper spray where she could reach it quickly. Bears this time of year were hungry and sometimes ill-tempered after a winter of hibernation. They were also mostly the larger, fiercer males, since females, especially those with new cubs, stayed in their dens till later in the spring. Chelle respected them and

would rather drive one away, if possible, than kill
it. Making enough noise to avoid coming upon one
by accident was her first line of defense. She knew
enough not to whistle—which could sound like a
cub crying, to a bear—and had learned to talk or
sing to herself as she hiked.

A lightweight, 25mm flare gun from the plane
hung from her belt, along with two extra charges. In
case of an accident, it would let a rescuer know
where she was. Also, discharged between herself and
an interested bruin, it would put out a lot of smoke
and fire, and would at least discourage a charging
one if fired into its fur.

The .375 Weatherby she hung by its sling from
the pack behind her right arm as last-resort insurance. Like many other bush pilots, Norm habitually
carried a model 600 Remington .350 Magnum, a
smaller rifle, just over a yard long and weighing only
six and a half pounds, as opposed to the more-than-
ten-pound Weatherby. He thought it too heavy for
her, but it had been a gift from the friend who had
taught her to shoot it well, and she felt its weight
compensated for upper-body strength, though it had
a wicked recoil that had set her on her fanny more
than once and still sent her home from the practice
range bruised and aching. She didn't usually tote it
for miles across the tundra, she had argued to Norm.
It was strictly a defensive weapon that could put an
aggressive grizzly in its place, on the ground, if necessary. Except for practice, she seldom had it out of
its case, but she was very good with it.

Now she considered the extra weight worth the
secure feeling it gave her as she climbed away from
the lake to the ridge and headed along it in the direction of Beluga River. An hour later, out of sight

of the small lake in a stand of evergreen that muffled sound, she did not see or hear the plane that came in low from the east without circling, landed, and taxied toward her plane, or the man who discovered and read the note she had left in the cockpit.

14

JENSEN AND CASWELL ALSO GOT AN EARLY START, but it didn't last long. Some days just don't configure themselves helpfully, and some seem to conspire to make it as difficult as possible to accomplish much. If Alex had thought Chelle really intended to go looking for Norm so soon, it would have taken them less time to discover she had gone. If he had known what awaited him at the Palmer detachment office, he would have at least considered going straight to Lake Hood and heading out immediately with Cas for somewhere . . . anywhere else.

The federal agent he encountered in Commander Ivan Swift's office was unknown, unexpected, and it was soon apparent, not inclined to be forthcoming with information, assistance, or courtesy. Keith Progers was enough a stereotype to make Alex wonder if the agency recruited by looks, then did its best to erase them, for he was the epitome of the average invisible man: of average height, weight, and appearance, wearing a dark, off-the-rack suit and a nondescript gray tie. His only memorable feature was a pair of ears that stuck out from the sides of his head like handles on a trophy cup, making his eyes look closer together than they really were. Still, he was so ultimately forgettable that anyone he met would have been hard-pressed to describe anything but his averageness the minute he passed from sight.

He did not rise or offer a hand when introduced to the tall trooper, but nodded once and remained seated next to a half-empty coffee mug on the corner of Swift's desk, staring at Jensen as if he expected little of worth from any law enforcement agency or individual so far out of the *real world*.

The frown on his commander's face, and the narrowing of his eyes at the discourtesy, told Alex that Swift was less than impressed with his visitor, and made him wonder what kind of conversation had preceded him.

"So, you finally found Randolph," Progers stated with obvious condescension.

Before answering, Jensen strode across the room to lean against a windowsill, determined to make his height a subtle point in retaining control and dignity in the situation. The only empty seat in the room was a low chair that would have put the knees of his long legs higher than his hips, and he refused to allow himself to be made to look like an awkward teenager. As he turned, he caught a gleam of recognition and amusement in Swift's eyes and the almost undetectable twitch of his lips.

Refusing to be nettled by Progers, he simply agreed with him, casually, in as few words as possible.

"Yeah, we found her."

"Took long enough."

"It was a long winter."

"Well . . . if you say so. In the United States, we work year-round. Just give me everything you've got and I'll get on with it."

Turning his head to look at Swift, who was sitting up very straight, and whose face had assumed a hue that indicated his blood pressure was rising, Jensen—wisely—swallowed hard and left the response to his superior.

"I . . . don't think so, Mr. Rogers."

"*Progers*," the agent corrected, with a frown that let it be known his name was mispronounced often enough to be a sore point and, unknowingly, gave the commander a bruise to prod. "Federal agent murdered . . . federal investigation indicated. Don't need assistance. I'll take over from here."

Swift leaned back in his chair to look down his thin nose at Progers and spoke precisely in what was for him a controlled and dangerous voice, but which hung in the air like the resound of a pistol shot.

"You may think you will, Mr. *Rogers,* but there's more than just one person involved in this case. The other probable homicide is an Alaskan resident. That puts this investigation squarely on our caseload and I don't intend to rely on an outsider for it. We know our own territory and people. We'll take the lead here. If you want to assist, we *may* be able to accommodate you, Mr. *Rogers.* I said, *may.* If you ask nicely and treat my people with the respect they deserve."

Progers, furious and fuming, shot to his feet as if his chair had suddenly turned red-hot. He opened his mouth to protest, but the commander cut him off short.

"Yes, I know. You'll make sure I regret this. You'll take it back to all those influential contacts you supposedly have back East and they will teach me all kinds of lessons, et cetera, et cetera. Don't bother with the threats, Mr. *Rogers.* Either get your act together with a little cooperative, interagency courtesy, or do your damnedest. By the time you round up all that support you seem to think you have, we'll most likely have this wrapped up for you anyhow. Now . . . unless you have something constructive to contribute, I have *important* things to do. Get out of my office."

Agent Progers had a number of things to say as he left, none of them constructive, or courteous, and he slammed the door.

Alex dropped into the low chair, letting his elevated knees remind Swift of a grasshopper's, and grinned as he shook his head.

"Run out of hot water at home, Ivan?"

"Naw. Self-satisfied bastard just pushed my Patriot Missile button. Hate that attitude."

"Half expected you to sing about how wonderful it is in the neighborhood. If you'd called him Mr. *Rogers* one more time, I might have."

Swift grinned with satisfaction, his eyes wide in the feigned innocence of an apprehended henhouse invader.

"Oh. Did I mistake his name? Well, you—with your *my-head's-higher-than-your-head* windowsill perching—shouldn't criticize my manners. If you see a cat with feathers around his mouth, never say canary, or he'll take offense."

As Jensen groaned at the pun, Swift grew serious.

"I put some pretty good pressure on your getting answers in this thing. Have we got some?"

"Not much, but a couple of ideas. I'll pull a Caswell and get back to you. Okay?"

"Yeah, but soon. Keep me up to date, so when what's-his-name makes the stink I know he'll try,

I've got something to toss back at them."

"Right. I'm gone."

But being gone took just a little longer. Stopping in his office before heading for Anchorage, Jensen sat down at his desk to make a couple of quick phone calls. Spreading out his notes on the insurance policy Chelle had shown him the day before, he thumbed through the phone book for the number of the company that had sold it to Norm, called it and asked to speak to the agent that had been listed on the policy.

"Nicholas Martin." The voice was pleasant and lightly flavored with a Texas accent.

Alex explained who he was and the identification of the policy about which he was calling, but the agent regretfully reported that information concerning specific policies was strictly confidential.

"Mr. Martin," Alex explained, "I have already been shown a copy of the policy by Mrs. Lewis, the benefactor. We know Mr. Lewis bought it. I don't need you to break confidence. But Norm Lewis disappeared in his plane last fall and we have reason to believe he may be dead. I can get a warrant if I have to, but all I want to know is what you remember about the purchase of this insurance. Did he give you any information about why he needed it, for instance?"

"Well, if it's not about direct details . . ." Martin replied, thoughtfully. "He told me that he was about to fly a few charters that were more hazardous than usual, and wanted to make sure that his wife was completely taken care of in case of an accident. He asked a lot of questions and finally took the policy you have because it could be dropped and prorated when he had successfully completed the contracts he was concerned about.''

"Did he seem upset or nervous about it?''

"Not that I remember. He was just seriously interested in protecting his wife and their business. Seemed pretty levelheaded to me. Listened carefully and made good choices.''

"So it wasn't an ongoing policy?''

"No. A short-term one.''

"How long did he want it to be effective?''

"Well, I think it was six months . . . usually is. I'd have to pull out the paperwork, but it was extra life insurance for no more than six. Less, if he came in to cancel it before it ran out. It's on the policy, second or third page.''

Alex found he had noted the dates.

"September twenty-first through March twenty-first?''

"Sounds about right.''

"So, if he was killed, or involved in a fatal accident during that time period his wife is entitled to the amount shown here?''

"That is correct. But you said he disappeared and that you believe he's dead. We would have to be certain of that, and the cause of death before paying the premium.''

"If he was murdered?''

"Yes, but not suicide, or if he was killed while committing a crime.''

"He knew that?''

"Yes. I explained all the contingencies to him carefully.''

"Anything else you can tell me?''

"Can't think of any. Just tell Mrs. Lewis she

should be in touch as soon as you know what happened.''

''I'll do that. Thanks a lot for your time.''

Hanging up the phone, Jensen sat staring at the insurance papers on the desk in front of him. So Lewis knew when he bought this temporary insurance that his death and its cause would have to be proved. It seemed to establish that he knew the flying he was going to do entailed more than average risk. Working with Karen Randolph could be the answer to that, and so could working with the poachers. But he had known crime would cancel out the obligation of the insurance company, and suicide was obviously not on his agenda. Credibility couldn't be stretched that far. Randolph's undercover work might have been part of his plans, however. That made more sense, if it could be proved.

Picking up the phone again, he called the Fish and Wildlife office in Wisconsin. In less than five minutes, he had what he needed, Karen Randolph's unlisted phone number: 608-264-5732. It matched the number Chelle had found in the box from Norm's closet. And established a direct link between the two.

Slowly he punched in the numbers and waited. ''Two-six-four-five-seven-three-two. Talk to me.'' The voice of a woman dead for six months seemed slightly unreal, even if the Fish and Wildlife officers had left it in service, hoping someone would leave a message with a clue to where and how she had vanished. When the beep sounded the machine's readiness to record a message, Jensen hung up and sat for a minute frowning at the phone as if it were haunted, before turning to the business at hand.

He was about to let Caswell know with a phone

call that he was on his way, when the instrument rang under his hand.

"Alex? Are you headed in?"

"Yeah. Just reaching to call you. An hour?"

"Better make it less if you can. I just tried to call Rochelle Lewis. She doesn't answer. APD says she left early and her plane's gone from Lake Hood."

"It's okay. She said she had a charter to fly today."

"I don't think so. She filed a round-robin flight plan, saying she'd report within a week. It listed Beluga Lake as destination."

"Damn it. I knew there was something she wasn't telling me last night, but I didn't really think she'd take off on her own this fast."

"She might have taken that brother of hers with her."

"Call and see if he's home. I'll head out right now. She's probably fine, but I'd like to make sure."

"On it."

The phone went dead and Jensen sprinted for his truck.

So, it was two hours later, just after noon, before they were finally aloft in Caswell's Maule M-4, heading for the other side of Mount Susitna, having established that Chelle was indeed alone and had not included Ed Landreth in her expedition.

There had been no answer to his phone, but repeated knocking on the door of his second-floor apartment had finally resulted in waking him to answer it, grudgingly. "Knock it off. Stop that pounding. Who is it? What do you want?"

A couple of locks snapped back and Ed opened the door to stand resentfully yawning and squinting in the bright morning sunshine, clearly suffering from a late night.

"What the hell do *you* want?" he snarled.

"Have you seen or heard from your sister?" Jensen asked him, taking a step back as the evil odor of Landreth's morning-after breath reached him in an invisible cloud. "Could have scorched the paint off my truck," he later commented to Caswell.

"Not since day before yesterday, when we flew out to where you found the plane."

"She hasn't called you?"

"No. Why?"

"She's gone with her plane. We thought she might have wanted to take you with her."

"Well, she obviously hasn't, has she? Didn't even know she was going anywhere. Probably had a charter booked."

"Her flight plan indicates Beluga Lake as her destination."

"Oh hell. Goddammit. Come on in." He turned and walked away from the door, leaving it open for the troopers to follow him inside. "Damn it. She's gone out looking for Lewis, hasn't she?"

"We think so. Did she say she was going to?"

"Not today. On the way back the other day. Told her I wouldn't help. She knows I think he screwed her over. She doesn't tell me everything, you know. We live our own lives. I don't need a mother anymore. She's had to get used to that. That clown, Lewis, wanted her to cut me out completely. I don't miss him."

"Would she have left a message? You have an answering machine? Your mailbox?"

"She knows I won't answer the thing in the morn-

ing. But . . . yeah. She might have left me a note.
She sometimes does.''

Landreth pawed through a bowl on a bookcase
near the door and came up with the downstairs mailbox key. ''Here. Check it out, if you want. I'm going
to make coffee.''

Caswell traded glances with Jensen, shrugged, and
took the key back through the front door toward
mailboxes they had passed near the street entrance
on their way up.

''Hey,'' Ed yelled after him. ''There should be a
paper down there. Grab it too, as long as you're
going down.''

The note was there, telling them what they had
already surmised. They left Landreth to nurse his
hangover as he pleased and headed for Caswell's
plane.

As soon as they were gone, Landreth went straight
to the phone and made a hurried call. Damn Chelle,
he thought, as he listened to the ring on the other
end of the line. Always giving me grief, one way or
another. An answering machine clicked in and he
slammed the receiver down. This was not information to leave for just anyone to hear. He picked it
back up and dialed a second number.

''Yeah.''

''Darryl?''

''Yeah. Who?''

''Landreth. You got any idea where I can find
Tom? Called his number and got the damn machine.''

''Haven't seen him. You leave a message?''

''No. I got to talk to him. I got some information
he wants.''

"Well, I don't know what to tell you. He's headed out of town."

"He going across the inlet?"

"What the hell do you know about that?"

"Hey, man. Nothing . . . nothing. He just said he had something going on over there. Okay?"

"Not okay. You better keep your fucking mouth shut about Tom's business, Landreth."

"All right. No problem. I don't care where he is. He wanted to know if my crazy sister took off to look for that missing husband of hers. Well, she did. This morning sometime . . . early. Just tell him that if you talk to him. She's headed for Beluga Lake with the cops right behind her."

"Oh fuck. He'll be *really* pleased with that information."

"I can't help that. She didn't tell me she was going, just left a note in my mailbox. Goddamn troopers woke me up looking for her. Somebody better let Tom know."

"No shit, Sherlock. He's got a client coming in on a noon plane that he's supposed to take right out there. The last thing he needs is the law."

"Where can I find him?"

"Stay out of it. I'll track him down. You'd just screw it up again somehow. Got that?"

"Yeah, I got that, you son of a bitch. Go to hell."

Landreth threw the phone back in its cradle and went to find something for his headache.

As Alex and Cas had driven around Lake Hood, they had passed Rochelle's Subaru parked next to the empty space for her Cessna. Two spaces from it, Cas pointed out a smaller aircraft rocking next to the bank.

"Hey, see that one?"

"Yeah." Jensen took another, closer look. "It's like yours, only a different color. Right?"

"Right. You remember asking me, when we were in Nome, who had taught me to fly? That time we barely made it in after getting blown all over the sky in that blizzard?"

"Oh . . . yeah. You said it was somebody really good here in Anchorage. I don't remember the name."

"Bunker. That's his plane. I bought mine because I liked the way his handled."

"Funny, it being right next to the Lewis spaces. But Johnny Raite said they were tight."

"Just a coincidence, but if he knew Norm Lewis, he probably knew Chelle, too."

"Wonder if he noticed anything before Lewis disappeared. Like, maybe, he would have seen Randolph, if Norm was flying her."

"Might be a good idea to ask, when we get back."

They drove on to Caswell's Maule and were surprised to find a rental car near it, parked considerately out of Ben's obvious spot. As they pulled up, a husky man in a tan jacket, blue denims, and heavy boots stepped out and came toward them.

"You Jensen?" he asked, reaching Cas first.

"Nope. Him."

"Ernie Tobias." He held out one hand with the introduction, flipping open his wallet with the other to flash his identification. "Wisconsin Fish and Wildlife."

The expression on Jensen's face as he shook the proffered hand betrayed his reluctance to have any more to do with federal agents at the moment—perhaps ever. Nevertheless, he nodded guardedly and introduced Caswell.

"I understand you investigated the location where Karen Randolph's body was found?" Tobias questioned, a concerned frown drawing two heavy lines in his forehead. There was no hairline to distinguish that forehead from the bald top of his head. A thick chestnut fringe covered the sides and back of his skull at a level with his ears, the same color as the modest mustache that concealed his upper lip.

"We did." Coolly. "As I told your partner at the Palmer detachment office, earlier this morning."

"Partner?"

Jensen kept his face straight. "A Mr. . . . *Rogers,* I believe."

"Oh . . . right. Well, not exactly." Tobias frowned, and from his uncomfortable expression, Jensen could tell he was not particularly pleased to be linked to the other agent, but didn't want to say so outright. Well, he couldn't exactly be blamed, could he?

Alex waited while he paused, looked at his feet, then back up, to explain.

"Ah . . . I'm not official . . . on personal leave. No one sent me. *Karen* was my partner. When we got word yesterday that you'd found her, I took time I had coming and hopped a plane. I just want to know what happened. Your commander . . . a guy named Swift? . . . said I might catch you here."

"You talked to Ivan?"

"Yeah. He didn't say anything about another agent, though."

"Wasn't too happy with the guy's attitude. I think he's trying to pretend he doesn't exist. You see Swift?"

"Telephone. He checked with your Fish and Wildlife people. They know me. I was here for the Brooks Range operation."

Jensen caught Caswell's attention and raised an eyebrow, alert to the possibilities of help from this man's personal knowledge of the sting that had obviously killed Randolph and had something to do with Lewis. Cas shrugged and continued to ready the plane for takeoff.

"Well, now," Alex said, lifting one booted foot to the front bumper of the truck and pulling out his pipe and tobacco. "That makes some kind of difference, doesn't it. We'd better talk. You ever hear of a guy named Norman Lewis?"

15

THEY SPOTTED CHELLE'S CESSNA AT THE SMALL
lake where Alex had suspected she would start her
search and were not surprised to see, as they flew
once over the lake before landing, that it appeared
to be solidly secured and there was no one in sight
on the bank.

Jensen shook his head in frustration and spoke to
Caswell through the second headset. "She's had
plenty of time to head out by now. Let's go down
and see if we can figure out exactly where she
went."

He pointed down, indicating the location to Tobias, who sat in a single seat behind them, but had
no communication equipment. Hearing they were
headed for the place Karen Randolph had been
found, he had asked to come along, and after talking
with him, Jensen saw no reason why not. Official or
not, he had *asked*, not demanded, and was plainly
more interested in any information that would forward the case and help him understand what had
transpired than in closing it. From their conversation
it was plain that he knew less than they did about
the wrecked plane, Norm Lewis, or exactly who
might have been inspired to shoot it out of the air.

167

"I was up north—undercover in Stoffel's Brooks Range camp, to hunt sheep, caribou, and bear. Karen was to go into a temporary camp on the bench the other side of Susitna for four or five days. They had promised her a record grizzly. I left first and was gone a week. She was supposed to go the next day. When I came back she wasn't there and we never heard a word from her after that.

"Stoffel's cover operation swore she never showed for the hunt and we couldn't prove otherwise. There was nothing—absolutely nothing. She just vanished. Some personal stuff left in the hotel looked like it might have been tossed, but we couldn't really tell. What worried me was that I couldn't find her notes. There *was* some pilot she was working with, but she kept his name to herself. I would have gone looking for him if I'd had any idea who he was."

"She kept notes?" Jensen had asked.

"Oh yeah. We both did. But she wouldn't have taken them with her out there. Her real ID was locked in the hotel safe, but not her notes, so we didn't even know who had flown her out . . . *if* she went. She might have been blown and snatched from Anchorage and never got out there at all. But she evidently did, since that's where you found her. I want to know what happened . . . for myself . . . and for her. She'd have wanted it for me, if I was missing."

He had looked very straight at Alex, then at the ground before asking his next question in a tone that had revealed to the trooper that the answer mattered a lot.

"Was she hurt bad?"

With a quick glance at him, Jensen had clenched

his pipe in his teeth and thoughtfully taken the time to light it.

"I'll go load the rest of the gear," Cas decided, and left them to the unpleasant discussion he knew was coming.

"Partner," Jensen mused, when he had gone. "She was your partner?"

"Well, sort of, as much as we have regular partners, and since we were the only two up here from Wisconsin. We'd been working together for years and were close friends, not partners like the police are partners, but . . . *you know*."

Alex *did* know what kind of caring trust that kind of relationship implied. Someone outside of law enforcement might have assumed that Ernie Tobias was referring to a romantic or sexual friendship. That could also have been true, but Jensen knew that what he really meant was something quite different. If romance *had* been part of the equation, it was not what Tobias was currently referring to.

Trusting your life to someone else created *partners* of the people involved in a way that was difficult to define to those who had never experienced it. Firemen understood. So did veterans of military combat, and emergency medical people spoke a similar language. When that kind of partner was hurt or killed, something of the other was injured or died as well. The question Tobias had asked was very personal and required a careful, honest answer. The man was not looking for information that would save his feelings. He already understood the violent nature of the world in which he worked, needed to know the truth, and deserved nothing less, painful or not. *Taking care of your own* was a phrase with as many meanings as the word *love*, Alex thought suddenly.

When he looked up, Tobias was patiently, watchfully waiting . . . understanding the trooper's reluctance as well as Jensen understood the nature of *his* earlier question.

"What was she like?" Alex asked.

For a second, Tobias's eyes narrowed, then he smiled, remembering.

"She was special . . . Karen was. And I'm not the only one who thought so. She was tough and not just smart . . . quick . . . willing to take risks . . . committed to her job . . . a very gutsy lady, who laughed a lot. Good . . . very, very good. But she was soft when it mattered, too. Her kids think she is just about the greatest thing that ever walked. So did I."

"She had kids?"

"Two . . . one of each . . . and an accountant husband, who was scared to death by what she did for a living, resented it. He should be here, but it's not his style. He's okay, though. Did right by her, is good with the kids and all."

"Will you tell him?"

"Only what he wants to know, which won't be the whole thing, will it?"

Jensen shook his head. " 'Fraid not." He took a deep breath and watched Tobias's face closely as he told him what he knew.

"A bullet went clear through the passenger door of the Cessna we found her in before it hit her. Heavy-caliber rifle. Coroner says it would have killed her almost instantly. She might not even have known she was hit."

He paused to light his pipe.

"But there's more," Tobias suggested.

"Yeah. She was beaten—badly—sometime before she was shot . . . before she got into the plane.

The index and middle fingers of her right hand were broken and she must have put up quite a fight, if Timmons is reading the position and location of the bruising correctly, and I'd be amazed if he's not. There was a lot of it. Whoever did it didn't mark her face, but the rest of her body had been pretty well worked over with a club of some kind—rifle butt, probably. Couple of ribs cracked and should have been more broken from that kind of abuse. A ruptured spleen is what killed her. Bled to death before the bullet ever touched her.''

Tobias's face was pale and his lips stiff, but he spoke in a quiet, reasonable tone that betrayed his anger and made his question appear the more ominous.

''This Norman Lewis she was flying with? He part of it?''

Alex shrugged. ''Honestly,'' he said, ''we don't know. His wife, Rochelle, says not, but I think she's not telling all she knows. That's why we're going out there—to find her. She took off early this morning, from the look of it—convinced his body's out there somewhere—or trying to convince herself it is—determined to find it if she can. It may be there, but he could also have taken off for parts unknown. That's less likely without his plane, but . . . who knows. Their house was broken into yesterday, and we haven't a clue. There's a lot we don't know yet. Maybe you can help.''

Headed for a landing, Cas had banked into a left-hand turn, bringing the Maule around to head south down the lake. Almost as still as it had been for Chelle, it made estimating touchdown difficult.

''Bad visibility,'' he commented. ''Glassy water

approaches always make me feel like there's nothing there to set down on.''

But set down he did, with an easy smoothness that all but lacked sign of impact. Alex momentarily reflected on how it almost always surprised him to find himself back on the earth, or water, when he was flying with Cas. The man was extremely good at what he loved best and prided himself on his flawless landings. It took a lot of weather, or adverse conditions, to give them any kind of bounce.

He was trying to remember the last time he had noticed a landing, when, just as Cas began to heel in the Maule's floats to slow the plane, Alex was suddenly and unexpectedly thrown against the door, as its pilot gave the craft a hard left rudder. There was a heavy thump from something hitting the right float, a long dragging shudder that could be felt throughout the plane, and the vibration of metal tearing, as much sensation as sound.

''Goddammit,'' Caswell's anger was loud enough to hurt Alex's ears. ''Damn it. Damn it.''

Jensen was dismayed to hear his partner's reaction. Not because he was inordinately adverse to profanity, but because Cas did not swear casually. When he began to spout four-letter words, he had good reason and meant every one of them. ''What the hell was *that*? What'd we hit?''

''A log, right below the surface . . . just as I came down off the step. Poked a hole in my float and feels like a big one. Hold on and make yourselves light. Got to get this bird to shallow water while I still can, or we're gonna take a swim we hadn't planned on. Damn it all to hell.''

Aiming the Maule at the bank, Caswell increased their speed while fighting the tendency of the craft to drift to the right, in the direction of the damaged float. The plane began to tilt slowly to the passenger side, a condition that grew more pronounced, causing Jensen to picture water dragging them into a roll that would result in an upside-down position.

The punctured and heavier float touched first, slewing the Maule hard to the right, grounding the left float higher in the mud of the bank. Cas shut down the engine and, yanking off his headset, threw open the door on his side of the plane.

"That float's partly underwater. You two're going to get your feet wet, so be careful, but get out quick before it goes in deeper."

Jensen complied, speedily wading the length of the partially submerged metal float and leaping less than a yard of water to the solid ground of the bank, with Tobias close behind him. He could see nothing of the damage, which had to be all on the underside, invisible. The plane shivered slightly and seemed to squat down a few inches in the back, thrusting its nose into a more acute angle.

Caswell joined them, carrying a winch, some cable, and two pairs of waders that he had hurried to retrieve from the aft storage compartment in the Maule, and they stood for a minute, assessing the situation and probable impairment to the float.

"Got to get it pulled up to be able to see," Cas said. "From the way it filled—fast—I think there's more than I can fix with hundred-mile-an-hour tape. Have to call for help to get it out of here and back in the air. We can take a look and get it drained, though."

Tugging on his waders, he started up the bank to where he could fasten the winch he had brought from the Maule. "Can you get some of that survival stuff out of there, Alex? Less weight we'll have to drag up.''

Looks like we'll be here a while, Jensen thought. Having learned from previous flights with Cas, he had brought his own hip waders. Pulling them on, he proceeded to empty the plane of survival gear, which he passed to Tobias, who piled it high on the bank, out of the mud. The winch placed and ready, Cas and Alex went into the water to turn the plane around to face the lake. There was still enough air trapped in the float to allow this and—by both lifting hard on the damaged side—to straighten it enough to lie at a ninety-degree angle to the bank.

With the help of the winch, the plane was soon high and dry on the lakeshore. Straining to lift again, little by little they managed to work two pieces of driftwood under the float, and were finally able to take a look at the extent of the puncture in it. The submerged log had ripped a long crease through the aft three of four compartments. From these, water had poured, and still dripped.

Ben Caswell muttered and grimaced as he examined the destruction, stepped back, and shook his head.

''Haven't a prayer with duct tape. Better get on the horn to someone up there who can call in and get us some help.''

Jensen knew that he meant it would be impossible to radio back to the Lake Hood tower. Their current position put them below and out of reach of its range. They could, however, from the radio in the plane, talk to anyone in the air overhead, who could then relay their problem directly to the Anchorage tower.

''We'll watch and see if anyone flies over.'' Cas

heaved a sigh of resignation. "I think it's going to be at least tomorrow before we can get some repairs. How you guys feel about a cup of coffee? There's makings in that pile of gear you dragged out."

"Sounds good. I'm going to check out Chelle's plane first, though."

"Okay. We'll get a fire going."

Alex found Chelle's Cessna locked, as he expected, and read the note she had left. As he stepped back onto the float from the step that assisted the pilot into the plane, he suddenly focused on the muddy footprints of someone who had worn boots when walking out onto it and back to the shore. The prints were larger than Chelle's waders would have made. Measuring, he could see that they were slightly larger than his own booted foot.

Carefully, he tracked them from the float to the bank and along it to where they had winched the Maule from the waters of the lake. There they ended, but, looking closely, he could see what was left of other marks, partially obliterated by their labor and footprints, where another plane had rested in the mud. The prints ended beside what would have been the passenger side, if the plane had headed in, seeming to indicate that someone in the pilot seat had stayed inside while the other went to investigate.

When he called Caswell and Tobias to take a look, they agreed with his assessment of the mark, but who?

"Couldn't have been her brother chasing her," Cas commented. "We already know where he was. He wouldn't have had time."

"More than one person. Could be a friend or pilot for hire. Maybe just someone curious about the plane." Jensen pondered. "Read the note and took off again.'' But it bothered him. Could it be connected to whoever had searched her house? And for what? ''Sure like to ask her a few questions about now.''

''At least we know where she went,'' Cas commented, when they had collected enough dry wood to boil water. He frowned, considering the situation, but at least half his sight and hearing were directed toward the sky, which, so far, had remained empty of aircraft.

''You guys do this often?'' Tobias asked, adding sticks to the small blaze. ''From the size of that plane, I hope we don't have to take turns sleeping in it tonight.''

''Hey,'' Ben rebuked him, with a grin. ''That Maule's a sweetheart. Don't hurt her feelings or we're in real trouble.''

He balanced a blackened and battered coffeepot on three rocks he had placed strategically around the flames, having filled it with bottled water and dumped in a handful of coffee.

''He's right about the sweetheart bit,'' Alex chimed in. ''Combination of that plane and its pilot have saved our hides more than once. I'm not sure about the bunk space in the bird, but Cas usually has enough survival gear packed for an army.''

''There's a tent, sleeping bags, and a couple choices of the freeze-dried semi-edible,'' Caswell confirmed. ''We'll survive.''

As they sat on a pair of logs near the fire and watched the coffee perk, Jensen was pleasantly impressed that Tobias did not push the conversation, as a new acquaintance was often inclined to do. The agent now had time to look around him and absorb the feeling of the country in which he found himself, including the broken trees on the ridge above them—almost the only evidence of the crash of the Cessna Norm Lewis had flown. Buds on the willows were beginning to swell and the warm sun on Jensen's back was a pleasant reminder that winter was over. He thought about the rapidly approaching fishing season for a minute or two before his mind returned to Rochelle.

Evidently, she had headed west, the direction she had said Norm would be most likely to go if he tried to hike out. He wondered how long she had been gone. The oversized boot tracks had not followed her, but he would have been happier had she not been alone and unaware that someone had checked out her plane, might be looking for her, and knew from her note where she was headed. It was time to go find her.

"You know . . ." With another glance at the still empty sky, Caswell thoughtfully broke the silence, "I've been kicking around the way Lewis's plane came in over the ridge, before it hit the lake. It's a better than good bet that, if it came from that direction, it was shot in that direction. He couldn't have flown very far, or had many choices of puddles to set down on. I wonder if we could find any sign of where those shots were fired. Would the shooter have bothered to pick up shell casings, for instance? Might be worth a try, as long as we're stuck here for a few hours."

"Good idea," Alex agreed. "But I'd like to locate Chelle. Those footprints, even if they didn't follow her, make me uneasy."

"You said she headed west?" Tobias asked, after a moment.

"That's what her note said."

"Am I off base in assuming that you feel it's possible someone else might be looking for her?"

"No-o," said Jensen, and described the current reasons for his uneasiness, along with the break-in.

"If *you* think she knows something she's not telling, couldn't that someone—maybe whoever landed here and read her note—think so too?"

"It's possible."

"Knowing she's headed for that other lake . . ."

"Lower Beluga," Cas interjected.

". . . couldn't they fly across and wait for her to get there?"

Jensen and Caswell looked at each other, knowing he was right.

"And we can't fly with that hole in the float," Cas stated in disgust.

Tobias nodded toward Chelle's Cessna. "Is it possible to hot-wire an airplane? I'm assuming she's got the keys, but you could fly it."

"Yeah, but I'm not inclined to break in on the strength of a possibility."

Jensen was on his feet, already moving toward the pile of items they had removed from the plane.

"That's it"—he tossed back over one shoulder—"let's get our gear and get after her."

Caswell used the half-perked coffee to put out the fire.

16

COLLECTING SURVIVAL EQUIPMENT AND FOOD, they quickly started west. Jensen carried Caswell's larger pack with a plastic rain fly and two sleeping bags. Tobias had shrugged on a smaller day-pack with enough food for lunch and dinner, a bottle of water, and some first aid supplies.

Alex had checked the Colt .45 he preferred as an off-duty side arm and had holstered it, as usual, within handy reach. He wished he had some heavier firepower in the form of a rifle, even though the likelihood of tangling with a bear was very small indeed, since though most of the browns avoided man if possible, blacks could be predatory. He did not ask, and Tobias didn't volunteer whether or not he was carrying.

For a while they quite easily followed Chelle's trail from the impressions her boots left on bare spots between rocks and vegetation. Though they traveled as fast as they could, hoping to catch up before she reached Lower Beluga Lake, at times they lost her tracks and were forced to search them out before moving on again. Still, she seemed to be going as directly west as was possible in difficult, uneven terrain, and clearly not trying to conceal her passage, so Jensen was not overly concerned with losing her completely. He knew her destination, after all, and would make for it if her trail disappeared completely.

Caswell had opted to stay behind at the lake with his damaged plane, where he would concentrate on reaching some passing pilot on the radio for help. It had been obvious that he was torn between the desire to come along and concern over his aircraft and their ultimate need to get back to Anchorage.

"Plenty to do." He had grinned ruefully. "Build another fire and make more coffee. Besides, what if Chelle came back on a different route for some reason and you missed her? I may even take a short hike in the direction those bullets that brought down Lewis probably came from."

Jensen had agreed that it made sense, but would rather have had him along on the hike. Tobias, an experienced outdoors man, wouldn't slow him down, was doing his best to be helpful while letting the trooper take the lead and make the decisions, but Cas knew both the country and Alex. They had worked together often enough to understand each other's methods and ideas. There was little he would have had to explain or justify to Cas, and could have turned his complete attention to the task at hand— or, rather, *foot*—terrain that made hiking difficult and required care.

All of Alaska was periodically covered with ice pack and glaciers during the Pleistocene Era. Three of at least five great rivers of ice that moved down into what would become Cook Inlet filled it to a depth of over two thousand feet. They advanced and retreated, leaving evidence in the rounded shape of Mount Susitna, and the moraines of glaciers that mark the wide plateau around and coast below the two Beluga Lakes. The remaining glaciers that still feed them water and silt, impressive as they appear, are only tiny remnants of ice from far earlier ages. Glacial erratics, enormous boulders carried by ice and deposited where it melted, and rocks of all sizes littered the plateau, as well as exposed bedrock scraped clean by glaciation.

Lumpy was the word Jensen used to describe it as he and Tobias traversed its rocky ridges, scrambled through brush and trees, and dropped down to splash in its boggy low spots. Crossing almost five miles of this in a hurry would not be a complete pleasure.

They found the place Chelle Lewis had stopped to change into her waders at the far end of the lake, at the edge of an extended swampy spot, and passed the moldering remains of an ancient log cabin against a bank full of alder just beyond it, facing south. He wondered who might have built the low-roofed, one-room structure and lived in it long ago, when it was new, and why.

A trapper, perhaps, spending silent winters in the frozen wilderness, subsisting on moose, beans, and sourdough, running his trap lines for marten, fox, hare, a wolverine or two—though they were notoriously wily and hard to catch—shooting the wolves that pilfered his take. Maybe he had died there, far from the slightest hint of civilization, with no neighbors at all. Whatever happened to him, his traveling would have been just as hard as theirs, except for winter, which would have frozen the soggy swamps and smoothed rough ground with an even layer of snow for sleds or snowshoes.

Though he suspected Chelle had walked along the edge of the creek and its marshy bed, wading when necessary, Jensen elected to climb a slope just to the north and work his way through the trees that covered it. Once away from the water supply, the brush thinned enough to allow him and Tobias, who followed closely, to make positive, if meandering, westward progress.

Looking up as he reached the top of a bare, rocky space that allowed him a view to the west, he paused long enough to appreciate the horizon full of spectacular mountains and glaciers that formed the Alaska Range. Spread in a long, rugged line of gleaming white, they *were* the west—everything else was either the line of dark spruce-green below or expanse of blue above. From where he stood, Jensen knew he was looking directly up the flow of Triumvirate Glacier, twenty miles away. This part of the range was crowded with dozens of glaciers, of which Capps and Triumvirate were the largest, flowing east, toward the plateau on which he stood. Their melt provided the water that created the Beluga lakes and River. He could identify Mount Spurr to his left, and two of the other peaks were Torbert and Gerdine, though he couldn't pick them out of so many.

Twice that far away, and directly north, he knew, was the bush community of Skwentna, first village stop on the Iditarod Trail, on which Jessie ran her dogs in the famous race from Anchorage to Nome each year. With few roads and most of the huge state still virgin wilderness, it always surprised him that so many people lived in the small towns and villages of its rural areas—had lived there long before the territory that would become Alaska was first claimed by the Russians, then sold by them to the United States—Seward's Folly or Icebox. Winter made travel possible—by dogsled or, now, snowmobile—

that was not even a consideration during the summer months. Then the rivers, with their wonderful, exotic names, became the only roads for any who did not fly: Kuskokwim, Tanana, Koyukuk, Nenana, Nushagak, Chilkat, Copper, and many others, among them the Yukon, fifteen hundred Alaskan miles long and mightiest of them all.

"Long way to the Brooks Range," Tobias commented, pausing beside him. "What a spread."

Alex grinned in satisfaction. "Yeah. I see so much of this kind of thing almost every day that I sort of forget it's there until something like this stops me and I remember that I *live* here."

They traded packs and Tobias led the way down the hill.

Chelle had not traveled as fast, searching as she hiked for any indication that someone else had passed this way, finding nothing. This did not discourage her. In analyzing the situation, she had decided that when Norm got out of the plane he would probably have gone as far as he possibly could toward rescue, which meant he would have gone too far to go back when he found he couldn't make it to the coast. Somewhere beyond Lower Beluga Lake was her best guess.

It concerned her that he had not retrieved any of the survival gear from the plane. It had not been deep enough in the lake to make reaching it impossible. It didn't make sense, unless he had been injured too badly to try for it, and if he were, would he have tried to hike out?

There were other things that worried her, including the fact that he had gone to so much trouble to hide the trail of information that led her to Bunker and the money. *The money.* Half the missing five thousand. The other half accounted for in the insurance policy from the bank. Standing at the breakfast bar before leaving that morning she had counted it out—twenty-five hundred-dollar bills, new and clean. Why? What did it mean? There was no explanation. The paper wrapped around the bills had been empty of writing, and all she knew was what he had told his friend: "*. . . someone else's confidence,* and *. . . if you are very certain I'm not coming back to get it.*" No message. No letter. Would she find anything when she found him—if she found him—found his body? Or would there be no body? Was he somewhere else in the world? Why and where? Was she only fooling herself with this search—trying to hold on to him?

Well . . . at least she would know . . . something. Doggedly, she forced her attention back to the task she had set herself.

Since it was her intent to go no farther than the lake, set up camp for the night, and go on the next day, she didn't rush. No need to wear herself out covering ground. The distance wouldn't be difficult, even with its rocky terrain. Wading through the swampy section after leaving the lake had looked reasonable on the map, but turned out to be a mile and a half long and had slowed her progress significantly.

Near noon, she climbed up and stopped on a higher, drier place to eat a sandwich and an apple she had brought from home. Taking off her pack, she sat on a large outcropping of rock in the sunshine. After lunch, she lay back against the rock, face turned to the sun and turned off her mind. Quite without meaning to, she fell asleep.

Forty minutes later, she gradually became aware of a familiar sound somewhere overhead and slowly opened her eyes to focus on a long, ragged V of geese beating their way north toward the interior. Most of the geese that came through south central Alaska were the dark-headed Canadians at the end of their long spring migration. The ones she saw now were snow geese, as pure white as the swans that were even less frequently seen in the flyway. Their honking cries drifted down faintly as they swept rhythmically past to vanish beyond a ridge.

Stretching to relieve a cramp in her neck, she sat up, startling a jay that had ventured close enough to collect the crumbs she had dropped. In a fluster of blue feathers, it sought the air, startling her in return. In apology, she crumbled up her leftover bread crusts and tossed them out on the rock, adding a bit of cheese and two crackers. Knowing jays, she was sure this one would be back before she disappeared from sight.

Groggy from her stolen nap, she returned to the creek and splashed water on her face, dried it on her shirt, reshouldered her pack, and hung on the Weatherby.

The part of the bank she walked on for the next quarter hour was dry but crowded with willow and spruce. Lacking a depth of soil in which to sink deep roots meant that any tree that grew tall and put out wide branches would find itself top-heavy and vulnerable to strong winds. Over the centuries, the Alaskan spruce had, therefore, evolved into a variety that did well in shallow soil, spread wide, horizontal roots, and survived in rocky places, or those where permafrost lay only inches beneath the surface. Never truly tall—perhaps thirty or forty feet at best—they grew narrow, though thick with very short branches that tended to droop toward the ground, hugging the trunk. They reminded Chelle of pipe cleaners, or drawings scrubbed onto paper by a child with a crayon, as she threaded her way through them. It was darker among the trees, and much cooler out of the sunshine.

Sometime after two o'clock, she had been walking through trees for quite a long way, trying to keep above and away from the creek, which had begun to wind back and forth like a snake and curve slightly to the south over flatter ground. The sound of her steps was muffled by a layer of spruce needles that covered the ground, and she was thinking that it couldn't be much farther to Lower Beluga Lake, when she distinctly heard a voice ahead of her and off, slightly, to the right. Stopping short, she listened carefully without moving. It was quiet, then the voice spoke again, far enough away around the curved slope that she couldn't hear what was said, or whether it was a man or woman who spoke. A deeper voice answered, which must be a man, she thought, and immediately she heard the first voice again.

The slope rose steeply to her right and the trees thinned as it opened up into a rocky point. Quietly, she climbed up till she was just below the rocks, in patches and lines of sunlight. Leaving behind the sound-deadening carpet of spruce needles, she paid careful attention to where she stepped to avoid making noise on the harder surface, or rolling rocks down the hill. Patiently, she moved forward till she could look around and down the other side of the hill.

In a small clearing, perhaps fifty feet below her,

stood a man wearing brown pants, a jacket of khaki camouflage print, and waterproof boots. The bill of a black baseball cap kept her from seeing his face. He turned away from her and spoke again. She could hear him clearly now.

"Hey. Come on," he called. "We've got to get going—get this stuff moved."

Piled around him on the ground was a variety of outdoor equipment, some covered with tarps, some that had been uncovered: tents, water cans, sleeping bags, boxes of food, half a dozen rifles, and cases of ammunition—what looked like everything to set up a camp for several people. A hunting camp, Chelle realized, the sorts of things she had seen in use when she flew hunters in for guided hunts.

"Yeah. Yeah. I'm coming," rumbled the second voice, and a shorter, heavier man walked out of the trees into the clearing, carrying a rifle in one hand, a box of ammunition in the other. "Hold your water. She won't be here for a while yet."

"Maybe not, but we don't know exactly when she left and it'd be better not to run into her accidentally. Besides, Farrell wants this stuff at the other lake and the tents set up by four o'clock when he brings in that guy. Got to get it out of here."

"Well shit. Get Gene back here to help carry this stuff to the plane. It'll take us at least an hour and I'm not doin' it alone this time."

"He's up there making sure she doesn't walk into this. We'll make the first couple of trips, then call him down to help finish."

She? Walk into this? Was he talking about her? Who was he? They? Chelle's hands were suddenly cold as ice. She shoved them into her jacket pockets and tried to think. What other woman could possibly be out here, now? As the first man turned back toward her, she drew back. Even if they didn't mean *her*, it was probably unwise to let them see her—a woman alone in this kind of place—with no kind of quick way out. It must not be her. How could they be looking for her? Even know she was here? Still . . . better leave. They clearly didn't want observers.

She was just taking a step back, when a third voice spoke, calmly, from just behind her.

"Hold it, Miz Lewis. We'd like to have a little talk with you." Then louder, to the two below in the clearing, "Hey, guys. Guess who's here."

Chelle swung around to face a tall man she had never seen before and didn't know. He stood a step or two below her on the hill, but his additional height brought his face almost level with her own. Raising a handgun to point in her direction, he grinned at her wolfishly.

She didn't even stop to consider. Continuing the movement she had used to turn toward him, she brought her hand from her pocket with the can of pepper spray and pressed the trigger, aiming it directly at his face.

The effect was instantaneous. He stumbled backward, dropping the gun, and clutching at his eyes, screamed, lost his footing on the steep angle of the slope and fell, rolling, tumbling, bumping into trees, out of her sight, still howling.

Careful to avoid the area she had sprayed, thankful there had been no breeze to blow the volatile cayenne concentration back into her own face, Chelle moved quickly back the way she had come, into the shelter of the trees with their muffling needle bed. As fast as she could, trying not to make noise, she fled east, to put as much space between herself and those behind her. The one she had sprayed would be useless, but the other two would soon find him and someone would surely follow.

Who were they? What did they want? Could she elude them?

In late spring, Aklak, already significantly heavier than when he woke from hibernation, would purposely make his way farther west and off the plateau to a series of low rapids in a small river that ran full of spawning salmon. There, as in years past, he would come in contact with a number of other grizzlies hungry for the large, fat-rich, roe-filled fish.

All of more than sixty-five thousand brown bears in North America—about forty thousand of which inhabit Alaska—are solitary creatures, living, hunting, and feeding in isolation for most of their lives, with the exception of mating and the raising of young. Only in a situation where a food supply is concentrated enough to feed many bears—large berry patches, a dead whale washed up on a beach, rivers full of spawning salmon—do they tolerate each other's company. Even then, they observe an established hierarchy, based mostly on size: largest, oldest males; females with young cubs; single, almost full-grown males; other adult males and females; less than adult males and females. This hierarchy, however, is constantly being challenged and adjusted, though this is mainly accomplished with threats and posturing, and seldom results in fighting that maims or kills. When battles do happen, they are usually between bears of equal size and position in rank.

The facial expressions of a bear are mostly limited to opening the mouth to display the teeth and curling a lip to accompany a growl or roar. Most communicate, and establish or challenge dominance, with significant body language or a variety of vocalizations: angry smack, chomp, growl, or roar; nervous grunt or woof; bawl of pain; cub-calling bleat; cough; contented hum.

Larger than all but one of the bears that would return to the river where he fished, Aklak would, as usual, claim a superior position close to midstream, where the salmon were forced into a narrow channel between two massive rocks. If necessary, he would chase away any bear that had usurped his place.

Each year that he came to that river he fished from the same location and had come to regard it as his right. There, for weeks, he would spend hours every day catching one fish after another, ripping off and gobbling up the fatty skin, licking up the nutritious roe, and letting the rest of the salmon go floating quickly away in the swiftly flowing water. Downstream, many of these would wash ashore on gravel bars and be claimed by flocks of seagulls and dozens of eagles waiting to scavenge the bear's leftovers. Other half-eaten fish would be snagged from slower eddies and wolfed down by smaller, younger bears less skilled in fishing.

In the middle of the day, full of rich salmon, Aklak would amble off into the thick grasses at the river's edge and fall asleep, curled up in a bed he would make by tearing several branches off a nearby spruce and dragging them into a small depression.

He would defend and consistently use this same bed with a commanding view of the river and the activity of the other fishing bears.

Late one afternoon of a previous summer, he had returned to his place on the rock to find it occupied by a younger male, somewhat smaller, but large enough to foolishly challenge Aklak's right to the good fishing it provided. At his grunt of warning, the younger bear had growled and clicked its teeth, then risen to stand on its hind feet, head and neck curved forward threateningly. Aklak had immediately risen in response, snarling and chomping, exhibiting his larger size to establish his superiority.

They had stood swaying back and forth, facing each other, growling and feigning attacks with teeth and claws, Aklak, with the advantage of height, able to look down on his rival. In only a few minutes, he had grown tired of the aggravation, dropped to all fours, and charged the young challenger, roaring in anger, mouth wide, upper lip extended, snapping his jaws. Lashing out with one paw, he had caught the already turning bear on one shoulder, tearing open a gash in fur and skin with a sharp claw.

It had been more than enough. The other had leapt from the rock into the river and splashed his way to the shallows, where he sat down facing Aklak, head lowered, refusing eye contact, in a submissive display. Slowly, he began to lick at the bleeding wound he had received.

Satisfied, with no desire to pursue or fight, having established his right to the rock and regained the respect of his position, Aklak had returned to his fishing, completely ignoring and, indeed, soon forgetting the interloper entirely.

A day would come, however, when such a challenge might not end in his favor. But, for the time being, he had been content to remain monarch of his particular rock.

17

AS SHE RAN, CHELLE TRIED TO MAKE SENSE OF what was happening and assess her options. It was at least four miles back to where she had left the plane and she had no idea how strong or fast pursuit would come. Perhaps there wouldn't be any, but, if there was, it would probably be just one of the three men she had seen. The one she had pepper-sprayed would not be able to walk blind, let alone chase her. One of the others would have to help him to wash his face and eyes. That left the third to follow her and she was not interested in waiting around to see if he did.

They had obviously been waiting . . . looking for her . . . knew she was coming. How? The *note* I left in the plane, she thought, but why and how would they know where to look for it, or the plane, for that matter? She stumbled over a fallen log as she attempted to jump it too fast, catching herself on the trunk of another. Slow down, she cautioned herself severely. You can't afford to sprain an ankle, or break a leg now.

As she paused to catch her breath, she heard someone crashing through the brush behind her. If she could hear him, he had been able to hear her as well. She moved on, fast. The most important thing was to keep ahead, out of range of the gun she must assume he had, at least out of sight.

With that thought, the trees began to thin and, in a minute or two, she was out of them and into a low, swampy clearing that held two ponds. The trees curved around its far edge to the right and a strip of land ran across between the two sections of marsh and water. She followed it, keeping to a narrow band of brown grass the snow had flattened that divided the mud of each bog enough so she could run faster. Close to a hundred yards in front of her on the other side were more trees. Could she make it into them before he saw her? What the hell did he want, anyway? What could make her so important? Whatever they'd been looking for in her house—if they were the ones?

Fifty yards to go . . . thirty.

"Hey! Stop."

Twenty . . . fifteen.

The sound of a single gunshot behind her and a feeling of air displacement to the right answered that question in her mind, but she felt nothing—was still moving—so he had missed. There was no way to dodge on the narrow strip of grass, so she ran on toward the trees, the pack she had no time or inclination to discard bouncing heavily, but protectively, on her back and shoulders, the stock of the Weatherby pounding her right hip.

And I thought the recoil was bad. I'll have a bruise the size of Alaska on my behind.

Ten yards . . . eight . . . five, and a downed log in the way.

She sailed over it and heard the second shot fired behind her as she was airborne. The frigid water-

filled hole, some three feet wide, beyond the log was
a shock as she went into it up to her knees, but it
saved Chelle's skull from the bullet that gently lifted
the wide-brimmed, gray hat from her head and deposited it in front of her, next to the beaver-chewed
stump of the log she had hurdled. She caught herself
with her hands as she fell against it and swung to
look back for the first time since she had left the
shelter of the trees. She had to stretch to peer cautiously over the top of the log, and found that the
lone man with the camouflage jacket and baseball
cap was heading her way along the far end of the
thin line of grass at a walk, gun in hand, a satisfied
smile on his face.

So . . . the fat one had elected to stay to help his
blinded friend. There *was* only one, and, from his
expression, he was convinced he had hit her.

He can't see this hole, or the water I'm in, any
more than I could, she thought. When I fell and disappeared, he assumed he'd got me.

But—only a few moments and he would be able
to see that she was anything but dead.

Quickly, she glanced around, while snatching her
hat from the water and replacing it, dripping, on her
head. Leading away from the hole, but parallel to
the trees, the water of a stream that fed the swamp
meandered away, surrounding several almost round,
grassy hummocks that were just a little lower than
the log. If she kept down, she could be hidden behind them. First, the Weatherby had to come off,
since its barrel stuck up above the pack, and would
be seen. She would feel better with it in her hands,
anyway, where she could use it if necessary.

Lifting it off the pack, she stooped over and, with
as little splashing as she could manage, half waded,

half crawled around the closest hummock, following the deepest part of the channel that ran between them, trying to keep low and still hold as much of her body as possible out of the ice-cold water. Around two more, fifteen feet from the log, she crouched behind a fourth, facing the way she had come, and waited.

"Goddammit," she heard Camouflage swear. "What the hell?"

What then followed was an odd kind of splashing, and she risked a look around the hummock, through a thin screen of dried grass, to catch sight of him bending over, poking to find the water depth with a long stick he had picked up somewhere. Finding the water too shallow for her to have sunk under the weight of the pack and be hidden beneath it, he began to lift grasses that hung down over the edge of the bank, attempting to see if she had rolled or crawled under them.

Eventually, all possibilities exhausted, he stopped, straightened, and standing still, seemed to look directly at her hiding place, a calculating expression on his face.

"Hey," he called. "Sister. There's only one place you can be hiding, and we both know where it is, don't we? I know you're out there somewhere, and you know I know."

Chelle pulled back behind the hummock and kept perfectly still and silent, the Weatherby held close, ready for action. Did he know she had the rifle? He might have seen it bouncing on her pack before she jumped the log. If he had, it didn't seem to intimidate him. She waited.

"You might as well come on out. Gonna get aw-

ful cold real soon. You stay in there, hyperthermia's
gonna get cha.''

He was right. Her teeth had already begun to chatter and she was shivering. Hyp-*o*-thermia was a
sooner-than-later fact if she had stayed in the cold
water. She was wet to the hips, her legs and feet in
the hiking boots, submerged under her. If only she'd
had time to put on her waders it would still have
been cold, but dry and less critical. *If onlys* were a
dime a dozen, she thought in disgust. If granny had
wheels, she'd be a bicycle. She wiped at her nose,
which had begun to run, with the back of a sleeve,
gritted her teeth to keep them still, and did not answer.

"Hey. I'm not goin' any place. You know? All I
gotta do is stay here. You'll have to give it up sometime—when you're cold enough.''

He paced back and forth, always looking in her
direction. The hummocks, too far apart to jump from
one to another, were the only thing that kept him
from coming to hunt for her, unless he cared to get
his feet wet, but the minute she moved he would be
able to see or hear her, and gain a target that was
too close to miss. Evidently thinking of this, he
pointed the pistol and fired three careless rounds in
her general direction. The second round thumped
into the hummock behind which she cowered, but it
was at least two feet thick and solid enough protec-
tion. Still, it was disconcerting to know that it was
all that stood between her and the destruction of his
gun.

She ventured another look, carefully, for only an
instant. He was sitting on the log, still watching in
her direction, reloading the pistol. She could shoot
him—kill him instantly. The powerful Weatherby

would blow a great hole through the center of his body, or take his head off. If she waited much longer, she would be shaking so badly with cold that it might be impossible to aim accurately.

Slowly, she lifted the rifle and, with infinite care, parted some of the dry grass and braced the barrel on the hummock, pointed directly at him. His face sprang into detail in the magnification of the scope, his expression sly and confident. As she stared at him through it, she noticed that he was chewing his lower lip and frowning slightly.

So . . . not quite as confident as he'd like her to think. It made him suddenly human, somehow, and she knew she couldn't put a bullet into him like a tin can on a fence . . . couldn't just dead cool shoot him as he sat, though she probably should, and might eventually wish she had. Unless he gave her no other alternative, she didn't think she could kill him. But what *could* she do? It was imperative to get out of the freezing water—soon—or she'd be too cold to be able to build a fire, thaw herself out, and get back to her plane.

Scare him. If he *thought* she would shoot him, maybe he would retreat back along the grass causeway, at least to the edge of the trees he had come from, and give her a chance to get away into those on this side. She could drive him away from her cover, she decided, as long as he had none, and there was none to be had.

"If you don't go back—get away from me—I'll shoot you where you sit," she called to him. "I've got a Weatherby three seventy-five here, and if you're a hunter, or familiar with guns, you know what it can do."

"Yeah right." He stood up again, feet wide apart,

and grinned. "Sure you do. If you had it, you'd of used it. Think I'm fuckin' stupid, sister? You got a can of pepper spray. Go ahead. Do your damnedest with it."

So . . . somehow he had missed the rifle—thought she was bluffing. Okay, she'd have to show him. Leaning into the weapon to absorb as much of the recoil as she could, Chelle aimed carefully and placed one shot precisely between his legs, hoping the scope had not been jarred loose in her desperate run. A ruined kneecap could be the result if it had.

His uncoordinated leap into the air and shout of surprise was totally satisfying.

"Shee-it. You goddamn fuckin' bitch." He shook a fist in her direction. "Whata you think you're do-ing?"

Without another thought, Chelle fired the Weath-erby again. This time just to the right of him. The bullet tore through his jacket sleeve and she thought she had hit or grazed him. Evidently, he thought so too, for he howled, clutched at his upper arm and turned to run like a scared rabbit. Unfortunately for Chelle, he didn't move back the way he had come, but leapt from the log across the water hole she had fallen into, and ran into the trees in the opposite direction before she could fire again.

She watched, openmouthed in dismay, as he van-ished, slipped out of sight and range. Suddenly she was vulnerable again. Should she move, he could locate her, and he had the advantage of cover he could walk behind to stalk her, to set up a clear shot before taking it.

Damn. What could she do? Wounded or not, he was every bit as much threat as he had been, if not more, and on top of that, he had to be furious, and

more determined than ever. And she must move—
if she could. Chelle realized with a sinking sensation
in the pit of her stomach and tightening of her throat
that she could no longer feel her feet.

Jensen and Tobias heard the first five unevenly
spaced shots from half a mile away, as they came
through a stand of trees near the rock where Rochelle had eaten lunch. Without a word, they both
began to run toward the sounds, Jensen in the lead.

"Handgun," Tobias panted, after a few minutes.

"Yeah," Jensen agreed, saving his breath, as he
slowed to climb over an outcropping of rock,
shrugged off the larger pack, which he was once
again carrying, and dropped it to the ground. Tobias
started to do the same, but Alex stopped him.

"You've got the food and first aid. We may need
it." He ran on ducking to fight his way through a
thicket of brush and alder, heading downhill.

When he could see that the trees were beginning
to thin out ahead, two more shots were fired, with a
short few seconds between them, as if they were
being carefully aimed.

"Rifle," puffed Tobias. "Different gun."

"Yeah." Jensen slowed to a walk and moved forward more slowly, lifting his .45 from its holster,
warning Tobias to spread out to his right.

As they crept down, watching carefully ahead,
there was the sound of running feet and a crashing
from the brush in front of them. Between the trees,
against the light of the clearing, Alex saw the silhouetted figure of a man in a baseball cap moving
with his back to them, a gun in his hand, peering in
the direction he had come. The figure hesitated,
moved another step, and stopped.

"Got you now, sister," he yelled at someone beyond the edge of the trees and raised the handgun.
"I can see you behind that bunch of weeds. Come
on out."

"Hold it right there," Jensen shouted, stepping
forward.

The man in the cap swung around, startled, gun
still raised, looking for the source of the unexpected
voice.

"Who the hell . . ." he started to say, when, from
Jensen's right, came the sound of a shot and he
crumpled.

Jensen turned to see Tobias step from between
two trees, a gun in his hand that still pointed toward
the now still form on the ground. The federal agent
continued on down the hill until he was standing
over the man he had shot, where Alex came to join
him. The man was clearly dead. Tobias's bullet had
struck him in the chest, killing him where he stood.
He lay in a crooked heap at the foot of a spruce, one
foot bent under him.

Jensen glanced at the federal agent and was startled by his frozen expression. Cold anger narrowed
his eyes and tightened his jaw. After a long minute,
seeming to suddenly become aware of Jensen's scrutiny, he took a deep breath and turned away.

"Didn't mean to kill him," he said, shaking his
head. "But he was getting ready to have a try at one
of us, probably you, and wouldn't have hesitated a
second. A real mean bastard."

"You know him?"

"Part of Stoffel's Brooks Range operation. We
couldn't make an arrest because he got out before
we picked up the others and the DA thought we
didn't have enough for a conviction. Not one of the

big guns—a nasty little errand boy—worthless shit.''

Jensen nodded, frowning. There was something more that Tobias wasn't saying, but he ignored it for the moment and moved on quickly to the edge of the trees.

"Rochelle," he yelled. "Chelle, are you out there? Are you okay? It's Jensen."

"Thank God," he heard her call back, in a strangely weak voice. "Help me, Alex. Please. I can't get up."

18

BACK AT THE SMALL, NAMELESS LAKE, CASWELL had built another fire and put another pot of coffee on to boil. When it was done, he added a little cold water to settle the grounds, sat on one of the logs, and poured himself a cup to wash down a late lunch of summer sausage, cheese, and crackers. Occupied in cutting another round from the sausage with his knife, he heard the faraway sound of an engine and, glancing up, saw a small plane heading east, high overhead.

In less than a minute, he had the door to the Maule open and its radio microphone in his hand, as he stood outside to keep an eye on the passing plane.

"Any aircraft on one two two nine, this is Maule nine eight six four mike. Do you copy?"

A crackle of static, then a female voice answered. "Maule nine eight six four mike, this is Piper Cub one oh four niner papa. I hear you. Go ahead."

"Four niner papa, you a white and red Super Cub eastbound on the east side of Lower Beluga Lake?"

"That's affirmative."

"Four niner papa, I have you in sight. I'm on the north bank at the west end of a small, narrow lake, at your three o'clock position, approximately a mile south. A blue and white Maule on floats—dragged out on the bank. Do you see me? Over."

"Roger, sixty-four mike. I have you in sight next to a red Cessna. Go ahead."

The small plane overhead began to circle over Caswell's location, keeping him in sight and in range of radio transmission.

"Four niner papa, I have a damage problem. Can you relay a message to the Kenai Flight Service Station for me? Over."

"Sixty-four mike, yes, I'd be glad to. Go ahead."

"Four niner papa, I have a punctured right float. Submerged log punched a hole in the aft three compartments that's too large to limp home with. I need assistance. Please request that they send someone out with the materials and expertise to get me back in the air. Over."

"Sixty-four mike, I copied all of that. Stay on this frequency while I switch to Kenai Radio. Hold on, I'll be right back."

Waiting with a dead radio, Caswell knew the pilot of the circling plane had switched to 122.2, the frequency for Kenai Radio, and was transmitting his message. In a short time, she was back.

"Maule sixty-four mike—Piper four niner papa. Are you there? Go ahead."

"Four niner papa, I'm here. Over."

"Sixty-four mike, relayed your message. Also gave them your Lat-long position from my Loran. They can't get to you before noon tomorrow. Are you okay till then? Go ahead."

"No problem, four niner papa. Got plenty of gear and food. Could hold out a week, if we had to. Over."

"Sixty-four mike, anyone injured? I'm a doctor, if you need medical assistance. Go ahead."

"Four niner papa, no one hurt. Appreciate the offer. Thanks for your assistance, friend," he told the helpful pilot. "Over."

"Okay, sixty-four mike. Anything for a smokey on the ground," the pilot tossed back, along with a grin Cas could hear in her voice. "Listen, be on the alert for grizzly. I've seen three good-sized ones on these flats today, just out of hibernation and probably bad-tempered. Four niner papa's clear."

"Thanks, four niner, we'll keep an eye out. Sixty-four mike's clear."

He watched the Piper Cub leave its circular pattern in the sky and head east toward Anchorage. Quickly it passed from view behind the ridge and all was quiet again.

So they were stuck where they were until tomorrow. It didn't surprise or frustrate him, since he had anticipated a wait for repairs, but he hoped nothing would occur between now and then to make him feel otherwise. When Jensen and Tobias came back with Rochelle Lewis, they would have the use of her plane if anything critical came up, but he had no way of knowing how long it would take them to find her, if there would be trouble at the other lake, or when he might expect them back.

For the moment, he had nothing to do but wait, and it was crazy to be concerned about things that were only possibilities. Ben Caswell was not the sort of man to waste his time on unrealistic worrying. He went back to finish his coffee and a Snickers bar for dessert while he enjoyed the surroundings in which he found himself. The sun was warm, the location pleasant and almost ready to burst into spring green. There were many revealing sounds of birds and small animals in the brush, and fish jumped periodically in the lake, making him wish he'd brought his rod and gear. A man could be forced to wait in a million less appealing places.

He had grown up in the Pacific Northwest and was used to the outdoors, but nothing that could compare to this, where a man could leave town and within an hour disappear into thousands of miles of wilderness for days, weeks, months, if he chose, and never see another human being, or anything man-touched. It satisfied some deep appreciation in Cas, struck a harmonic chord in him that he knew he would never hear so clearly anywhere else. He was hooked on the far north and his addiction bothered him not in the slightest.

For ten minutes he watched a whiskey jack do touch-and-go's for pieces of cracker he tossed on the ground for the big blue bird. He had lured it in within five feet when a second jay showed up and he ended the game.

"You guys would pick me clean of anything edible, given half a chance," he told them, and went to put what was left of the food back in the plane, along with his trash. The coffeepot, he emptied of grounds, filled with clean water, and left near the fire, which he banked carefully inside its circle of stones and left to slowly turn one thick piece of driftwood into charcoal. Usually he extinguished fires anytime he left them, but he didn't intend to go far and thought it might be a good idea to have this one ready for quick use. Also, there was nothing in the area dry enough to spread a fire.

For the next hour, he created a tidy camp, setting up the tent and sorting out the equipment they would need for the night, putting the rest back in the plane for the time being, locking it up where it would be protected and out of the way. From the banks of the lake and slope of the ridge, he collected a good-sized pile of firewood and placed it far enough from the smoldering fire so that a random spark would not set it ablaze. Satisfied with his efforts he looked around and mentally nodded to himself. All set.

Pulling on his jacket and picking up the Remington Springfield .30–06 he had taken from the plane, he started up the ridge to see if he could find the place where someone had shot Lewis's plane out of the sky. He knew his chances were extremely thin, but anything was possible. With no accurate knowledge of how much altitude the Cessna had gained or how fast the engine had died, he couldn't estimate how far it could have traveled after being hit before crashing. But if it had gone in a relatively straight line, trying for the waters of the lake, and if the shooter had, as Cas speculated, picked a high spot from which to shoot, he could even the odds somewhat.

As he climbed steadily up the slope, he slung the Remington diagonally across his back, to have both hands free. At the top, where Chelle had stood two days before, near the trees broken by the floats of her husband's plane, he paused and assessed the landscape in front of him. To the left lay a marshy area, slightly lower than the ridge and quite flat, full of hummocks, mud, and standing water. To his right the ground rose for a half mile into several rough hills, between fifty and a hundred feet higher, covered with bare rock and trees. He remembered seeing from the air that there were two or three small lakes among them, one almost as large as the one on which he had landed earlier, but shaped like a crooked, flattened letter W. The rocky summit of the hill closest to him was the most free of trees and seemed a good possibility. He headed for it, hiking along the ridge, then up through a stand of alder and spruce to come out on top, where he could look down to see a roundish lake below it that had been hidden by the hill itself. The crooked lake was still out of sight beyond other hills. This summit was bare and empty of any sign of occupation.

Farther east, across the tops of another thicket of trees, he could see another hill, perhaps a hundred feet higher than the one on which he stood. Its summit was flatter, seemed a little bowl-shaped, with a rocky prominence rising up above it. Heading down the slope, he started toward it.

Half an hour later, he was examining the remains of a small fire just under the highest, rocky point. It was old, had probably been there all winter, but the rocks behind it were smoke-blackened by more than one blaze. A couple of faded aluminum beer cans and a small amount of other trash, including the plastic rings from a six-pack, the box from some kind of heavy-caliber ammunition, and dozens of cigarette filters, lay scattered around. Someone, perhaps more than one someone, had spent time here. Hunters? The hill was high enough to be a good lookout sight for game, if you wanted to spend your time waiting rather than tracking. About half of the W-shaped lake could be seen clearly below. He found no shell casings of any kind.

Would anyone pick up shell casings and leave an ammunition box in their trash, Cas wondered. It might make sense if they wanted them to reload. Could they be reloaded? Never having been a hunter, he didn't know, but perhaps the brass casings were

worth something. Someone might retrieve what
might incriminate them in the shooting of the Lewis
plane, implicate a shooter with fingerprints or other
identification. Perhaps the absence of shell casings
implied almost as much as their presence. Still it
gave him no location.

Disgusted with the litter whoever had used the site
had left, Caswell searched his jacket pockets for
something in which to collect it, and found an evidence bag. He and Jensen usually carried some
along, finding them handy for more than evidence at
times. This one was large enough for the trash, and
he set about picking it up. Around one side of the
rock prominence, he came upon another handful, including more beer cans and a cracked water bottle.
Next to it, with two plastic produce bags from some
grocery store, was a single playing card.

He picked it up, turned it over, and grinned. The
ace of spades. Playing cards without this ace would
certainly have unbalanced their game, whatever it
was. He hoped some litterbug had lost a bundle.
Maybe it had dropped out of a sleeve and gone un-
noticed. Whatever. He flipped it into the evidence
bag with the rest of the trash.

As he was closing the top of the bag containing
his collection of trash, the sound of another plane
drew his attention to the western part of the sky.
Flying much lower than the Super Cub he had spoken to earlier, a silver Cessna was gaining altitude,
apparently from a takeoff on Lower Beluga Lake. It
headed north, then leveled off and banked in a large,
sweeping turn, altering course till it was coming
straight in his direction.

Feeling suddenly exposed, remembering the
tracks they had found on the bank leading to

Chelle's plane, Caswell stepped back against the prominence of rock and froze under a slight overhang. With luck, in the absence of motion, whoever was in the plane wouldn't detect his tan jacket against the variety of colors in the rock. They passed slightly north of him without a hesitation, close enough so he could see the white face of a person in the passenger seat, too far away for recognition.

As soon as they were gone, Cas moved to the eastern edge of the small bowl and leaned against a boulder to watch as the plane lost altitude and made a landing on the crooked lake, taxied to the eastern arm of the flattened W, and grounded the floats on the shore. A figure got out of the passenger side and walked the float to the bank, soon followed by the pilot at his side. The passenger went directly to the edge of the lake and splashed water on his face, over and over. Then he stood rubbing at his eyes.

The pilot, a shorter fatter man, waved him to help and together they heaved the plane higher on the bank. For several minutes they appeared to be discussing something heatedly, for the pilot waved a hand in broad, directive gestures, while the other man seemed to be shaking his head.

Cas pulled out a pair of binoculars from his pack to get a better look, but when he had them in focus the argument seemed to have been settled for they began to quickly unload a large amount of equipment from the back of the Cessna, the taller man moving more slowly and awkwardly, pausing frequently to splash more water onto his face. For the next hour, as he watched, they organized a camp, set up three tents and a rain fly over a fire pit that was quickly dug, lined with stones, and covered with a grill. Into one of the tents went a dozen boxes that seemed to be canned food, four large plastic coolers, water containers, fuel cans, several rifles and a large amount of boxed ammunition.

They had just finished their work and were building a fire, when another plane flew in to land and taxi to the bank. Three men got out and approached the two at the fire. As Caswell watched, the shorter of the original two walked away from the fire with the pilot of the second plane, and they stood talking far enough away to be unheard by the others. Energetically, he waved in the direction of Caswell's hill, which also included their camp at the small lake, and Lower Beluga Lake. The pilot, who seemed to be in charge, and whose face was partially hidden by a pair of dark glasses, exhibited signs of frustration and anger—kicking at a rock and grabbing the neck of the fat man's jacket to shake him roughly. Cas could almost hear him swear. Something was unmistakably not to his liking.

Dragging the fat man by one arm, he shouted something in the direction of those at the fire and went hurriedly back to his plane, thrusting the fat man toward the passenger side. Another man came running, got in and the plane was quickly in the air.

As it passed overhead, Cas once more froze against the sheltering rock and watched as the plane disappeared below the ridge of the small lake where his Maule and Chelle's Cessna were left unattended.

Time to be getting back, he thought. Whatever they were up to, it had a bad feeling.

It was late enough in the afternoon for the sun to have begun its downward slide toward the horizon as Cas went quickly down through the trees and onto the flat space between the hills, hiking in shadow, a little farther south than his original route. As fast as he could travel, he hurried toward his camp and three angry men, one of whom he thought he had recognized through the binoculars.

19

IT WAS ALMOST DARK BEFORE JENSEN, TOBIAS, AND Chelle Lewis made their way back to where Caswell anxiously waited. They walked single file, Rochelle between the two men, needing no assistance, though Jensen had insisted on taking her pack. Tobias carried both the others, having consolidated them by hanging the day-pack outside the larger one. Chelle wore the Weatherby slung over her left shoulder, which felt slightly awkward, but did not aggravate the bruise it had inflicted on her hip during the chase earlier in the day.

She was once again warm and dry, though it had taken time swaddled in her down sleeping bag, huddled near a fire they had hurriedly built after hauling her from behind the hummock in the marsh. It had taken several cups of coffee and a complete set of extra clothing to still the chattering of her teeth. Because her hiking boots were drenched beyond usefulness, she wore her waders over three pairs of wool socks, which made hiking more difficult on the way back, but allowed her to cross marshy spots without having to change footwear.

While she was recovering from her soak in the swamp, Jensen and Tobias had gone on across to

Lower Beluga Lake, where they found evidence that a plane had landed, but nothing else. The other two men Chelle had described had apparently departed, leaving their comrade to his fate.

"Probably heard the shooting and, when he didn't come back, figured they'd better cut their losses," Jensen calculated. "Either that, or they came close enough to see us before they took off."

"May have thought he would chase her clear back to the other lake," Tobias suggested. "Might have gone there to see and never even heard the shots."

"Possible. Caswell will keep a good lookout, and he's a pretty good shot with that thirty oh six he carries. He'd hear a plane before it landed anyway. Still, we'd better get back over there and it'll be dark if we don't get moving."

Unable to remove the body of the man Tobias had shot, they had hoisted it into the tallest tree they could find, hoping no black bear would happen along to notice or smell it. They were not so concerned with grizzlies that lose their climbing ability as they mature and gain weight, are limited by their fixed wrist joints, and lack the sharp hooked claws that blacks retain for climbing, but they picked a tree that was not small enough to be chewed or pushed over by the big browns. They buried what little blood had resulted from the wound that killed him, emptied the coffee grounds over it, along with wet ashes from the fire.

By the time they had finished, Chelle was able to move and they started back the way they had come. There was little talk on the way, for Jensen, wanting nothing more than to make sure that Caswell had not been somehow surprised, moved as quickly as possible over the rough terrain and they were all wearing thin on energy when they neared the lake where they had left the planes.

As they approached the remains of the ancient log cabin at the west end of the lake, Caswell stepped out to meet them with a grim, angry expression.

"Ben," Jensen said, catching first sight of him. "What're you doing here? What's wrong?"

"Thought I'd better keep you from walking into an ambushed camp that some determined strangers spent an hour tearing apart a while ago. Almost everything we had was trashed, dumped, cut apart, broken, or burned. Damned lunatics made a bonfire of the tent and some other stuff, which almost torqued me into putting a bullet into one of them. They seemed to be looking for something as they worked, but most of it was deliberate vandalism.

"If that wasn't enough, you're going to hate what comes next. They smashed the radio in the Maule, which they couldn't fly, of course. But when they left they took both their plane and Rochelle's Cessna."

"They took my plane?" she broke in, eyes wide.

"Yeah. Sorry, Chelle. But that's not the worst of it. The guy who flew it had a key to unlock and start it and—I wasn't sure till I got back to the ridge, close enough to get a good look, but—it was your brother."

"Ed?" She simply stared at him, stunned with the information.

"You said *got back*. Where were you?" Alex asked. "How'd they manage to miss you?"

"They flew in, but earlier I took that hike I was thinking about and got back just in time to watch the last part of the destruction from that ridge above the planes. They've got a camp set up on a lake west

of ours that we should check out, I think. I'd be
willing to bet we've stumbled onto part of that
poaching ring of Stoffel's. If so, we could be in trouble, with no transportation or communication. They
obviously don't want us leaving to talk to anyone
from the look of it. They left the third man waiting
with a rifle for whoever came back. Far as I know
he's still over there, hidden in the brush. I went
around him and came here.''

Jensen didn't say anything for a minute, glanced
at Tobias, then at Chelle, who stood, still silent, listening to Caswell with an expression that grew in-
creasingly angry.

"This probably involves the one you sprayed and
his fat friend," he said to her. "And a few others,
it seems, including Ed."

"But why? What's he got to do with it? What the
hell do they want?" she asked.

"This is more than revenge for the guy Ernie shot.
It sounds like some kind of illegal hunting activity
all right."

"Shot?" Caswell's eyebrows lifted in questioning
surprise at this piece of news.

Jensen nodded a confirmation to him, as he continued his assessment to Chelle.

"Something they want pretty bad that they think
you have? Something to do with Norm, or the Randolph woman? You said they knew you were coming, used your name. Could be the same ones that
searched your house."

"I'd guess this is more complicated than it first
appears," Cas said slowly. "Waiting for you, I've
had time to think it over some, and from our two
planes, they obviously know there's more of us than
one. It appears they expected Chelle, but not the rest.

They don't know where we are, or how many. On
the other hand, with Landreth along, they probably
know we're the law. Taking the only operational
plane and smashing my radio is a pretty clear statement they don't intend anyone to leave. I'd like to
know exactly why and what they have in mind now.
We can't fly and have no way to contact anyone for
help. The guys to fix my float won't be here until
tomorrow.''

"You got a call out?''

"Yeah, before any of this happened. They showed
up well over an hour later.''

"But how could they have known I was coming
out here—who I am?'' Chelle asked, her forehead
furrowed with the effort of trying to figure it out. "I
didn't tell anyone, but . . .'' Her eyes widened in
sudden realization, then she shook her head em-
phatically. "No. Not possible. It doesn't make
sense.''

Jensen assured her it did . . . somehow. "He knew
where you were headed before we left town to come
after you. We were at his place and found your note
in his mailbox. He must have called someone after
we left.''

"What note? Oh . . . you mean *Ed*? I left a note
for Ed.''

"That's not who *you* meant?''

"No. I meant Jeff Bunker. I told him last night
that I was going to look for Norm. He offered to
come, but I wanted to do it alone. What's going on?
I don't understand any of this. Why would Ed . . . or
Jeff . . . have told anyone where I was going? How
is Ed connected to this?''

"That's what I'm beginning to wonder,'' Alex answered, thoughtfully.

Tobias was frowning in confused concentration. "Who's Bunker?"

"Look," Cas suggested. "Before it gets completely dark, let's get ourselves settled for the time being. While I waited for you, I cleared out a section of this old cabin. The roof's gone, but there's a sheltered corner. You've got that plastic rain tarp we can put up and two sleeping bags, right? Chelle, you've got another one? Good. If we keep it small, I think it'd be safe to build a fire, make some coffee, and cook that freeze-dried stuff you took along for dinner. It'll keep four of us from starving. Then we can answer each other's questions, pool information, and decide what to do."

The corner of the cabin Cas had claimed was ramshackle, disintegrating with age, and overgrown with moss and weeds that clung to the narrow logs that had been used to build it. With only small trees available as material, none of these logs was much larger around than ten or twelve inches at the widest, and though the cracks between them had at one time been stuffed with moss and grasses, most now gapped emptily, allowing breezes and insects free access. Luckily, the night that fell was windless and the mosquitoes that would later in the season swarm in such a marshy area were still unhatched and dormant.

When they had moved in, before the light was completely gone, Alex noticed something roughly carved in the log that was the lintel over the doorframe now lacking its door. Going close enough to trace it with one finger, he deciphered it, then couldn't decide if he had satisfied, or added to, his curiosity. "Small house, great peace" it read in

Latin. Apparently, a man with a classical education had lived here, alone and isolated from the rest of his kind. The tall trooper wondered once again what had determined this unknown hermit's solitary choice.

It interested him how as few as four words could provide an insight into the person who cared enough to carve them—for whom they were meaningful. He wished someone would carve a few words to give him a handle on the happenings of the day and who was responsible for them. It clearly had some kind of associations with Norm Lewis, Karen Randolph, and the illegal hunting activities that had connected them. Whatever these links were, someone was conspicuously concerned that they not be uncovered. And just how did Ed Landreth fit in?

By the time they were settled, it had grown dark enough to make Ben Caswell's small fire glow brightly and cast flickering shadows on the old, gray logs of the nearest partially standing wall. They crouched around it, warming their hands at its crackling flames and appreciating the appealing smells bubbling from the kettle of freeze-dried stew he had simmering over it.

Chelle had sunk immediately to a spot where she could lean against the wall, propped the Weatherby against it, and gratefully accepted the mug of hot coffee he offered her. The first sip brought a questioning smile to her face. "What . . . ?"

"Just a little medicinal brandy." He grinned back. "Thought you might need a lift after trying to swim the swamp. Thank Alex. He packed it. You okay?"

"Yes, thanks, Ben, and you guessed right about the brandy. You, too, Alex."

He tipped his laced coffee mug at her in response and nodded.

Clutching the mug, she warmed her hands as she sipped again and sighed with appreciation, clearly glad to have reached their current destination. "I'm pooped."

"Hungry, too, I bet. We'll eat in a couple of minutes."

There was enough to satisfy them all, and after the trials of the day, freeze-dried or not, it tasted like a banquet.

"So, who'd you contact on the radio?" Jensen questioned, firing up his pipe to go with another cup of coffee.

"A high-flying friendly Piper. Woman doc, who got through to Kenai Flight Service Station for me, and offered medical assistance."

"And now we haven't any way to contact anyone else."

"Right. But, at least, we know someone will show up around noon tomorrow. What are we going to do meanwhile?" Caswell had begun to collect the odds and ends of trash from the meal and hauled a large plastic bag from Jensen's pack to put it in. Remembering, he retrieved the evidence bag full of litter he had collected that afternoon on the hill and threw it in with the rest.

"Where'd you get all that stuff?" Alex asked, always observant, and aware of Caswell's penchant for picking up what others left behind, a habit he cultivated in himself as well.

Cas told them, pulling it back out to exhibit, as he continued, "I think some people leave it on purpose. The arrogance is astonishing." As he turned it over, the ace of spades, face flat against the plastic, was momentarily visible in the light from the fire.

Rochelle jerked upright, pointing. "Wait. Stop. What was that?"

He twisted it back into view. "Just a lost playing card that someone dropped with the beer cans."

"Let me see it. Give it to me. Please." The strain in her voice caught the attention of all three of the others.

"What is it?" Alex asked, but she didn't answer, intently focused on Ben as he opened the bag, felt for the card, and placed it in her impatient, grasping hands.

Carefully, with shaking fingers, she turned it over, examining both front and back. When she raised her eyes to look across the fire at Cas, tears were streaming down her cheeks, which were white with shock. "He was here," she stated tensely, through stiff lips. "This was Norm's. *Where* did you find it again? Wherever it was, he was there. See?"

"What do you mean, Chelle? How do you know?"

Her intensity was matched by the infinite stillness with which Jensen asked and then waited for her explanation.

"It was his symbol . . . like a motto . . . kind of a trademark. You know? He carried one all the time, had one on the instrument panel in his plane. It was sort of for luck, but it meant him, too. Other people, pilots, called him Ace half the time—gave him things with the ace of spades on them. I think his friend Bunker started it a long time ago. He bought these kind of cards and saved the ace of spades, threw the rest away. Only this kind." She turned it over so they could see the red and white back with its complex, common pattern. "No one else would carry around just this ace. Don't you see? Just Norm. He was alive. Where *is* he?''

Months of fear and not knowing filled her last question with shrillness and anguish. The rush of words stopped suddenly and there was stillness as they all sat looking at her, startled into silence. It was too big a coincidence not to be true, but could it be? And what exactly did it mean that Lewis had parted with his trademark ace?

20

EXCEPT FOR NORMAL NIGHT SOUNDS—THE SUB-
dued hoot of an owl, something small in the bushes
near the cabin—the makeshift camp was quiet, fire
burned down to a few smoldering coals. Alex sat
outside the remains of the old cabin in the dark between two trees, bundled in practically all the extra
clothing they had, hands in his pockets, his jacket
collar turned up around his ears, and an old fishing
hat—rescued from the bottom of his pack—pulled
down on his head, keeping watch. He was all but
invisible in the dark.

With only three sleeping bags, and just in case
their acquaintances of the afternoon decided to make
an uninvited visit, the men had agreed that trading
off as lookouts would be prudent. Jensen had volunteered for first shift, wanting to think more than
he desired sleep, though it had been a long day for
him, as well as for everyone else.

Shortly after Caswell had given Chelle the ace,
she had grown silent, her thoughts turning inward.
In a little while she had yawned and, suggesting
sleep, had headed for a nearby stream with a towel
and toothbrush. Alex had soon followed, not comfortable with letting her go alone, given the possi-

bility of unpleasant company. He didn't think anyone would come looking in the dark, but told himself it was better to be overly cautious than regretful.

An almost full moon had risen and shed a pale but definite light. His eyes quickly adjusted, so it wasn't hard to walk, most obstacles clearly visible.

He met her coming back and stopped to ask a couple of questions.

"You're sure about that card, Chelle?"

She looked up at him, her pale, oval-shaped face distinct in the moonlight, and nodded.

"Yes, Alex, I am. It's Norm's. Has to be."

They were both silent for a minute, then Alex cleared his throat and gave her a long, level look, filled with sympathy and a hint of suspicion.

"You think he's alive, don't you?" he said gently. "Why?"

She said nothing at first, didn't make a sound, just stared at him with wide eyes that slowly filled with tears again. Turning her face to look toward the dark within a stand of spruce to her left, she swallowed hard, clenched her teeth, and took a deep breath.

"I think he might be," she replied carefully. "But, if he is, where is he?"

"You *really* don't know?"

Her attention jerked back to Jensen with a gasp.

He watched her reaction closely, hoping to discover the truth about what she knew and didn't know. She watched him watching her.

"You think I'm part of some conspiracy, Alex? What? What am I supposed to know?"

"I have no idea, Chelle. But I do feel there's something you're not telling me."

Resentment showed plainly on her face, and anger, while she thought before she spoke.

"I *do not know* where Norm is. But if he's dead, where's his body? And why did he leave?"

"What makes you think he's not dead?"

She frowned and broke eye contact, staring unseeing over his left shoulder, concentrating on her own thoughts. Uncertain.

"Just tell me, Chelle. Whatever you think you know, tell me. Maybe we can put this thing together, if you do."

She sighed and suddenly gave in.

"Okay. There are a couple of things. Number one. If Norm was injured too bad'y in the crash to get his survival stuff out of the plane, how could he hike out? Why haven't we found his body? He must be somewhere close. But your people looked and didn't find it, right? And I didn't find any trace between here and Lower Beluga Lake, did you?"

"No, but there's a lot of space out there. In this wilderness he could be ten feet away from where we looked and we'd never find him. It's too big."

He shook his head.

"Number two." She hesitated and glanced up apologetically. "I should have told you this before. He left a lot of money with Jeff, for me. I don't know why. Just told him to give me the envelope if he was sure Norm wasn't coming back for it. Those were his words . . . *if he wasn't coming back for it.* Not if he was dead, but '. . . *if he wasn't coming back.*' "

Alex thought about that for a minute.

"Anything else?"

"No. Well—yes, sort of. Small stuff. I have a funny feeling that he's been around. I smelled his pipe tobacco once when I got home and opened the front door. The milk was in the wrong place in the refrigerator. Somebody else may have been in my plane. Nothing, really. Just odd things like that. Like he was trying to tell me . . ." She stopped speaking and whirled around, turning her back to Jensen, but not before he had heard the sob and seen her face crumple.

Her unexpected reaction startled him into silence, but he reached out and swung her back around by the shoulders to face him. She refused to look at him, staring blankly into the trees again—then she wrenched herself out of his hands and stumbled away into the dark.

As quickly as he could move, he followed and caught up where she had stopped to lean against a tree, struggling with great, shuddering sobs.

"Chelle?" He laid a hand on her arm and she immediately turned into his arms, clinging like a child, burying her face in his shoulder.

All he could do was let her cry, get some of the pain out, knowing from personal experience that if Norm Lewis *was* dead, this was not only an ending, but also a beginning of something she would never completely forget or get over, and only come to accept slowly, a piece at a time, as she was ready. If he was alive—had chosen to leave her and go somewhere else, whatever the reason—she would have another kind of guilty agony to come to terms with, one that she would identify with personal failure, rightful or not.

As long as there was hope—any hope at all—she had been able to psychologically crouch behind it, huddle down protectively and shut out other possible outcomes, or look at them obliquely. Now she was close to being forced to face a much harder reality, one that could not be pretended or wished away, that must be looked at directly . . . and alone.

Sadly, there was absolutely nothing he, or anyone, could do or say to her that would truly make a difference in what she was feeling, or how she would cope with it. So he simply stood and held her, murmuring meaningless sounds of security and understanding against her hair, wondering why life seemed to be so hard for certain people.

After a long time, as her sobs gradually grew less intense and finally stopped, he slowly became aware of the living warmth of the woman he was holding. Arms around his waist inside his jacket, face against his now damp shirt, her utter stillness told him she had also realized that—to his confusion and embarrassment—his response had become unmistakably more than emotional.

He also knew that, though the timing and circumstances were inappropriate and awkward, he was not completely surprised at his body's betrayal, that he had been aware of Chelle Lewis as a woman for some time, and had refused to acknowledge that awareness. How much of the equation was empathy, he had no idea. What did surprise him, when he attempted to step away from her and try to apologize somehow, was that she refused to let him. By merely clasping her hands behind his back, she held him against her and prevented their separation.

"Chelle . . . ah . . . no," he stammered. "I'm sorry . . . didn't mean . . ."

She lifted her face, details of her expression hidden in deep shadows, with the moon behind her, letting him sputter into silence as she waited. Then, raising herself on her toes, she kissed him full, if briefly, on the lips. "Thank you, Alex," she breathed in his ear, let her arms fall to her sides, and stepped away from the embrace. Then, with a hint of resignation and bitterness, "Life just won't quit, will it? It's all right. Don't worry. Thanks for reminding me."

She dug a couple of tissues from a pocket, blew her nose, dried her face, and that was the end of it.

As they walked back to join Cas and Tobias, Alex wondered if Jessie would understand what had just happened . . . if he told her. He wasn't sure *he* did, but thought that he didn't have to and could live with the small amount of uneasy guilt he had brought on himself. He was ridiculously glad it had happened in the dark and would require no explanation.

But, reaching the shelter of the ruined cabin, he suddenly realized that, with the abrupt change of mental and emotional direction, he had not satisfied himself that he knew all of what Chelle was keeping to herself. In uneasy confusion he wondered if she were smarter than he had given her credit for. Not for the first time, a thread of suspicion floated through his mind. Was it possible that she was not just keeping something to herself, that Rochelle Lewis was somehow calculatedly involved in her husband's disappearance? Had he just been very skillfully manipulated into abandoning a line of inquiry she would rather not pursue?

By one o'clock, Alex had still not come to a conclusion about Rochelle. He had quietly made a new pot of coffee and reviewed everything he had discovered or knew about the case in light of the recent events. He was ready to talk it over with Ben Caswell, when the pilot woke and came to take his turn as watchdog.

Cas, however, had something else on his mind. Filling a cup from the half-empty pot still warm on the remains of the fire, he came, yawning, to where Alex huddled, sat down on a rock, and leaned his .30–06 against one of the trees.

"You get everything straight with Chelle?" he asked casually.

"Mostly, I guess. Who knows?"

"Sure you're not a bit less than professional in that direction?"

"How do you mean?" Alex asked a little too quickly.

"Don't get defensive on me now," Cas warned. "This is your friend here. I know you pretty well, remember? I just feel like I have to say it seems there's more to your concern for her than usual. You two were gone for quite a while there, and you came back looking slightly scrambled and red around the ears. Thought I might mention it, that's all. I like Jessie a lot."

He took a sip of coffee and ignored Alex's scowl to glance at the two figures still quiet in their bags near the dying fire.

"Look . . ." Alex started. "You're wrong. Besides, it's none of your . . ."

"I know that. Probably none of yours either. Chelle's pretty fragile these days."

Jensen hesitated, thinking. Then tried to honestly explain his feelings to the friend that he knew cared enough to risk his anger.

"Okay. Here it is. I hurt for her—know what it's like. I've been there—in the pain and anger because you hurt and the one you've lost is responsible for it—in the guilt because of your anger, because you know it wasn't their fault . . . or, maybe this time it was. I know how she feels—crazy. You don't know what to do—or what you *will* do next. I wish I could help. That's all.''

"Yeah," Cas agreed. "I think that's true—except for the last part. I see how you look at her every so often. How your voice changes when you speak to her. Different from the way you usually deal with people in her kind of situation. Come on, Alex. We can talk about it. You think she doesn't know it? Sure she does. It's instinctive. But what does it do to your other feeling that she may be involved in this? If she is, your interest may be useful to her.''

Alex, angry and embarrassed, also had to nod and give in.

"Damn, you're good at getting to the point, aren't you? You just take it all in, like a sponge, and knock it around till it makes sense.''

"Well?"

"Well . . . yes. You're right. I think she may have done that tonight. But I also think she needs support.''

"Oh, I agree with that. I think she's attracted by your attention and sympathy. The problem is that it's all mixed. The way we guys deal with almost any kind of emotion involving a woman seems somehow to usually include sex. That's not bad. People alone and in trouble tend to reach for security and healing support. Touching another warm human's part of that. You know how people fall into bed with each other when their lives are threatened? Like in a war? I think she's compensating for Norm with you. But I doubt she'd put it like that.''

"It's more than that," Jensen said, slowly. "I think she may be using the way I respond to her to keep me away from whatever she doesn't want to talk about—whatever she's not telling."

"Well, I'm glad you've got far enough to figure that out. Don't make mistakes with that urge to take care of a female in distress. *Big, brave trooper saves poor, helpless . . .*"

Before he could finish, Alex had to laugh. It fit, at least part of it fit. "She's not the most helpless of people, is she?"

"Nope. Neither is Jessie, if I dare mention her."

"Also true."

"Good. Enough said."

Silent for a minute, Cas then changed the subject completely.

"That guy Tobias shot that you left in the tree. Who was he anyway?"

"Nothing on the body to say. Wish Ernie hadn't shot him dead, before I had a chance to ask him a few questions. He was evidently in the Brooks Range camp, but we still don't know for sure exactly who's involved in all this—except Ed, if he is—or if they're the same people who shot Karen Randolph, though I'd be amazed if they weren't. Right?"

There was no answer from Caswell for a minute, as he turned it over in his head. When he spoke, it was in a tone so low it was almost a whisper. "What do you make of Tobias?"

Instantly alerted, Alex lowered his own voice accordingly.

"Hadn't thought too much about him. Why?"

"You think he's on the level?"

"You think he's not?"

"Well, maybe. Maybe I'm just jumpy. But there's something about him that keeps me all the time aware that he's watching everything that goes on and picking up a lot of information.''

Alex paused thoughtfully.

''Tobias was pretty quick on the trigger this afternoon. But he obviously knows all about that sting and who was in on it.''

''Does he? From which side—stingees, or stingers? We only have his word that he spoke to Ivan, or that he's who he says he is, for that matter. Did you get a good look at his ID?''

''Just a glance, upside down. Damn, Cas. You suppose he shot that guy *so I couldn't talk to him*?''

''What I think is that we better watch him close and take turns staying awake tonight. There's nothing we can prove—not a good idea to start something now—he's got a gun over there—but I'm not inclined to trust anything at this point. Are you?''

''Nope.''

So they kept watch, or meant to. But the day had taken its toll on Alex. When Cas woke him again for his next two-hour shift, he was so groggy he walked around for the first fifteen minutes, afraid to sit down for fear of going right back to sleep. Quietly, he checked that Tobias was snoring and Chelle was also asleep in her bag. When he finally went to his post by the trees, he was unintentionally snoozing within half an hour.

When he woke with a start and looked at his watch with the small flashlight he carried in one pocket, it was a quarter past four. Damn. Listening intently, he heard nothing. Not even Tobias snoring. Maybe he had rolled over.

Getting up, he went to look, and came back to ungently shake Cas awake.

''Hey, sorry. I nodded off, damn it. You better get

up. Tobias is gone. Took off sometime in the last hour.''

''Yeah . . . well. Thought he might,'' Cas said, pulling on his boots and jacket.

They went together to look and stood over the empty space where he had slept, or seemed to. He was definitely gone, as was the sleeping bag Cas had loaned him. He didn't intend to be cold, wherever he was. It suggested that he, too, waited somewhere for the sun to come up, and it was already growing light.

''Chelle?''

''Still asleep.''

''Better get her up. One way or another, we've got to stay away from whoever these guys are, at least until we get help at noon.''

''I think we should move nearer where we left the planes,'' Jensen suggested. ''There's more cover up beyond the ridge and we'd be closer when that someone shows up to fix the float. Besides, Tobias knows where we are, so we better not stay and take a chance on him bringing them back here, if he's part of their game.''

In a very short time the small ruined cabin was as abandoned and as peaceful as it had been before they came.

21

By the time the mountains on the eastern horizon were edged with gold from the rising sun, Alex, Cas, and Chelle had made a wide circle north of the lake and found a place from which to watch the section of the lakeshore that held Caswell's disabled plane. In a stand of brush and trees about half a mile east along the ridge, they settled in quietly and used the binoculars to carefully examine the area. It didn't take Jensen long to locate a half-hidden man with a rifle who was evidently tired and restless from his fruitless, all-night watch, for he revealed himself by carelessly shaking the concealing bushes when he stepped away from his ambush site to empty his bladder. Jensen surveyed the slope behind him leading to the top of the ridge and thought it might just be possible . . .

"Bastards," Chelle interrupted his assessment, distinctly angry and upset at the sight of the empty space where she had carefully secured her plane the day before. She said little more, but had a few choice names to call her brother.

"Look," Jensen said, when he was satisfied that there was only one man guarding their landing site. "If we're careful, I think we could get the drop on that guy before he knew we were coming. He doesn't know we've spotted him and won't be expecting a surprise. What do you think, Cas?"

After also studying the layout, Caswell nodded agreement. "From two directions, one from the top and one lower down. It's worth a try. It'd be good to make sure he doesn't get a chance to shoot our repair crew and we might get some information out of him." He yawned, then grinned. "Besides, I'd like to see if they left him anything edible. My spine's rubbing a hole in my empty belly."

"You okay to stay with this stuff, Chelle?" Alex asked, indicating the packs they had slipped off.

"No problem," she said, leaning back against the pack she had carried herself, stretching to relieve sore muscles and bruises that had tightened during the night. "I'd just as soon stay here, anyway. Yesterday was pretty hard on the bod."

It wasn't difficult. The man on guard was absurdly lacking in alertness.

"Police. Don't do anything stupid," Jensen calmly instructed him twenty minutes later, after a stealthy stalk along the ridge and down its slope to a spot ten feet behind the sleepy guard. "Toss out the gun, then come out of there with your hands on your head."

Following directions, the stranger soon stood facing the lake, with Jensen's .45 semiautomatic against his ribs. Caswell rose from a covering position and moved quickly to join them. Searching through the scattered supplies and damaged equipment near his plane, he located a roll of duct tape and proceeded to securely fasten the ambusher's wrists and elbows behind him, then taped his ankles and knees together.

"There. He won't be going anywhere soon. We'll tape him to a tree and cover his mouth before we go."

"We going somewhere?"

"We've got hours until anyone comes with help. There's no sense in sitting around here waiting for them when we could head over and take a look at that camp on the other lake. Right?"

Alex nodded agreement. "True. I'd rather know what we're up against than stay here doing nothing. This one out of the way cuts the opposition down to four. Now"—turning to their prisoner on the ground—"who are you? And who're you working for?"

Though they questioned him for the next ten minutes, they got nothing. He said not a word, just sat, staring at them, stubborn and insolent, periodically spitting on the ground. Long, greasy hair held away from his face with a filthy strip of bandanna; small, piggy eyes narrowed to slits with incongruously long lashes; he kept his chapped lips tightly closed and wouldn't even give them a name.

Taking his rifle, they finally gave up in disgust. Cas wrapped a long strip of tape tightly around his mouth and head, including his long hair, so there was little chance of his rubbing it loose. He would not appreciate its removal later. Lifting him by the armpits, they sat him up against a tree surrounded by brush, where he would remain unseen, and used the rest of the tape to attach him to it, chest to waist. He glared and swallowed the saliva he would have expectorated had he been able.

From the wreck of their belongings, Cas had

sorted out three small cans of peaches, a box of pilot bread—mashed to crumbs by someone's boot—and a crushed but still wrapped Butterfinger bar that had not been doused with the charcoal lighter. Searching the watchman's hiding place, he came up with two ham sandwiches and a bottle of water.

"You can't eat them anyway," he told the tape-imprisoned guard. "Hate to see them dry out and go to waste."

Trekking back to where Chelle waited, they divided the sandwiches and canned fruit three ways and washed their improvised breakfast down with water.

In half an hour they were on their way to the lake on which Cas had spotted the other camp.

"I want to know what Ed's doing with this bunch," Chelle stated, as they headed northeast off the ridge. "I don't understand it at all."

Jensen let it pass, but considered and found himself wondering again about her motives for what happened the night before. Were both she and her brother involved? What did this have to do with Lewis? Or had they stumbled into something completely unrelated? It was all happening so fast there didn't seem to be time to figure it all out, put the pieces together. Where was Tobias, and why? For that matter, *who* was Tobias? Were he and Cas the only people on the plateau not somehow connected to the Lewis case, which seemed to be expanding exponentially with very few useful clues. How did it all fit together—as it must, since every new piece to the puzzle seemed to be at least partly the same color as all the others, though they differed in shape, and none quite matched in configuration?

Leaving the rain tarp, and several other heavy

items hidden in the brush, along with the two sleeping bags they still had, they now traveled with more ease and speed. Cautious, Jensen insisted that they assess the route and stay near some kind of cover just in case they needed to escape the searching eyes of anyone flying over. For this reason they avoided the ridges and wide expanses of rock, and instead, also avoiding soggy sections, they picked their way across the uneven ground along a crooked course that eventually, over an hour later, brought them to a location directly across the lake from the camp. From this observation point, they could watch people moving purposely between planes and tents, and pulled out binoculars.

"Sure wish I could hear what they're saying," Cas commented.

"Yeah," Alex agreed, glancing at Chelle. "They seem to be getting ready to go somewhere in your plane."

Pale and scowling, she was clearly infuriated to see her plane sitting half out of the water on the bank of the lake. Through her own glasses, she could see that the man she had pepper-sprayed the day before, now seemingly recovered, was filling the tanks of the Cessna from five-gallon cans of fuel. It took two, twice as much as she would have used flying to the lake from Anchorage. They must have flown the Cessna somewhere else since they had stolen it.

As she was informing Alex of this fact, through the binoculars he saw Ed Landreth step out of one of the tents, followed by another man. Landreth was not answering his companion's apparent questions, but stalked across to a fire that burned in the center of the camp, stubbornly shaking his head and refusing to engage in conversation. Picking up a metal cup, he poured coffee into it and stared at the lake as he raised it to his lips. With a quick, impatient motion, the man slapped the cup to the ground, grabbed Ed's shoulder and shoved him around, yelling loud enough so that the sound, though not the words, could be heard faintly from where Jensen stood. For a minute, Jensen thought he was going to hit the younger man.

Chelle caught her breath in a mixture of concern and irritation. "What the hell is Ed doing over there?" she questioned. "Where did he get a key to my plane? I'd like to smack him myself, but I'd rather not watch somebody else do it for me."

"Does he ever fly it for you? Could he have had a key made?"

"Never. I don't trust him. He can't be bothered to learn the basic safety procedures . . . has no patience. After he wrecked my car I quit letting him borrow anything I'd have to pay for if he screwed up again, made sure he couldn't get hold of my keys."

"Were there extra keys? Did Norm have one?"

"Ye-e-s," she said thoughtfully, "but it was on the same ring as his. It was with him last fall. How could Ed have it now?"

"Well, he got a key somewhere, and if I'm right, these guys are about to use the Cessna for illegal hunting. Look, they're loading tarps and a couple of rifles. He could lose the Cessna for you if they're caught. Maybe that's the idea—lose yours, not theirs."

"Damn it. I bet you're right. But how would they get him to steal it?"

"Don't know, but it's pretty obvious that he's in on it with them some way, Chelle," Cas told her frowning. "Nobody's holding a gun to his head over there."

She turned back to peer across the water, trying to see. "What's he doing, Alex?"

Taking another look through the glasses, he answered her, slowly. "Still arguing. Looks like Ed wants to fly your plane and the other guy's refusing to let him."

"Can't imagine why." The note of cynicism in her voice betrayed her irritation and disappointment.

The confrontation across the lake was soon settled, it seemed, but not to Landreth's liking. He turned away, kicked the cup that had been knocked from his hand, and disappeared into the tent.

The man with whom he had argued, crossed to the plane, now evidently fueled, helped shove it into the water and climbed in, shouting something to his helper, who went back up the bank in a hurry and into another of the tents. In a couple of minutes, a fourth figure, carrying a rifle, came hurrying out to join the pilot in the plane. He appeared to be a client, from their attitude of deference and congeniality, and the look of him—expensive clothes and firearm. While Chelle and the troopers watched, the Cessna taxied and took off, disappearing to the east almost as soon as it was airborne.

"Come on," Jensen directed, lowering the binoculars and turning to head around the end of the lake. "Let's get up on that ridge behind the camp. I want to see what's going on. They're after something."

Hustling to keep up with his long strides, Chelle and Caswell followed, taking less care to look for cover now that the plane had vanished and they couldn't be seen from the lower level of the lake. It seemed to take a long time to gain the ridge above the camp, but, as they headed away from the lake, the vegetation thinned until they left behind the tangle of willow and alder that impeded progress. Once they reached the first ridge, the terrain on the other side swept eastward in a smoother, flatter slope, interrupted only by low rolling rises and scattered patches of scanty brush and bare rock—easier hiking, but almost none of it provided cover.

Fifteen minutes later, moving quickly and carefully, they found limited shelter behind one such patch and saw the Cessna lifting off another small lake perhaps a mile away, where the hunter waved from the ground as it circled, gaining altitude.

"What the hell are they doing?" Cas wondered aloud. "Why take that guy out there and dump him off?"

"Wait," said Rochelle. "Let me take a look."

He handed her the binoculars, but the plane, flying very low, had disappeared once more, beyond another low ridge.

Waiting for it to reappear, none of them was prepared when, without warning, it suddenly rose up very close to them on the left, banked steeply back toward the hunter, and passed almost directly over them.

"Get down," Jensen barked. "Cover your faces and don't move."

All three immediately threw themselves to the ground, all wishing they could dig a hole to crawl into. Caswell's tan jacket blended well with the colors of the earth and Jensen's dark green was fairly good camouflage, but the forgotten red bandanna around Chelle's neck was an unmistakable contrast against the natural colors surrounding her.

In less than a minute the plane swung back, completing a circle in the sky that brought it around in an angle that allowed the pilot to look directly down on the three still figures lying with their faces in the dirt.

"Damn it," Chelle heard Jensen mutter. "So much for them not knowing where or how many we are."

But, as she raised her head, the pilot straightened his path and once again headed east till the Cessna dropped behind a ridge.

"He spotted us, didn't he?" she said. "There's not enough brush to hide in if we'd tried. Why did he leave?"

"Don't know, but he's gone for now. Let's get away from here and back over that hill. We can't risk getting caught now and there's two or three miles between us and the Maule. I don't want any running gun battles."

Almost at a run, they started back the way they had come, covering ground quickly. When they had hiked three or four hundred yards and were nearing the crest of a small rise, they once again heard the sound of the plane and gained a small amount of cover in some brush before they looked back. It came into sight, but not flying a straight line. With dips and circles it seemed to be playing some kind of game in the air, swooping low over the ground, then rising to turn and swoop again.

"What the hell are they doing?" Caswell asked.

Quickly, Rochelle again retrieved her binoculars from the day-pack and planted her feet solidly to look back toward the ground below the plane. Eyes wide with concern, she handed the pair to Caswell.

"I've seen that maneuver before. Watch the brush

where the plane comes closest to the ground.''

"Da-amn. Take a look." He handed the binoculars on to Jensen, who took his turn.

For a few seconds Alex saw nothing, then a large, brown, furry animal, moving swiftly in a powerful, rolling gait, came into sight, headed fast in their direction.

"God, a grizzly, and a big one."

Chelle nodded. "Yes, and by now it's plenty mad. I've seen them stand up and reach, trying to snatch at a plane that's harassing them. What he's doing with those dips is drive it right to us, assuming we'll be forced to move . . . try to get out of the way, or in position to fire at it. What the bear doesn't get, he wants to be able to shoot. He saw us when he flew over, all right, and knows we're here, between the bear and the lake.

"It's called hazing, a technique they use to make sure hunters get their trophies. Find a bear with the plane and herd it into range. If the hunter can't kill it himself, one of them will even do *that* for him. These hunters *get* what they pay for, one way or another, and *another* is usually faster and easier."

"We'd better pick our spot." Jensen decided grimly. "We can't possibly make it to the lake in time. That thing's coming too fast."

Without a word, they turned and increased their pace toward the lake, looking for any place they could defend. Trees within reach were too small to climb, there only were rocky outcroppings and a few insufficient scattered shrubs. Picking the best of what little was available, they selected a depression surrounded by a pile of rocks and settled in as best they could, facing what they knew was coming that they could not escape.

Very few minutes later, the bear that could outrun a horse in rough terrain and cover fifty feet a second in a charge, burst through the low scrub brush and over the top of the closest ridge, coming at them like a freight train. This one was huge, a mature animal, running full out, intent on escaping its airborne affliction.

Though Rochelle and the two troopers lay perfectly still in their hollow behind the rocks, they had no real choice in position and the breeze blowing from behind them carried their human smell and anxiety straight to the bear. As it topped the ridge and caught the scent, it came to an almost sliding, complete halt and paused, its head weaving back and forth as it attempted to determine the location of this new threat, the distinctive hump of muscle over its shoulders clearly visible. From forty yards away, they could distinctly hear the rumbling growl reverberate in its throat and massive chest.

Without further hesitation, it rose on its hind legs for a better view and stood, close to seven feet tall and just over a thousand pounds of awesome, angry Ursus arctos horribilis, Alaskan grizzly. It was golden brown in color with darker brown fur on the feet, legs, and exposed underparts. The swaying head was lighter brown and well over a foot across, so broad its eyes appeared small and piggish in relation to the rest of the slightly dished face. Six- or seven-inch-long, curved claws on the forefeet hung, wickedly sharp and yellowed, before its gigantic body, ready for instant, tearing action. Opening its jaws, it exhibited a mouth full of teeth capable of crushing rifle barrels. Then it roared, a sound that was a tactile sensation, so loud it almost drowned out the sound of the plane passing overhead and Jensen thought he could feel it in the rock he lay against to aim his .45.

Gradually, the bear seemed to settle on their position, possibly, though its eyesight was only average, catching a gleam from one of their guns, for the swaying motion of its head stopped, though it still rocked slightly from side to side. It roared again, sending chills through Rochelle, who held tight and sighted carefully with the .375 Weatherby Magnum, waiting.

Maybe it would avoid them, go away, just go away. Probably not. This kind of bear, already angry, would welcome something against which to vent its wrath. It could tear a man apart, puncturing lungs and breaking ribs with its claws, ripping body flesh with its teeth, tearing at scalp and skull in its jaws, dragging a body off to bury in a pile of dirt, leaves, and brush. She could be its next victim, as could Jensen and Caswell. The idea brought shudders and shaking hands, sweaty palms.

She wished Jensen had a rifle, and Caswell was, admittedly, no hunter. How good a shot was he? She knew that, without a doubt, her Weatherby was their best hope.

Swallowing hard, she forced the terrifying images from her mind, wiped her hands, one at a time on the shoulders of her jacket, and concentrated on what Norm had taught her. Relaxing her grip on the rifle slightly, she drew a deep breath and focused on the job at hand, banishing fear with facts. Take the head shot. Only hunters out for trophies should shoot for the heart, to avoid crushing and spoiling the skull for the taxidermist. Also, grizzlies, even with bodies full of bullets and hearts blown apart by exploding slugs, had been known to complete their charge and savage the shooter. In this situation, she aimed directly at the face, where she knew a hit in the eye, nose or forehead could stop the bear instantly.

Then there was no time for further thought. Dropping to all fours, the monster charged straight at them, so fast they could hardly react, and the incredible sound it made seemed to fill the world and shake them in it.

As the snow receded, the abundance of green edible plants increased along with the daylight hours as each day crept closer to the summer solstice. Aklak soon found it unnecessary to be so far-ranging in search of food, though he still often covered more than a dozen miles between sunrise and the time it set, late in the purple haze of evening.

Years of feeding had taught the great bear exactly where to find the most prolific sources of tender young shoots and bulbs. Like all bears, he was a creature of habit, returning again, year after year, to locations most likely to provide the best food. Though he did not recall it, he had first grazed in some of these places as a cub, but it was second nature that drew him back, not memory. He did not even remember that he once had a mother to watch and from whom to learn. It was simply repetition and results that made him respond to what accorded the most gain for the least effort.

It was repetition and the instinctive promise of reward that drew him down among the small lakes of the plateau beyond Mount Susitna, to the rich sedges that grew thick in the swampy spaces between rocky ridges and lakes of varying sizes. There, he was content to stay for days, regularly filling his belly and napping when he was full, only to wake and feed again.

But this year there was something else that drifted ever so lightly through his mind: not a memory, more of an expectation of something he would soon find that was good to eat—not plant but animal— something for which he had intended to return. Something buried? If only he knew what—and where. So, slowly, as he consumed huge amounts of the satisfying, nutritious sedges, he gradually, unconsciously moved west, toward a larger lake, without planning, decision, or awareness.

Habit must offer security to brown bears, for they repeat actions not only independently, but as a species. Grizzlies are influenced enough by their customary inclination to make trails in certain locations that are used over and over for decades, perhaps longer, by large numbers of bears. Each walking precisely in the paw prints of the others, stepping exactly in the same spot, always with the same foot, they create depressions in the ground in a regular rhythmic pattern along a track. There is no mistaking it for anything else. Only the consistency of browns, one after the other, can create and maintain this particular mark on the earth, and it speaks better than words the significance of their habitual presence.

Aklak became conscious of the sound of the flying thing when it was very faint and far off, but when it grew louder, he growled deeply and unhappily in his throat. It was almost familiar—and not a thing he anticipated with pleasure. It was bad, unpleasant, threatening even. As it came closer and he could finally see it moving in the sky, he stopped eating and focused his attention, waiting to see what it would do.

It drew an arch and dived toward the ground, directly toward him. He ran, feeling that if he did not it would hurt him. He slowed when it retreated as it circled, then came at him again, roaring a challenge. He roared back, stopped, and raised himself to a standing position, reaching skyward, trying to drag it from the air, and failing.

Dropping back to all fours, he ran again, on and on, angry, uncharacteristically afraid, and frustrated, needing something on which to vent his fury, to reestablish his superiority, to inflict punishment. The flying thing followed, falling at him out of the air whenever he slowed, coming ever closer, but never, never within reach.

For several miles it chased him steadily over the plateau, until at last he crested a low ridge and suddenly became aware of something else—a smell. It was the smell of the animal he had subconsciously expected to find. Aklak stopped and searched with his eyes, but his nose and incredible sense of smell told him what he needed to know, that it was somewhere very close. Rising again to stand on his hind legs, he waited, watching and—there, to the left— saw the flash of something that moved.

He roared a challenge, but it did not rise to meet him. Though he waited, no stick spit fire in his direction. The flying thing in the air was not nearby, its sound only a whine in the distance, growing slowly louder. He ignored the increasing sound. Once again it had directed him to an animal that would be an easy kill, one he could drag away and bury. He sniffed the air and realized that it was not

*just one animal. There was more than one, all pow-
erless and for him.*

*He was still furious and hostile, ready to rend, to
tear. Dropping down, he waited no longer. Roaring
his anger, he charged straight at the prey in the
rocks.*

*Then the sticks he had not been able to see, had
not thought dangerous, barked at him and fire filled
his consciousness—fire and an agony of confusion.*

*He could not see. For what seemed like a very
long time, he fell as his forelegs and paws crumpled
under his weight and would not move. Searing pain
filled his huge head, but his body, flat against the
ground he could not feel, was numb. He tried to
growl, but only a gurgling sigh escaped his ruined
throat. It seemed darker, and suddenly, cold, and the
only thing he could smell was his own blood.*

*Then, slowly, there was nothing, and Aklak, the
great brown bear—fine young chief, elder brother,
lord of the woods, the unmentionable one, real
bear—as unconscious of dying as he had been of
being, was no more.*

22

ROCHELLE, WEATHERBY STILL CAUTIOUSLY AT THE ready, stood looking down at the huge, shaggy carcass of the bear on the ground where its charge had ended, conscious of fear gradually ebbing in her system. The hair on her arms still stood up and her skin felt icy, as if adrenaline had heated the blood that ran through her veins, forcing terror instead of sweat to rise and chill as it evaporated. No wonder they refer to fear as cold, she thought, shivering as she relaxed. Sure that the bear was dead, she sighed in relief and lowered the rifle. Somewhere, nearby, a bird called, and the sun seemed exceptionally bright, making her eyes water.

Jensen stepped up to lay a hand, wordlessly, on her shoulder.

Two bullets from the Weatherby had struck the animal, one full in the mouth, wide open in the roar of its charge, one splitting the skull just above the left eye. Destroying the huge throat, the first had passed on into the neck, cutting the spinal cord, paralyzing the enormous brown as if it were a marionette with suddenly severed strings.

Caswell's shot had taken out the other eye, passed through the brain, and out the back of the skull. As they stood over the carcass of the incredible animal, his hands still shook as they clutched the Springfield. Chelle's were steady, but her white knuckles matched her pale face. They couldn't tell what Jensen's shot had done, because the monster bear rested belly down, covering the chest at which he had aimed. Later they would know that he had missed the heart by less than a finger's width.

"I've never seen one so huge," Cas said, taking a deep breath, "though it looks smaller now than it did standing up, coming at us. Thought we'd never be able to stop it. A few more feet and I'd be wishing for clean underwear."

"A few more feet and you wouldn't have to worry about clean underwear," Jensen said, calculating the distance between the dead brown and the rocks from which they had fired. "Couldn't be more than a dozen feet."

"Have you ever seen one this close?" Chelle asked him.

"No, and I don't intend to ever again, if I have any choice in the matter. You're one hell of a shot with that Weatherby, Chelle. Don't let anyone ever tell you it's too big."

She smiled, shakily. "Thanks. It's a good gun, but there really wasn't a lot of choice, was there?"

Once more she looked at the bear and acknowledged that part of what she was feeling was sorry. Blood-soaked and lacking dignity in the position of its sprawling body, still, even in dying, it was beautiful, awesome. She knew and understood something of why Norm had so loved the great brutes, with their rich, colorful pelts and savage strength. This death, however, was an unnecessary waste. She felt herself growing angry at its cause and, somehow, again, with Norm, for inspiring these feelings—and everything else.

"Where's that plane gone?" Jensen asked, suddenly, beginning to think about something besides the bear they had just killed. "We've just been damn lucky. But, whoever these guys are, they're serious. Someone from that camp will be heading this way shortly. We'd better get ourselves away from here."

"You're right," Cas agreed. "But what about the bear?"

"Well, you can stay and skin it, if you like." Alex grinned. "Me. I'm making tracks."

"No way. I'm with you. I meant we'll have to report it."

"We'll report all of this, so let's make sure we get the opportunity. I'd like to know what happened to Tobias. He's the only one we haven't seen, and I expected him to show up in their camp, didn't you?"

"Yeah, I did. That's another thing we've got to watch out for."

"What are we going to do about Ed and my plane?" Chelle asked, when they were well on their way, cutting east around the end of the lake, the way they had come. "I want my plane back. Whoever that guy is, he hazed that bear with *my plane*. That really ticks me off."

"We'll get it for you, Chelle," Jensen promised, as they reached the top of the ridge above the crooked lake and skirted a thick stand of spruce and willow. "Just not right now. But, if I knew where that guy in the plane has gone, and that he wouldn't be back for long enough, I'd be tempted to try a hostile takeover of their camp. There's only two of them left, and one of those is Landreth."

"You know, that's not a bad idea." Cas stopped

to comment. "Let's take a look over the ridge and see if they've brought the Cessna back yet. It can't hurt to look."

When they reached a space to peer between the brush, the bank of the lake held only the poacher's plane, no sign of Chelle's 206.

"Well? What do you think?" Cas questioned.

In only a second Jensen's frown of concentration vanished as he glanced at his watch, his decision made. "I'm going down there. It's time for some answers and I want them now. This may be the best and only opportunity we get, and anything could happen in the couple of hours before your repair crew arrives. We've got the element of surprise and there's two of us to two of them."

"Three," Chelle reminded him, reloading the Weatherby.

This time, however, things were not so easy or so smooth.

They crept in quietly through the brush until they were directly behind the camp on the low shelf that separated the plateau from the lakeshore. There, they split up, Chelle flattening herself on the ground between two rocks to cover the other two, aiming her rifle down into the camp. Jensen slipped away to the left, Caswell to the right, where the slope was somewhat steeper, in an attempt to climb down and reach the rear of the tents without being seen.

They were almost halfway, moving with great care, when a rock shifted and the ground avalanched from under Caswell's feet. Flailing the air with both arms, one hindered by the Springfield, he attempted to retain an upright position, lost it, sat down hard and slid to the foot of the incline, rocks bouncing noisily around him. As he scrambled for cover behind a boulder of barely adequate size, the man Chelle had pepper-sprayed bolted from the nearest tent, rifle in hand. Close behind him, Landreth followed, his hands empty of anything but a cigarette. Without hesitation, the man with the gun swung it to his shoulder and fired a shot at Cas, which hit the rock just as he disappeared behind it, missing him by inches.

Alex had ducked behind the only trees of any size, two narrow pipe-cleaner spruce, minimal cover, which forced him to stand very straight in order to avoid revealing large portions of himself. He had, however, a limited view of the camp between the trunks that formed what amounted to a loophole through which to fire his .45.

"Throw it down," he directed from this vantage point. "We've got you covered. Don't fight it or you'll get hurt."

The rifle in the camp below was swiftly turned in his direction and a second bullet whanged into the earth of the hillside.

"Give it up. You must know there are three of us, all armed."

"Yeah," a snarl of a voice returned. "You've got the Lewis woman, right? Big deal."

"No-o," Alex heard Chelle shrill, as he shifted to get a look at the shooter. The man, he saw, had stepped back, grabbed Landreth around the neck from behind, and was using him as a shield. Ed struggled for a moment, but became more cooperative as the chokehold tightened.

With a crack, Chelle put a shot just to the right of the gunman.

"Let him go, you bastard. I'm very good with this

thing. The next one goes into whatever part of you I can see, and there's more of you than there is of him. Stand still, Ed.''

"Shoot me, you get him," the shooter yelled back, beginning to move slowly, cautiously toward the water, dragging Landreth with him.

The roar of Chelle's Cessna coming in for a fast landing drowned out whatever else he said, but did not halt his determined, step-by-step retreat. As the plane taxied swiftly toward the camp, Jensen could see that the pilot was alone and wondered, fleetingly, if the client hunter had been left to claim and skin out their bear. The unspoken question floated quickly out of his mind as his attention was caught by the floats of the Cessna coming to rest against the bank of the lake.

"What the hell is going on, Pete?" the pilot yelled, getting out to stand on one and starting forward to jump off.

The other waved his rifle in a warning gesture. "Stay back. They're up behind the tents with guns— the Lewis woman and those two troopers that shot Gene.''

So, Jensen thought, they know we're troopers, and they've been back to the other lake, where we got the one who tried to shoot Chelle in the swamp. Wonder if they pulled him down out of that tree.

"Shit. How'd they get by Darryl? Where is he?"

"Don't know. Haven't seen him. Stay out of range and turn that thing around so I can get to it and we can get out of here, damn you.''

"You think I'm leaving now, you're crazier than I thought. Mortinson's still up on the flat, waiting for me to come with another skinning knife.''

"Look. I don't give a damn about your fuckin'

bear, Tom.'' He stopped moving backward and glanced back to see what the pilot was doing behind him. ''I'm not interested in getting blown away here.''

Tom. This had to be Stoffel's cousin, Alex realized. The pieces were beginning to come together. Greeson was, as the Fish and Wildlife agent had suspected, running what he could of the illegal business as a big-game guide. They had accidentally stumbled—thanks to Rochelle's determination to solve the question of her husband's disappearance—onto what could have taken months, if ever, to investigate and find. The guy was doing the best he could to play it safe by using a plane he considered a throwaway if he were caught in the act of illegally hazing game. And he might very well have got away with it if they hadn't shown up to complicate what he must have thought easy money with this standoff.

However Ed Landreth had become involved with this bunch, it was clear that they considered him expendable. What could be done now to gain the upper hand without further endangering Chelle's brother? Perhaps some negotiations were possible. They had to assume that Greeson's main objective would be to eliminate as many of them as possible. They were witnesses that could tumble his whole operation. He needed to establish control of the situation and it wouldn't be long until he thought of using Landreth as a hostage, knowing his sister was part of the opposition. How could they act quickly to prevent that?

Jensen could see that Caswell, with very little maneuvering space in the shelter of his boulder, had somehow rearranged himself to be able to rise up and shoot quickly if required. A glance upward told him Chelle was also primed for action, but before he could decide exactly what to do, she suddenly stood up out of her protected position.

Pete immediately swung the rifle in her direction, but before he could fire, she was once more out of sight.

"Put it down and I'll come out."

He lowered it.

"Chelle," Jensen called. "Don't. It won't work."

"I said put it down," she said, ignoring his warning.

"Do it, Pete," Greeson said from behind him.

He did, to one side and within reach, managing to remain behind Landreth.

"Now," she called, once more in view. "A deal? You let him go, and I come down there. I'm the one you want anyway. Right?"

The pilot had stepped up behind Pete and, from where Jensen was located, he could just see him pull a pistol from under his jacket.

"Chelle, get down," he shouted. "The pilot's got a gun you can't see."

She was invisible in an instant, but not before a shot was fired in her direction from around Pete and Landreth. Shoving the other two back up the bank in the direction Chelie had appeared, Tom, the pilot, called out. "Okay. Deal. But *my* deal. You come down. Right now. Before I start with your idiot brother's right kneecap. Hey, Ernie. Get out here, take this rifle, and hike your butt up behind her on that ridge to keep those two cops in line. Ernie. Goddammit."

With a sense of increasing disaster, Jensen saw the flaps of another tent move, and Ernie Tobias stepped out and grinned, stretching as if he had merely been napping, despite all the noise of gunfire

and shouting. Damn it. Damn it. So he *was* part of
their illegal poaching party.

"Hey, Tom. Keep the noise down, huh? I'm trying to catch up on the shut-eye I missed last night
getting over here in the dark. What's the problem?
Can't take care of a couple of troopers and a female
by yourself? You never had trouble with women before."

"What the hell are you talking about? Get up that
hill and let's get this over with. You know the
score."

"Oh, I don't know," the big agent answered
thoughtfully, and Jensen began to glimpse a thread
of cross-purpose in his slow-moving, relaxed attitude. There was a subtle tension and watchfulness
under his seemingly easygoing exterior. He yawned,
and ambled toward the pilot, tucking his thumbs in
his hip pockets, but, as he turned his back to the
hillside, he wiggled the exposed digits of one hand
in Alex's direction, then held out one singular index
finger. Wait.

Walking up to the two taking shelter behind Landreth, he dropped to sit on his heels and pick up the
rifle Pete had laid down. Then, with a motion so
casually smooth that it was graceful in its simplicity,
he stood up and jammed the barrel into the soft flesh
under the pilot's chin.

"Drop that thing," he told him in a sharp, commanding voice. "Don't even twitch. Just open your
hand and toss it out in front of Pete and old Ed
here."

"Hey. What the hell're you doing?" Tom asked
him, annoyed and confused. "We've got an agreement."

"Wrong. You *thought* we had a deal. Don't assume I'm a fool, Tom. Drop it, or I drop you. Believe me when I say there's absolutely nobody in the whole goddamn world that would rather see you dead—would actually *enjoy* killing you—more than me.''

The gun dropped.

''Now, Pete, turn Landreth loose. Then you and Tom step back, slowly, about five feet.''

''Do what he says, Pete,'' Greeson said in a strangled sound, the gun barrel jammed hard against his throat.

Landreth staggered forward as the chocking pressure was removed, tripped, and fell to his hands and knees, gagging.

''Come on down here Jensen—Caswell. You too, Chelle. It's okay.''

They did and as soon as Cas located another roll of Alaska's omnipresent duct tape—good for solutions to almost every need or problem—secured the two remaining poachers in neat silver packages.

By that time Landreth had recovered enough to talk.

''Thanks,'' he said eagerly, holding a hand out to Cas, who simply stared at him without responding. Taken slightly aback, he turned to Jensen. ''Sure glad you guys showed up. I don't know what they would have done to me if you hadn't rescued me in time. They kidnapped me and forced me to come out here. Bunch of bastards. I had nothing to do with this. Nothing . . .''

''How'd my plane get here, Ed?'' Chelle asked in a low angry voice. ''Tell me that, will you? How'd they get my plane and what'd you have to do with it?''

''Hey, Chelle. Don't sound like that. It wasn't my

fault. They made me fly it from the other lake. Honest. I didn't want to. They forced me. Threatened to kill me.''

Greeson, immobilized and sitting on the ground, made a disgusted sound in his throat. ''Don't you forget what I told you, Landreth,'' he growled. ''This changes nothing.''

Ed cast a nervous glance in his direction and shut up.

''What do we do with this one,'' Caswell asked Jensen, nodding in Landreth's direction. ''Take him in with the others, or not?''

Landreth lost it.

''No. They made me . . . Tell him, Chelly, please. I didn't really have any part in this. They forced me . . . It wasn't my fault . . .''

She stood very silent, watching him panic, until he ran out of words and merely begged her with his eyes. Then she turned to the troopers with an unspoken question and a shrug of the shoulders.

''Oh hell,'' Alex said, shaking his head. ''Take him back with you. We'll pick him up later when we need him. Maybe you can get something worthwhile out of him.''

''Thanks,'' she said. ''We can discuss it back in town.''

''Chelly . . .'' Landreth started.

''Just shut up, Ed. There're a lot of things I want to know, but not now. I'm tired of bailing you out.''

Sniveling and whimpering, he gave up.

One more exchange was particularly significant concerning Jensen's questions about Ernie Tobias. The agent volunteered to go with Chelle, in her plane, to pick up Darryl, taped and waiting, and transfer him back to the poacher's camp. He chuckled when they described where and how he would find the last poacher. While airborne, Chelle would call the Anchorage office for assistance from Fish and Wildlife and the troopers in investigating Greeson's camp and illegal operation.

As he started for the plane, Tom had a parting shot in his direction. "I'm gonna get you, Ernie, you fuckin' shit. I wanna tell you that you better not turn your back on anything. Ever. I'm gonna get you. And if I can't, I'll make sure somebody does. I wanna tell you, you son of a bitch—"

"So. Write me a letter," Tobias told him, turning to pick him up by the shirt front and shake his dark glasses from his face. "I'll be retired back in Madison long before you even think about getting out of jail. You'll be an old—very old—man. So will I, but, if you *ever* come looking for me, I won't hesitate to dead-cold kill you.

"You bragged to me how you beat Karen bad enough to murder her when you found out she was a federal agent, then watched the plane she was in go down, and checked to make sure she was dead before you walked away. I'll make sure you pay for that. Karen was a partner of mine and a very good friend. You didn't know that, did you, Tom, old buddy. Never put two and two together. Gene might have recognized me and told you, but he tried to off someone else and gave me—not an excuse—a reason, but I might have killed him anyway.

"So—for Karen—please, Tom. I ask you. Do something stupid and give me the chance. Just for Karen, you filthy bastard."

Chelle stared at him, mouth open, eyes wide, face pale, but Jensen kept his astonishment to himself. The intensity of Ernie's anger was an awesome contrast to his usual soft-spoken polite manner. Wouldn't want to be on the receiving end of it, he thought.

There was a pause, then Cas spoke up in his usual practical way.

"When you get back with Darryl, we better go tell the Texan just who that bear really belongs to."

"Naw," Jensen suggested. "Let's wait till he gets it skinned out."

23

"WHERE *DID* YOU DISAPPEAR TO, ERNIE?" JENSEN
blinked in confusion below a frown that brought his
eyebrows together close enough to almost match his
full handlebar mustache. "We couldn't figure out
where you'd gone. Had to assume you were involved
with the poachers, when you didn't come back."

They sat on a log near the fire, waiting for assistance from Anchorage to show up to gather evidence
from the poacher's camp. On the way to the other
lake, Chelle had relayed Jensen's message. She returned to report their estimated arrival time and that
the repair crew for Caswell's plane had arrived at
the other lake and was in the process of fixing the
float. Cas had hurriedly gone off on foot to meet
them, refusing an airlift in favor of some peace and
quiet, and a last chance to enjoy a hike. They had
all, however, appreciated a huge second breakfast
from the camp's supplies. Ernie commented that it
was the first time he had eaten fried *poached* eggs.

When they were satisfied, and Cas had headed
west, Jensen filled his pipe, made himself comfortable, and asked questions, filling informational gaps
with Ernie.

"I started out to see if I couldn't find out something about who these guys were and what we were up against,'' Tobias told him. "Just got thinking about it and couldn't sleep. Thought I'd come over and find a place to watch them for a while. One person would make less noise.

"Then, I recognized Tom—he *is* Stoffel's cousin—and figured, since I had already set myself up undercover in the Brooks Range as a dirty agent to them, that I'd go on in, play it up and see what I could find out about Karen. It worked.'' He paused, and took a deep breath. "I didn't like what I found out, even if I'd suspected it, but at least now I know what happened . . . who was responsible. By the time you guys showed up, I was almost ready to make a move anyway—just collecting facts—waiting for them to bring that bear back into camp—hoping they'd give me some idea what happened to Karen's notes.''

"Did they?''

"Nope. Only that they don't have them and were looking. You were right about the break-in at the Lewis place. It was Tom. I watched her house all night that next night, thinking he might come back to finish the job, but he didn't show. Should have told you, I guess, but it didn't seem necessary. I'm too used to working on a 'need-to-know' basis. Sorry.''

"Same thing happen last night? You could have said something before you took off, you know.''

"Yeah . . . well. Started to. But, you looked so comfortably asleep under those trees, I decided not to wake you up. Thought I'd be back before too long. Changed my mind. You got my apology, okay?''

Alex nodded.

"So—he admitted beating Karen Randolph?"

All humor left the large agent's face as he answered.

"Yeah. Swears he had nothing to do with shooting down the Lewis plane, though. We'll get it out of him eventually. But, if not, I don't think it makes much difference. Your forensics man said the beating was the cause of death. Right?"

"Right. They say anything about Lewis?"

"No. Just that a pilot showed up to pick up Karen and managed to get airborne with her before they could stop him. They were about to go after them in another plane, but saw them go down and assumed they were safely dead."

A fragment of a question skipped through Jensen's mind and was gone. But Ernie *was* right. They had a tight enough case to convict the guilty and would probably never find where Norm Lewis had crawled off to die in this rough country. Still, he'd like to have tied up that particular loose end. Would have made it easier on Chelle, emotionally and with the insurance. It was clear, though, that she was—would be—all right.

Suddenly, he had a great desire to get back to town and home to Jessie—wanted to talk it all out with her till it fit and the lid could be closed.

As he climbed steadily up the slope of the hill where he had collected trash, including Norm Lewis's ace of spades, Caswell slung the Remington diagonally across his back, to have both hands free. At the top, where he had stood the day before, near the fire-blackened rocks, he paused and assessed the landscape in front of him. The marshy area, full of hummocks, mud, and standing water, and the now

familiar rough hills, covered with bare rock and
sparse trees, spread out in front of him again. Turning slowly, he reviewed the lake he had just left,
shaped like a crooked, flattened letter W, and the
rocky summit of the first hill he had climbed, headed
the other direction.

It was now near noon, and as Cas went quickly
down through the trees and onto the flat space between the hills, hiking mostly in sunshine, he moved
a little farther south than his original route. Almost
across, he noticed a ravine that cut away to his left.
Probably the start of Olson Creek, he thought, pic-
turing the map in his mind. If he went down it a few
hundred feet, he thought he could walk around the
base of the hill and come out on the ridge above the
lake, reducing the amount of climbing he would
have to do and saving time.

He altered his direction accordingly, and soon
found himself on an uneven sort of trail, full of
lumps and depressions. A minute or so later, he
frowned, hesitated, and scrutinized it more carefully,
as an uneasy realization set in. He was walking on
a grizzly trail.

He remembered reading that, singular and unso-
ciable, roaming where they pleased, over decades, in
a few particular places, enough bears travel the same
route often enough to create specific depressions in
the ground. Stepping in each other's footprints, they
wear out cup-shaped depressions in regular, alter-
nating patterns: right forepaw, left hind paw, left
forepaw, right hind paw.

Though he had heard of such bear trails, Caswell
had never seen one. As he moved a few steps along
it, he thought of the enormous vitality of the bear
they had been forced to shoot earlier in the day and

wondered if it might have used this track. He recalled that no one knows why bears do this. They have their own hidden reasons, and do for themselves alone what has meaning only to them. But, inspired by the depth of the depressions, he decided that they could not leave a more unmistakable sign of their passing, or a greater impression on any witness to the mute record of their sheer numbers and perseverance. It was almost more awe-inspiring to stand in the path of generation upon generation of this species than it had been to meet the great bear himself.

The grizzly trail made walking difficult, for the depressions were awkwardly spaced for the length of a man's stride. Cas stopped a moment to look more closely at them and felt the hair rise on the back of his neck. A grizzly had passed here recently, for no rain had blurred the huge prints of his feet, larger than dinner plates. The forepaws were easily recognizable, for an inch and a half in front of the toe prints were the sharp marks of each individual claw.

Squatting beside one print, Caswell examined it in detail and noticed that, in the damp dust of the track, the print looked very clean. He could see whorls and ridges that he knew were as unique to the bear as fingerprints were to every human. He shivered. This bear had to be fresh out of hibernation and hungry. Not pleasant to meet this time of year and he had already had one encounter on this day. Standing up, he took the Remington from his back, ducking under its sling, determined to carry it at the ready for the moment.

Since the trail curved along the hillside in the direction he wanted to go, he trotted along it a little farther, till it turned down the ravine and he continued on along the slope toward the lake, keeping careful watch and speaking to himself to make enough sound for any bear in the area to hear him. When he ran out of nonsense to say, he began to recite poetry.

"Oh, I am a cook and a captain bold and the mate of the *Nancy* brig . . ." he had started, when he saw something blue and covered with dirt next to a tree ahead of him. Reaching down, he lifted it, and found he was holding a torn piece of a plaid cotton shirt, with a ripped sleeve and pocket attached, covered with dark brownish stains.

"Oh God," he breathed, wanting to drop and forget it, knowing he could not.

Instead, still holding it, perhaps twenty feet farther, he found another piece, along with the similarly stained and ragged waistband of a pair of denim pants. Around a curve, he was suddenly standing in an almost circular clearing, where every bush and small tree, every bit of vegetation, dirt, the roots of trees, and old dead leaves had been raked from the ground and was scattered around a ragged pile in the middle.

Adrenaline pumped into Caswell's body along with fear that straightened his spine and brought him to an abrupt halt, for he knew he had stumbled onto a cache created by one of the grizzlies that used the trail he had just left. As he looked, however, it became evident that the cache was an old one, long abandoned from the look of it. Snow had flattened and washed the clutter.

Slowly, he stepped forward and, among the brush and dirt, several white bones came into view. Scattered in disorder over a wide area was what the bear had dismembered—ribs, vertebrae, pelvis, broken long bones of the arms and legs, and the fragmented pieces of a human skull. A few red hairs, probably from the tail of a fox clung to the bark of a stick on the ground.

There was no doubt in Caswell's mind that he had found Norman Lewis. He could not prove it, or identify the man with anything he now held or saw, but he knew it as surely as he knew that the bear had not been solely responsible for the man's death.

Walking forward a few feet, he picked up part of one of the long thigh bones he knew had separated the knees of this man from his hips. It was broken, as was another like it that he could see not far away. And within the break was the unmistakable mark a bullet makes when it hits living bone, and still imbedded in that broken bone was a slug that could have come from one of the casings he had searched for on the hill by the fire-blackened rocks.

Someone had shot Lewis before the bear found him. Shot and made it impossible for him to escape his four-legged attacker. It didn't take much to figure out who, he thought.

Cas moved nothing else, but took the scraps of clothing he had found and the incriminating piece of bone he still held, and headed for the lake with long strides, forgoing his poetry recitation, oblivious to the possible presence of bears. Concentrating on what he had learned, he simply forgot to be afraid or watchful, wanting only to be able to put the grief he carried away somewhere before he rejoined Jensen, Tobias, and Rochelle—before she could see what he had found and carried back.

24

CHELLE TAXIED HER CESSNA INTO ITS SPACE ON
Lake Hood and got out, ignoring her brother, Ed,
who had flown back in the passenger seat, saying
nothing. When he was also out on the bank, she tied
the plane down and began to move the camping
equipment from the back of it to her Subaru station
wagon, still waiting where she had parked it the day
before.

Just a day? she thought. It seemed she had been
gone a week, a month, as if everything should be
different; as if she stopped at the grocery store, there
would be new magazines on the rack that she hadn't
read yet, or maybe the bills she thought she had just
paid were due again. It was a strange and unsettling
sensation.

"Chelly?" Ed said, as she closed up and locked
the plane. Picking up the few things she would leave
in the shed, she crossed to it and worked the combination on the lock, opened the door and deposited
them inside, along with the waders she took off and
replaced with her street shoes.

"Chelly?" he entreated, again.

She whirled to face him, anger distorting her face.
"Stop it, Ed. Don't whine. You're not a child, and

neither am I. It's time you stopped acting like one and grew up.''

"But, Chelle . . . hey. It *wasn't* my fault. I told you.''

"Whose fault was it then, Ed. I don't believe they just picked you and forced you out there. There's more to it than that. But you always blame someone else. You're never at fault and I'm sick of it. Take some responsibility for yourself, won't you?''

"But, I . . .''

"What did that Greeson mean when he said you should remember what he told you and that it didn't change anything that he was caught? I want to know. What did he mean?''

Ed looked down and kicked at a clump of grass, obviously trying to think of a fast answer that might satisfy.

"Don't bother making something up,'' she told him harshly. "Just tell the truth for once. What won't change? And why did you steal my plane?''

"Borrow, Chelle. I only borrowed it. Never stole it, not once.''

"Steal, Ed. The word is not *borrow*. It's *steal*. What do you mean *not once*? Oh''—her eyes widened as she realized—''this wasn't the first time, was it. You've taken it before. That's why I kept finding the radio turned to the wrong frequency. It was *you,* not me. Why? Spit it out. The truth, damn it.''

Surprisingly, he did.

"Tom helped me—loaned me money . . . a lot. I owe him. I'm sorry, Chelle. Really sorry. It'll never happen again, I promise. Honest.''

For a long moment she was absolutely still and silent with the shock of it, the total betrayal and lack of loyalty. When she finally spoke there was almost no expression to her voice. It was cold and distant, but there was no question that she meant every word she said.

"You're right. It won't. You could have lost my plane—my living—for me. Did you ever think of that? Ever care? All you cared about was your own problem."

"I brought it back. Nothing ever got hurt." Angrily he still tried to defend himself.

"But if it had, you would still have maintained that it wasn't your fault."

"Well . . . it really wasn't."

"Whose then?"

"Ah . . . if you'd ever let me fly it, I wouldn't have had to borrow it. Right?"

She stared at him, in wordless astonishment. Then, slowly, she began to laugh. There was little humor in the sound, but she laughed until she had to sit down on the step of the shed, and was suddenly silent.

"So," he asked, hopefully. "It's okay, then?"

For another long moment she looked up at him.

"No, little brother, it's not *okay*. But I'm through with talking about it. Here's how it's going to be, just so you're very clear and understand. From now on you take care of yourself. Don't come to me for money. There won't be any. Don't ask for favors. You've never earned them. You go your way and I go mine."

"But, Chelle. I promise . . ."

"Your promises mean nothing, Ed. I'm through with you getting everything your way. I think it's my turn for a change. This time I'm not bailing you out. Norm was right. I don't help you by making things okay."

"Norm was a . . ." He started to interrupt.

"No. Don't say it, not ever again. Just go. I won't listen to anything about Norm. You never even knew him. I'll let you know when and if I want to see you. Right now, just go away."

She sat and watched until he was out of sight, walking east down the road. Two blocks away was the Cockpit Lounge and she thought he would probably go there and con someone for a ride home, if he didn't spend the evening in a bottle.

She simply sat until he was gone and did not make the effort to start her car and drive home. There was something else she had to do.

When she was sure he wasn't coming back, she leaned forward and reached back under the edge of the shed, to the left of the door, where there was a narrow space, just large enough to admit her hand to the wrist.

Confidently, she took hold of a thin metal box, held by a magnet fastened beneath the shed floor, and pulled it loose. Lifting it out, she opened the lid and removed the envelope that she had known would be there waiting for her.

"*So,*" Ernie Tobias had said. "*Write me a letter.*"

And she had known.

As suddenly as she had realized what numbers would open the metal box she had found in Norm's closet, she had known the only place he would have left her a letter that no one else could find. It was where they had left notes for each other before they married, and after, when they were both flying charters and needed a way of communicating without going back to the house. Norm had thought of it and attached the box to the underside of her shed. They had checked it on a regular basis, but, after he disappeared, she had not looked once, knowing there would be—could be—nothing.

But there had been. The most important letter of all. Dumb, she thought. Dumb of her not to have remembered, figured it out.

She tore the envelope—a manila one like the other, the one he had given to Jeff—open and took out the contents. There *was* a letter. Unfolding it, she read the salutation: "Dear Chelly-love." It *was* for her. Thank God. And there were two small, rubber-banded notebooks: one plain, and one with the name Karen Randolph at the top. These, she ignored for the moment in favor of the pages he had written . . . for her:

Dear Chelly-love,

If you are reading this then you will have figured out and found where I am going to hide it. Sorry about not leaving directions, but I have to make sure that only you will be able to find it—and someone might come looking— so you can do what will need to be done with it and be safe. It is very important that this not be found by the wrong people.

Bunker will probably have already given you the money that was left after I took out the insurance policy you may also have found, I think, with the key in the box in my closet. He will have told you what I told him, and not coming back is what I regret most of all, but it is possible, considering that the things and peo-

ple I am about to tell you about are pretty unfriendly. I apologize for not telling you before,
but it isn't all mine to tell and up to now I have
promised silence. But the most important thing
to me is that, for now, you are safely without
knowledge and not involved. Now that you
have this, know that it is dangerous. Get these
notes to the right people as fast as possible,
now. Don't go looking for me or anything else.
Someone may be watching you and waiting to
see what you do, as I think they may have been
watching me.

It all started last spring, when I flew an early
tourist out for a couple of days of camping and
photography. Remember that time in May
when I got weathered in with Harry Ward at
Beluga Lake and we wound up spending two
days before I could get us back? It snowed,
sleeted, rained, and was generally too miserable to fly. Old Harry was a retired construction
sort in his late sixties, from Florida, who had
always wanted to come to Alaska, and did, and
got stuck with me in a very wet camp, with
little to see. I hacked out a decent space in one
of those infernal alder thickets, we put up his
tent, used the emergency stuff I carry in the
plane, and stayed as warm and dry as we could,
ate his steaks, my pork and beans, drank his
bourbon, and swapped lies.

I liked old Harry a lot, partly because he
didn't seem to really mind at all, never complained a bit. It was the wilderness experience
he wanted, whatever that turned out to be, so
we got along just fine. He had a wicked sense
of humor and a hundred good stories. I think

he sort of felt that getting stuck like that with me kind of took the tourist quality out of it.

The third morning, when it cleared up, he was like a little kid at the sight of all those impressive glaciers and mountains filling the whole western landscape. So I shooed him off down the lake a bit to get some of Capps and Triumvirate and the Alaska Range on film while I packed up our gear and loaded the bird. We had tied up and camped near that little stream next to the hook on the east bank— where you and I set down that afternoon over a year ago, remember? The lake was its usual muddy self, so I had been getting clean water from that creek to boil, and when I went for some to wash out a couple of frying pans, I found a red plastic jug that had floated down from somewhere upstream.

You know how I feel about people who leave their trash in that kind of place, so you can understand that at first I was pissed off. But it was kind of odd. The jug had just enough engine oil in the bottom so it seemed a funny thing for someone to throw out. I poked on upstream a bit and began to find other things: a plastic foam cooler cover broken into several pieces, pages from an account book of some kind, a water bottle—you know—small stuff that would float. Well, I wrestled my way up and came to a place where the spring thaw coming down that creek had washed out someone's cache.

I just stood there like a dummy for a minute because there was so much of it. Seemed like they had left just about a whole camp's worth of gear, airplane fuel, engine oil, tools, tents, sleeping bags, and some sealed dry supplies, like flour, beans, and rice. I was amazed the bears hadn't got at it, even sealed. Whoever left it had packed it all in camouflage tarps, stacked some of it under some brush, and tied the rest up as high as they could in a couple of the tallest trees, but the stream had changed course just enough to underwash one of them until it fell over from the weight of that stuff.

Well, my first thought was to be neighborly and clean up the area, salvage as much as I could for whoever would obviously be coming back for the gear sometime fairly soon now that warm weather was back. So I rescued the tarp that was still tied to the fallen tree and started filling it with everything I could find and pick up. Halfway through the job, I came across eight boxes of shells that would have fit my Remington 350, and figured it was a hunting stash. But, it seemed like a lot of heavy ammo, and after thinking about it a while, I got real curious. So I skinned up the other tree and cut loose that second sling of gear.

Besides more supplies, there were a couple of big hunting rifles in it, carefully greased and wrapped to survive the winter, and they weren't there for potting squirrels. But the thing that really caught my attention was a camouflage jacket that had been packed in with the rest. In one pocket was a note to somebody called Darryl, telling him to "hold off till Thursday and keep an eye on the sky," that there was "a fed nosing around" according to "our source." There wasn't a date and it was

signed with just the initial T. Whoever Darryl
is, he must have forgotten it was there when he
left the jacket.

After thinking a little, I put everything back
the best I could, wishing I hadn't hauled all the
stuff out of the creek and made it obvious
somebody had stumbled onto that cache. They
wouldn't know who, though, so I went back to
where Harry was whistling for me by then, and
we got out of there. I didn't tell him anything
about the stuff I'd found—but I took that note
from the jacket pocket with me.

For about two weeks I thought about it off
and on, and wondered if I should do something.
When I flew over, I kind of kept an eye on that
area.

Then one afternoon, on my way back from
a Lake Clark run, I was over that same bench
between Beluga and Mount Susitna when I
caught some peripheral motion below me and
looked down to see a plane doing some pretty
fancy loops and circles close to the ground. I
went around once to see, but it was pretty clear
what was going on—the pilot was hazing a
bear—or maybe a moose. I was too high to see
the animal, but there's no other activity I know
that makes a pilot fly that way. It made me
furious, but there wasn't a thing I could do
about it from there. It was a Cessna, like ours,
but I was too high to get an identification number off it.

The next day I went to Fish and Wildlife,
gave them the note and told them where and
when I had found it, what I had seen the day
before—the whole thing. They had me pin-

point the location of the cache on the map, thanked me kindly, warned me to keep it to myself, and I left and pretty much forgot about it.

You know that all through June and July we flew our normal summer gaggle of tourists here and there, and were so busy I hardly gave it a passing thought. I don't think you noticed that I was going ahead and flying the hunter types I usually give to you. I thought I might learn something else if I kept my eyes and ears open, but nothing came of it.

The federal agent showed up in August. You were gone down to Homer with a load of halibut fishermen when she found me at the lake cleaning out the plane. I was tired, hungry, and in need of a shower after an overnighter to Prince William Sound, so I took her back to the house and aimed her at a gin and tonic while I sluiced off the two-day crud. Then I threw some meat on the grill and we talked— a lot.

Her name is Karen Randolph. She's an F and W special agent from Wisconsin who's here undercover for a sting operation aimed at catching a bunch of jerks they have a line on, who're making sure their hunters get what they pay for any way and anywhere that works. The big part of all this is happening other places in the state, in the Brooks Range, for instance, but they are convinced something pretty sordid is going on out there near Beluga Lake. Back then she was just looking for a local pilot on tap to fly her a few places she needed to get acquainted with before the deal went down. The big charter boys are too well known and she wanted someone who didn't fly off the Hood docks where visibility and recognition would be a risk. But she asked a lot of questions about the things I had told the local office. Dale Stoffel's name came up more than once, to let you know how serious it is. They are convinced his bunch is running the game.

So, the short of it is that I agreed to do the flying for her and we've gone out a couple of times—once to the place where I found the cache, but everything was gone by then. The deal is set to go down in a couple of days. She has arranged a hunting trip with these guys that they think was set up through a contact of theirs back East. I don't know much about it and don't want to. She's asked me to fly her out to a lake this side of Beluga and leave her in their camp. She's ordered up at least one brown bear as close to record size as possible, and they assure her it's no problem. While this is happening, she will try to collect enough evidence to convict them. I will go back after her in five days.

Now comes the part I don't like at all. If you are reading this letter you know something went wrong. Maybe I'm just paranoid, but I've had an uneasy feeling for the last few days. Somebody broke into my shed at the lake, but nothing was taken. Several times I've seen a green pickup drive by out there, and once I think I saw it near the house. Karen hasn't picked up anything questionable and thinks I'm imagining things—that everything's okay.

She's probably right, but if she's not, you know it now.

Once I drop her off out there on the plateau I'll have no way of knowing if she is blown, as she calls it. They could make her just disappear and, unfortunately, me too, when I go back. But I'm to circle and identify her before I land, and we've worked out some signals. Whatever, hopefully it will all be over soon and I can tell you all about it.

I'm sorry, Chelle. I'm thinking now that I should have told you, I guess. When it's all done I will—or, I will have in this letter. Don't worry about the money. It's okay. As you probably know by now, I've set up an insurance policy so you'll have everything you need and then some.

I can hear you saying, "Why, Norm? Why did you do it?" I can't exactly answer that. I'm not the hero type. I guess maybe I just got mad when I ran up against it personally. But somebody has to do it, don't they? Even when it's risky? I'm worried, but kind of excited and proud to be in on it at the same time. Can you understand? This sort of thing has got to be stopped. But then you already know that I think all the trophy hunting should be stopped, even the legal kind. It doesn't make sense anymore. There's too many of us and getting to be too few of them—the animals—and especially the bears. Hardly anyone's paying attention— wolves get all the press—but the grizzlies are extinct, or about to be, everywhere but here and Canada. They are my favorite animal, monarchs of the wild, the largest carnivores on

earth today, descended in a straight line from
the cave bears that were around with the di-
nosaurs. I've enjoyed watching too many of
them just living their lives, hurting no one, to
be able to condone the random unnecessary
killing of them for something to hang on the
wall. Subsistence is another thing. People have
every right to eat. I've done enough hunting
myself in the past, but for food, and I'm even
beginning to question that's the answer either.
No one really needs to eat bears. But enough—
you've heard this before.

What I want to say—just in case—is that
whatever happens I want you to know I love
you much more than you believe I do, and that
the last thing I want to do is leave you. I know
you still think that someday I will, but I won't,
Chelly-love, not if I have even an ounce of
choice in the matter. I want to stick around for
a long, long time yet, until we're both brushing
our teeth out of a glass. I want a rocking chair
and slippers with you, and finishing each
other's sentences, and walking arm in arm the
way people do who have walked together for
years and years. But there are some things that
just must be done. If I said no to this one,
somehow I would think less of myself, and
maybe you would too. So this has nothing and
everything to do with you and me. The only
thing I regret right now is not letting you in on
it. I never would again.

If you get this letter, then there is one thing
I'm asking you to do for me—for us—and you
are the only one I can trust to do it, Chelle.
These are the notes I made about everything,

every detail I could, and Karen's notes too, so they will have her side of it. Take them to Fish and Wildlife and let them use them however they can to nail these bastards to the wall. I've put in all the names and places and everything I know about it and she put in the rest.

If all goes well, as planned, we'll be able to do it ourselves, but if not, you must please do it for us. I've done everything I could to make sure the notes survive. I'd leave you my ace for luck, but I'm taking it because right now I need it more than you do.

If anything happens to me, don't be angry or bitter. It isn't your fault any more than it is mine. I won't ever leave you, not really, you know.

> I love you,
> Norm

She didn't read the notes, but carefully put the pages of Norm's letter back in order, lined them up neatly, smoothed them carefully back into their folds around the notebooks, and put it all back into the envelope. Then she sat, unmoving, staring at nothing beyond and through the water. Seeing, hearing, feeling . . . nothing. She frowned a little, but there were no tears, just a total emptiness where her heart had been such a short period of time before.

Then she stood up, stiff from sitting, closed the shed door, walked across to where she had noticed that the space beyond Norm's was empty, and sat down on the log to wait for Jeff, as she felt she should.

In a little while, a raven swooped down to land a

few feet away, strutted around, cocking its head this way and that, inspecting her, commenting with a series of quarks. But there was only silence and nothing to eat, so he soon flew away.

25

IT WAS ALMOST SEVEN O'CLOCK THAT EVENING when Jensen turned off Knik Road into Jessie's long driveway, now almost dry of the mud and water that had filled the potholes. Still, they would be back with more spring rain; it was a rough, uneven two hundred feet to the space in front of her cabin, and would soon create billows of dust. As he pulled in next to the empty space that Jessie's blue pickup should have occupied, he decided that a load of gravel would be a good thing before much longer.

Without going to the door, he knew the sturdy, two-room log cabin was empty, and felt disappointment draw his brows together. Where was she? It hadn't crossed his mind that she might not be there to meet him.

Stepping out of the cab, he stood for a minute, comparing his feelings to the pleasure and anticipation he had felt a few days earlier, and remembered her standing at the top of the steps, smiling down, drying her hands on a dish towel, the yeasty scent of drunk roast floating from inside out into the cool evening air. He had been reluctant, that evening, to have to tell her about finding the Lewis plane. Now, he knew he was reluctant to go into the cabin, empty and silent of Jessie's vitality and presence, having looked forward to sharing the end of this case.

Procrastinating, he extracted his briar pipe from the pocket of his wool shirt, packed and lit it with a usual kitchen match, puffing till the taste of tobacco filled his mouth and smoke rose in a cloud around his head.

Looking down, he saw that Tank again stood in silent confidence, patiently waiting to be recognized and petted. Again, this attention earned Alex an affectionate face washing.

"Well, old man," he told the husky, "it's just you and me. Where's your musher friend? Huh?"

Tank's tail beat a tattoo in the air, but gave no clue to Jessie's absence. So, unfolding himself from a crouch, Jensen went resignedly up the stairs and opened the front door.

The room he entered was comfortably warm from the potbellied stove softly glowing on the other side of it, but no appetizing smell of dinner cooking greeted him. A light, however, was on over Jessie's large, cluttered desk. Removing his boots and hanging up his coat, he crossed to it, but no note lay waiting for him in the spot she often left one, nor was there a scrap of paper on the dining table.

Feeling slightly abandoned, and a little depressed, Jensen found a bottle of Killian's in the refrigerator, opened it to take a long, satisfying swallow, and stretched his lanky frame out on the sofa, without switching on another light. He remembered that he wanted a shower, felt grubby from clambering through hills and swamps in the bush for two days, but hadn't the energy to do more than lift the lager to his mouth and feel the tension begin to melt away from his neck and shoulders. Vaguely, he wished he had thought to turn on the radio before lying down. This, too, seemed beyond his ability to accomplish, and he forgot it as he emptied the bottle, set it on the floor beside the sofa, and closed his eyes, hands folded over his chest.

The dogs in the yard had stopped barking. It was totally still . . . and . . . lonesome. It was, he imagined, what Chelle Lewis had experienced all winter and would, now, every day—unless she found someone to replace Norm . . . sometime . . . later, maybe. Unexpectedly, the idea of Ernie Tobias slipped into his mind. Big, inherently gentle, dependable Ernie, single and attracted to strong women. Interesting . . . and premature, he was sure. Still . . .

He liked Tobias, was glad to find him on the right side after all. There was a cold, unexpected, deadly streak in the agent—surprisingly exhibited in his cold fury at the poacher's treatment of Karen Randolph. But what had highly impressed Alex was the man's unconditional, absolutely unbreakable loyalty. Cas had a lot of the same quality, he knew, but Ernie's was expressed in a much more physical manner—no more effective, perhaps, but more immediate. It, or the threat of it, if you were a criminal, would certainly get attention—results.

He thought of the expression on Caswell's face as he handed over the evidence he had located on the way back to the lake to meet the repair crew. Revulsion had been part of it. So had pity, and anger. Particularly anger. It took a lot to inspire that kind of anger in Ben.

"What is it?" Alex had asked.

"I found something you need to see."

"On the ridge."

"Not exactly. Farther east, in a gully that cuts south from it." Silently, stiffly, he had handed Jensen one of two evidence bags. The remnants of the stained clothing he had found showed up unmistakably through the clear plastic.

He had explained, quickly and in detail, under what conditions and where he had found them, describing the bear trail and cache, as well.

Jensen had examined both closely and nodded. "It's got to be Lewis. You think a bear got him?"

"Might . . . if it weren't for this, and another, similar, still at the scene." He had handed over the other bag containing the broken thigh bone with its damning slug.

Jensen had turned it over and examined it through the bag, and his reaction had been what Cas had expected, knowing the tall trooper well, his whole attitude one growing outrage. He had said nothing, until he had pulled his pipe from his pocket and was puffing anger into the air in a fragrant cloud. Then he had taken it from between his clenched teeth and hissed, "God damn the miserable bastards straight to hell."

"My feelings exactly," Cas had agreed. "It seems pretty clear that they shot his legs from under him and left him to the grizzly."

"I'll bet they didn't just hope the bear would show up—leave it to chance," Alex had growled. "No more than they did for us this afternoon. Whoever did this undoubtedly drove the bear onto him." He tapped the slug in the bone with one long finger. "This made sure he couldn't get away and the smell of his blood would be as good as bait."

"Yeah, I've been thinking about that, too. Ever since I found it this afternoon. Any bets on which one of the Stoffel gang's rifles this slug would fit? What do we do about Rochelle?''

Jensen had thought about it for a minute or two before answering. With the stem of his pipe, he had rubbed at the full blond mustache on his upper lip and looked up at Caswell wearily.

''She's got to know. If she doesn't, she won't give up on this idea that she's going to find him.''

''Just show her the piece of shirt. It's the easiest to identify. She doesn't need to see, or know about, his legs, just that a bear got him.''

Jensen had disagreed. ''No. She'll have to know it all. I promised and . . . no matter how hard it is. She doesn't need to see it, but I'm going to tell her.''

Caswell had slowly nodded. ''Okay. Your call.''

And Chelle had looked at him warily, waiting in silence, intuition telling her that what he had to say would not be pleasant.

Silent for a minute, Alex had cleared his throat and given her a long, level look, filled with sympathy. ''You don't have to go on looking for Norm,'' he had told her quietly. ''Cas found his body this afternoon. I'm sorry, Chelle, but we've all expected it . . . even you.''

Reaching into his jacket pocket, he had removed the evidence bag containing the stained shirt and handed it to her.

''Was this Norm's?''

She had said nothing at first, made no sound, had just stared at the bag with wide eyes that slowly filled with tears that spilled over and ran down her cheeks. Raising her eyes, she had swallowed hard, clenched her teeth, then had taken a deep breath before she nodded.

"Yes. So he really *is* here. Didn't . . . Where? Where is he?"

She had started to rise from the log she was sitting on, looking at Jensen, but he had waved her down.

"Up along the ridge in a ravine of some sort. That direction." He had pointed east with the stem of the pipe. "You can't . . . don't want to . . ."

"Tell me, Alex. Just tell me. Was he hurt bad in the crash?"

She had handed back the evidence bag, which Jensen had repocketed.

"I don't know. Ben wasn't able to tell. Chelle . . . a bear got him . . . last fall. A grizzly, from the look of it."

"Jesus!" Her face had twisted with repulsion and horror. "How—?"

But he had cut her off before she could ask more than he wanted to tell her, and she had watched closely as he told the rest.

"Someone . . . one of them . . . shot him and he couldn't get away when . . ."

"Oh . . . God . . . no."

Her reaction had startled him into silence as she abruptly stood up, staring blankly, her face a kaleidoscope of shifting emotions—aversion, grief, anger, refusal, a few others he couldn't separately identify . . . guilt and resignation, perhaps—then she had turned and faced the lake, trembling. "My fault," she had said. "My fault."

"Chelle." Jensen remembered how frustrated he had felt with her insistence on guilt. "Damn it. It *was not* your fault. You had nothing to do with it. One of these guys shot him along with Karen Randolph, and it won't be long till they admit it. There's no reason for them not to. But even if they don't, we know, and we've got enough evidence to convict them. Let it go. He never meant to leave you. You must know that now."

Her face a mask, she had listened and finally nodded once.

"Can . . . can I go up there to see?"

He had hesitated. "You don't want to do that, Chelle. Will you take my word for it this time."

There had been quiet for a few seconds while she thought about it, ending with a sigh. "Yes. I think I will . . . this time. I don't really need to go, because . . . I already knew he was dead, Alex . . . before, without seeing. It's like something just stopped. You know when you hear a bell ring, then it stops and there're vibrations in the air that seem to go on for a while? It's like that. Like the winter was sort of vibrations for me. Now they're gone—he's gone. I know."

She had looked up at him, the need for confirmation clear on her face. "But, you're right, he didn't mean to leave me, did he?"

"No," he had said, wanting very much to reassure her. "No, I'm sure he didn't, Chelle." Not intentionally, he had thought, but that doesn't make him any less gone, the space he filled any less empty.

And now, in Jessie's small, quiet house, lying on her big sofa, he thought about all the empty space and days that had made and would make up Chelle's life for a long time.

When she moved, she had walked as if her legs felt strange, as if she had been ill and wasn't quite well yet. She had walked away with a nod of thanks in his direction, and he had watched her go toward her plane, beyond which the Kenai Service repairmen were patching up Caswell's Maule. Twice, she had glanced around as if it seemed odd that everything was so normal—lake water lapping softly at the bank, the damp mud smelling slightly musty, a thousand sparkles from sunshine on the wavelets, a cool breeze ruffling a few blades of new, brilliant green grass at her feet. She had frowned a little, but there were no more tears, just an empty, slightly haunted look on her face.

He had no way of knowing that, as she went and reached into a pocket, she found the ace, among other things, and that she was holding it as she climbed into the pilot seat to start the engine of the Cessna that, recovered, was ready for her to fly it home.

Where the hell was Jessie? he wondered, and immediately felt ashamed of his irrational irritation. She was not, after all, his personal chief cook and bottle washer, nor would he want her to be, would he? There were dozens of things she could be doing, places she could be. She might share his life, but had her own to live as well.

Yes, he thought, as he drifted off, *but, oh, how well she fits into mine.*

There was the fresh smell of soap and outside air, just before Jessie kissed him softly awake, before he opened his eyes to find her on her knees by the sofa.

"Hi, trooper. Where ya been for days at a time?"

He didn't say anything, just reached to pull her up with him, knocking over the empty Killian's bottle in the process, and held her close for a long time.

She was dressed in denim pants and one of his own soft, old, flannel shirts that he could get his hands under to feel the warm, smooth skin of her back, and he couldn't get enough of the smell of her honey-blond hair. He wanted to tell her a hundred things, but couldn't find the words for one, could only feel the tears behind his eyelids and the lump in his throat.

Finally, she raised her face from the hollow of his shoulder to say, "Hey. It's really only been two . . ." Then she saw his expression and stopped, losing her smile.

"What, Alex? What is it? You're scaring me."

And he could move again, speak to reassure her.

"Nothing. It's all okay. I just missed you. I love you, Jessie."

She sat up, turned on the reading lamp at the end of the sofa, above their heads, and looked at his face for a long, still minute, seriously assessing what she found there.

"Yes," she said, at last. "Yes, I *think* you really do."

"I . . . ah . . . haven't been very . . ."

"If you mean only part of you's been coming home at night lately. It's okay. All of you's here now. You get that way when you're focused and working a case sometimes."

"Yes, but this was different. I . . ."

She paused to give him a searching look.

"I know," she said slowly. "But *was* is the operative word now. Right?"

"Right. But I want you to know . . ."

"It's okay, Alex. Really. You don't need—"

He interrupted her flow of words with a finger against her mouth.

"No, Jess. It's not quite okay until we talk. I want to talk about it. Want you to know . . ."

"And maybe I don't want to." She almost leapt from the sofa to stand, looking down at him.

"Maybe I don't want to hear it—help you clear your conscience by listening and feeling hurt. Don't be selfish, Alex."

"No. It's not like that."

"Isn't it?"

He remembered the night in the dark with Rochelle Lewis, and was silent, trying to decide. Was she right? Was he trying to share, or assuage some guilt of his own?

"No."

"Does what we're not talking about here have anything to do with trust, Alex?"

"Trust?"

"Yes. The word does keep coming to mind."

He stared at her, startled wordless. It had not come to his mind.

"I've had a fair bit of it to do lately, Alex. And, just so you know, it hasn't been easy."

He could see she was close to tears. Things were happening—fast—that he did not understand.

Standing up, he went to turn on the lights so he could see her clearly, try to learn whatever it was she was feeling that he needed to know. What he learned was that it was a lot.

"Come."

Taking her hand, he walked to the table and pulled out two chairs. She sat in one while he continued to the kitchen and put on the kettle. While the water heated, he took out mugs, tea, milk, and sugar, and when it was hot, made them each a cup. Jessie watched in silence.

"Now," he said, sitting down to face her across the table. "Tell me."

"I think . . ." she started, then stopped. "No. I've got to preface this right, get it in perspective. We're coming from two completely different places, Alex.''

''What places?''

''Well, to start, I don't think you've ever been in a position to lose trust in the painful way I did. *Losing* is different than *losing trust in.* Do you see?''

''Yes,'' Alex said thoughtfully. ''I do. You had it the other way around, you mean.''

''Yeah. I've told you what happened with Grant. I didn't lose Grant, I lost trust in Grant. He knowingly stole it by lying to me. He meant one thing and let me think he meant another. What scares me is I know how much it costs. For the better part of a week you've come home either talking or thinking about Chelle Lewis in a way that has scared me to death . . . afraid it would cost me . . . you—but, worse, everything else. Now you want to talk about it.''

''No, Jessie. It's not . . .'' . . . *that way,* he started to say. But he knew that—in all honesty—part of it was, or had been, and that she knew it. He heard himself start to lie, to make it easy, to reassure her. And she was waiting for him to finish, an apprehensive look in her eyes. He suddenly knew that if he lied to her now, about this, it would never be the same.

''I tried to make it go away, too,'' Jessie said. ''When I could see that you had walked around it and really come home, I tried to shut it out. Doesn't work, does it?''

''Nope.''

''Is it over?''

''Never really started.''

''Yeah?''

''Yeah. You can partly thank Cas, maybe. Nothing that matters to us happened, Jess," he said carefully, trying hard to put into words the shape of what he understood and had felt. "A little more sympathy than I counted on inspired a little more interest than I recognized. I was trying to find a way to express that when I said I wanted to talk."

There was a long moment of silence, then she smiled, shakily.

"It's time you stopped doing penance," she said suddenly, without thinking, and stopped, appalled.

Alex thought for a minute, then nodded, slowly, with an odd, lopsided half-regretful grin. "Funny. I was thinking something like that on my way home. Will you help?"

"Only if you'll help remind me that you are not like Grant."

"Deal."

They made dinner together, took a shower together, and found their way to the big brass bed in *their* house, feeling more together than they ever had before.

"She seems very alone," Jessie murmured, just before falling asleep with her head on Alex's shoulder.

"Chelle?"

"Um-m. Very singular. Always has. It's like Norm's disappearance . . . death, didn't change her much . . . since she seemed that way when he was still alive. I mean, sort of self-contained. You know?"

Alex thought about that out loud. "I thought she knew, somehow, that he was dead. To know, she had to have been involved, had something to do with it. You just explained it, I guess."

26

THE MORNING SKY WAS CLEAR, WITH ONLY A FEW small clouds to the east, as Chelle Lewis lifted her Cessna from the waters of Lake Hood, and turned north, heading one last time for that small lake where Norm had died, on the far side of Mount Susitna.

She did not turn on the music of the radio, preferring to float along in the white sound of the plane engine as she passed over the familiar waters of Knik Arm and altered course to the west, passing from controlled airspace. It was good to be back in the air alone after everything that had happened, and with a destination, a reason all her own to be going.

Two months had passed since her last flight in this direction, and the green velvet of summer had spread itself over the slopes of the Sleeping Lady. In the long hours of daylight particular to the far north, every growing thing had seemed to explode into life at once. Contrasted against the white of ice and snow that never left the highest mountain peaks, the colors of nature seemed exaggerated: dark, rich greens, deep, intense blues, and a riot of wildflower hues invisible from the air: magenta fireweed, blue-purple lupine, yellow marsh marigolds and monkey flowers, pink roses, dark brown chocolate lilies, bright white

daisies and miniature dogwood. After a winter filled
with whites and grays, it was like going from black
and white to Technicolor.

Crossing over Ch'chihi Ken, the long ridge of the
Sleeping Lady's hair, Chelle could see the plateau
beyond, with its many small lakes reflecting blue as
if liquid sky had fallen to fill dips and depressions
between the rolling hills. It was easy to pick out the
nameless one for which she was headed; its shape
was so familiar she would never forget it.

Nameless, she thought, and wondered briefly if it
would be possible to have it named Lewis Lake for
her husband. No. Better to leave it undesignated. He
had always liked the anonymous quality of the wilderness, with its thousands of unnamed mountains,
lakes, and rivers. He had thought it pleasant to be
able to answer "west" or "that way" when asked
where he was going. "It leaves all kinds of possibilities, instead of a specific destination—leaves
your options open."

Chelle smiled, remembering, and glanced at the
passenger seat next to her. A small, plainly wrapped
box sat on it—all that was left of Norm—ashes and
chips of bone—all Alex and Cas had been able to
find and retrieve. It seemed incredibly small to hold
such an important, unforgettable part of her life—of
their short life together.

Its size had startled her when she had picked it up
the day before from the crematorium, and surprised
her still. She had been offered an urn, but it hadn't
seemed appropriate when she already knew where
the ashes belonged, and that it wasn't a place an urn
would be useful. The lake where he had died was
where he should be returned, and she knew he would
have been pleased with that idea. They had talked

about it once, knowing their profession was one of risk as well as satisfaction, and he had been adamant. "Don't let anyone dump me in a hole in the ground. Just have me burned and scatter what's left over some uninhabited part of Alaska that I like, or would have liked. Okay?" So that's what she would do— the last thing she could do for him to make . . . amends?

Bunker had offered to keep her company, but she wanted to go alone. To complete it all, she knew she must be by herself, with no one else watching, or waiting. It was a simple chore, could be done quickly, with little trouble, and she would take care of it herself, picking the spot and the time that felt right.

Dropping out of the sky, she banked the plane into a turn and leveled off for her landing, drifting gently downward. A light breeze rippled the surface of the lake, making it easy to see the water. She touched down, allowed the plane to gradually lose speed, and heeled in to bring it to a controlled run, watching carefully for floating logs.

Taxiing to the middle of the lake, she slowed the plane to a stop and allowed the engine to idle. Then she reached for the box and climbed carefully out onto the float. Removing its lid, she slowly emptied the ashes it contained onto the already cloudy water, and watched them drift slightly toward the rear of the plane. She imagined them moving with the water to the stream at the west end of the lake and down to Lower Beluga Lake. From there some of Norm would be carried along the Beluga River, from the plateau into Cook Inlet far below and, eventually, on the tides, out into the Gulf of Alaska, making him one with the country he had loved.

"I'm sorry, Norm," she said, softly, for the first and last time. "I should have trusted you. I was mistaken about Karen Randolph . . . about most of it. If I hadn't come back from Homer a day early and seen her with you at our house, I wouldn't have thought . . . If I hadn't followed you out here and seen her again in your plane, when I knew there wasn't a charter on the books . . . If I hadn't expected you to leave me . . . Hadn't assumed . . . Hadn't made so many mistakes . . ."

She paused, and raised her eyes to the sky over the lake. A solitary hawk drew circles in the air, looking for unwary rabbits or squirrels. Everything was warm and still, within the hundreds of small wilderness sounds. The Cessna rocked slightly under her weight, as she tossed the box back into the plane. Now there was only one thing more to do.

She reached into a pocket, then stretched her arm out over the water on which a few of Norm's ashes were still slowly sinking.

"I'm sorry, love. Thank you for taking care of me . . . for not leaving me . . . no matter what."

Opening her hand, one at a time, she allowed two brass shell casings from the Weatherby to fall into the murky, silt-filled water, and watched them vanish forever into its depths.

Back in the cockpit, she throttled up and let the plane pick up speed until she felt it rise onto the step, gliding powerfully on the surface of the water, ready to lift off—going up to be part of the sky.

If you enjoyed *Sleeping Lady*,
then read the following preview
of the next thrilling
Alex Jensen Alaska Mystery,
DEATH TAKES PASSAGE,
coming soon in hardcover from Avon Books.

8:30 P.M.
Saturday, July 12, 1997
Skagway, Alaska

"IT MUST HAVE LOOKED A LOT LIKE THIS A HUNDRED YEARS ago," Jessie Arnold said to Alex Jensen, as they paused in front of the Red Onion Saloon to look up Broadway, Skagway's main street. It was just after dark on a clear evening, and there were few modern streetlights in the historic gold rush town. Most of the warm glow between blue shadows came from the doors and windows of the small shops and boutiques that lined the street. Several of these had false fronts, and a couple—including the famous Golden North Hotel, where Jessie and Alex had registered—sported round tower rooms on one corner, but most were boxy, single-story frame structures intended to look as if they had weathered a century, as many of them actually had. Most of the businesses that occupied them had already closed for the day, and the rest would soon follow suit.

303

A few tourists were still wandering the boardwalks, heading slowly back toward their giant tour ships at the town docks, or looking for some appealing place to have a late dinner. Silhouetted against the lights, they could have been gold rush stampeders from the late nineteenth century.

A pair of women laden with bulky plastic bags walked past, discussing their purchases with enthusiasm. Alex thoughtfully watched them head west toward the harbor, his mind still drifting back to the old Skagway, jumping-off point for the Klondike.

Someone whistled. A laugh rang out from down the street. The muffled ragtime rhythm of a piano drifted from the saloon, growing abruptly louder as someone flung open the door, releasing the sounds of conversation and the music.

"It's like stepping back in time," Alex agreed.

Jessie looked up and down the street again. "If you add a few more people, some horses and muddy streets, this would seem pretty much like 1897."

"Like it?"

"Even more than I expected. It makes me feel connected. Just imagine coming all the way from Seattle, or Portland, or San Francisco ready to start for the Klondike, excitement and fortunes in gold. It's no wonder they called it gold *fever*."

Alex agreed. "It was contagious all right. But they hadn't a clue how hard it would be to make it to Dawson. A lot of them turned right around, came back here, and went home."

"Well, I wouldn't have quit and neither would you. I still think it would have been great."

"Yeah, but *you*—who think nothing of thousand-mile sled dog races—would have fit right in. I'd probably have been at the top of the pass, freezing my tail, and helping the Mounties make sure everyone who went into Canada had enough equipment and supplies for a year."

Jessie laughed and turned toward the Red Onion. "Well, speaking of supplies . . . come on, trooper. Let's get something to eat before we die of starvation."

Closely followed by Jensen, she moved through the door into the immediate contrast of a large and well-lit room, full of cheerful sounds and the mouthwatering aroma of hot pizza. Aside from its thoroughly modern crowd of local and visiting customers, not to mention its twentieth-century cuisine, the Onion would have been right at home in the gold rush. In fact, it had been built in 1898 and was later moved to its current location. In the process, the movers had somehow turned it around, so that the back of the structure now faced the main street.

A long antique bar, backed with large mirrors and details carved with scrolls of fancy woodwork, extended along well over half of one side of the long room, accommodating twenty-some people on tall stools. Another thirty or forty souls were seated on a collection of mismatched chairs at square tables only a little larger than checkerboards. The walls—except for the large windows facing the street—were decorated with an interesting assortment of artifacts from the 1890s.

"During the gold rush the second floor of this place was a bordello," Alex informed Jessie, as they quickly claimed the only empty table in sight. "It's supposedly haunted by one of the former working girls."

"You're joking, right?"

"Nope. She has a reputation for not liking men—scares them if they try to go upstairs. She sticks around to take care of the place."

A piano player in a collarless shirt, gartered into puffs at the elbows, teased an infectious honky-tonk from the yellowed ivory keys of an old upright piano, keeping patrons' toes tapping on the scuffed wood floor as they sang along with his old-timey tunes. Jessie and Alex did some toe-tapping of their own, but there was little singing as they hungrily worked their way through a combination pizza and drafts of pale Alaskan ale in thick glass mugs.

When nothing remained but crumbs, they moved to tall stools at the bar, where they had a better view of the piano player, who paused now and then to add humorous comments to his music. Contented, they sat, enjoying the entertainment and sipping the last of their ale.

Alex drained his mug, lit his pipe, and looked questioningly at Jessie in response to the bartender's suggestion of another brew. She nodded. Then her attention was caught by a person claiming the empty stool next to hers. Jessie smiled at the woman, who responded with only the slightest of nods and a twitch of her lips, and turned quickly away to lay a ten dollar bill on the bar.

The newcomer was short and had dark eyes and dark hair combed tightly into a knot at the back of her head. Small

unruly curls of it escaped and stood out vigorously in a not
unbecoming frame for her oval face. She was delicately built,
and her expression was not particularly open or welcoming.
Her thin lips were set narrowly together and she looked tired
or worried—it was difficult to tell which.

Before Jessie had time to ponder the all but nonexistent
acknowledgment she had received, the bartender set two ales
before them with a flourish.

"Hey," he demanded with a self-satisfied grin, "Jessie Arnold—the Iditarod, right?"

"Right." Jessie reached to accept the hand he extended to
her across the ancient, scarred surface of the bar, skillfully
avoiding a collision with the full frosty mug he had just set
down.

"Welcome to Skagway. We all cheered you into Nome a
couple of years ago in the *gutsiest-ever* finish, and another in
the top ten last year. Congratulations."

"Thanks," she smiled, pleased with his enthusiasm and the
recognition of her effort.

"You going along on this big centennial boat run to Seattle?"

"Yeah," she confirmed, turning to introduce Alex. "This
is Alex Jensen. He's the formal representative for the Alaska
State Troopers on the trip."

"Don Sawyer," he offered, as the two men shook hands.
"I'll be going along, too, as a extra bartender. So stop by
Soapy's Parlour on the dining room level and say hello."

"We'll do that. It's really a vacation, since I'm just along
to show off the uniform in the ceremonial parts, and not assigned to chase bad guys this trip." He laid a bill down to pay
for their drinks.

"Naw." Sawyer shook his head. "These are on the house.
Nice to have you both in town. Running this year, Jessie?"

"Planning to."

"Good luck then."

As he moved away to mix a drink for the woman sitting
next to Jessie, Alex couldn't resist a comment.

"Glad we aren't supposed to be undercover. Why didn't I
make you wear that fake mustache? Is there anybody in this
state who doesn't know you?"

She grinned. "It's kind of nice that a few Alaskans know
who I am—sort of a reward for all the work that goes into

running the race. Besides, a fake mustache would make me look like a trooper. Right?''

Alex's reddish blond handlebar mustache was one of his few vanities. It was wide, with a half-curl at each end and he had worn it for so long he couldn't imagine what his face would look like without it. Periodically Jessie waved a pair of scissors and offered to cut off half, so he could compare and see if he liked himself better without it. Pressed, however, she cheerfully admitted that she liked it and would prefer that he keep it.

They made an attractive couple. He was tall and slim, with the beginnings of smile lines around his mouth and eyes. She was a bit shorter, tan and fit from days spent running dog teams through the Alaskan wilderness, her hair, a short honey-colored tumble of waves and curls, her eyes a calm gray.

The piano player stopped for a break, which initiated a loud vocal disappointment of the impromptu, semi-harmonious chorus surrounding him. Soon a quieter hum of cheerful conversation filled the room. The chess players didn't even glance up.

Don returned with the drink for the dark-haired woman, and was reaching to pick up her money when a new voice interrupted him.

"I'll take care of that."

Jessie turned her head to see a stranger swing himself onto the stool beyond the other woman.

"Hi," he said. "I'm Bill Prentice. Don't want to sound like I'm just hitting on you, but I know you from somewhere."

The approach did seem sincere, but it was hard to tell. He paused, smiling quizzically, and waited for her response.

Plainly startled, she frowned slightly and gave him an uneasy glance before turning her eyes back to Don.

The bartender waited, still holding her money, giving her a very straight and level look, communicating silently that if she wanted this person gone, he would see to it. She raised her eyebrows, soliciting his opinion. Was he personally acquainted? He pursed his lips slightly, cocked his head, and with a barely perceptible movement, shrugged his shoulders. It was up to her, he didn't know the guy.

Giving her uninvited companion one more contemplative look, with a tiny half-nod and answering shrug, she allowed Sawyer to set up the drink. Without accepting payment, he returned to the tap to draw a beer for the newcomer.

Good man, thought Jessie, who had closely followed both the spoken and silent exchange. She was beginning to like this Sawyer person. A quick look at Jensen's amused twist of lips told her that he, too, had observed the byplay to their right.

"Thanks," she heard the woman say, "but I don't think you know me. I'm not from around here. Judy Raymond."

"Oh, neither am I," he answered. "Nice to meet you, Judy. Where're you from then?"

The bartender set up the beer and smiled. "These are on me," he told her.

Another bit of good, subtle work. Without being conspicuous, he had succeeded in giving the guy notice that anything out of line would not be tolerated, and he had explicitly canceled any obligation she might feel by making the beer on the house. As the couple resumed their tentative conversation, Sawyer met Jessie's watchful eyes, and she smiled appreciatively at him; another small conspiracy of silent communication. He grinned and went on down the bar in response to a customer waving an empty mug.

Jessie turned back to Alex, who was watching the piano player wend his way through the maze of tables back to his instrument.

"You about ready to go?" he asked. "I've had enough of the noise."

"Sure." She pushed back the last of her ale and slid off the stool to stand beside him. "The boat will be in by eight tomorrow morning and I'd like to see if we can get our stuff on board early. Then we can enjoy the day before we have to dress up."

"Great." Jensen laid a generous tip on the bar for Sawyer, who raised a hand in a brief farewell wave. "I'm tired. Too much bouncing around in the air between here and Juneau."

"Were you airsick? We weren't airborne very long and you fly in small planes all the time with Caswell."

"No, I just don't like it rough, and it's always rough over the Lynn Canal."

Jessie yawned as they stepped out the door. Alex took her hand, tucking it snugly under his.

The street was empty. They did not notice a figure that exited the Onion a few seconds behind them and slipped immediately into the dark shadow of a doorway to watch them stroll in step along the boardwalk toward the hotel.